PRAISE FOR AUC

"Hilarious, fast paced, and madcap."

—*Booklist* (starred review)

"Another amusing tale set in the town full of over-the-top zanies who've endeared themselves to the engaging Mira."

—*Kirkus Reviews*

"[A] hilarious, wonderfully funny cozy."

—*Crimespree Magazine*

"Lourey has a gift for creating terrific characters. Her sly and witty take on small-town USA is a sweet summer treat. Pull up a lawn chair, pour yourself a glass of lemonade, and enjoy."

—Denise Swanson, bestselling author

"A fun, fast-paced mystery with a heroine readers will enjoy."

—*The Mystery Reader*

PRAISE FOR KNEE HIGH BY THE FOURTH OF JULY

Lefty Finalist for Best Humorous Mystery

"*Knee High by the Fourth of July* . . . kept me hooked from beginning to end. I enjoyed every page!"

—Sammi Carter, author of the Candy Shop Mysteries

"Sweet, nutty, evocative of the American heartland, and utterly addicting."

"[The] humor transcends . . . genders and makes for a delightful romp."

"Mira . . . is an amusing heroine in a town full of quirky characters."

"Lourey's rollicking good cozy planted me in the heat of a Minnesota summer for a laugh-out-loud mystery ride."

PRAISE FOR *JUNE BUG*

"Jess Lourey is a talented, witty, and clever writer."

"Don't miss this one—it's a hoot!"

"With just the right amount of insouciance, tongue-in-cheek sexiness, and plain common sense, Jess Lourey offers up a funny, well-written, engaging story . . . Readers will thoroughly enjoy the well-paced ride."

PRAISE FOR *MAY DAY*

"The first-person narrative in *May Day* is fresh, the characters quirky. Minnesota has many fine crime writers, and Jess Lourey has just entered their ranks!"
—Ellen Hart, award-winning author of the Jane Lawless and Sophie Greenway series

"This trade paperback packed a punch . . . I loved it from the get-go!"
—*Tulsa World*

"What a romp this is! I found myself laughing out loud."
—*Crimespree Magazine*

"Mira digs up a closetful of dirty secrets, including sex parties, cross-dressing, and blackmail, on her way to exposing the killer. Lourey's debut has a likable heroine and surfeit of sass."
—*Kirkus Reviews*

PRAISE FOR *THE TAKEN ONES*

Short-listed for the 2024 Edgar Award for Best Paperback Original

"Setting the standard for top-notch thrillers, *The Taken Ones* is smart, compelling, and filled with utterly real characters. Lourey brings her formidable storytelling talent to the game and, on top of that, wows us with a deft stylistic touch. This is a one-sitting read!"
—Jeffery Deaver, author of *The Bone Collector* and *The Watchmaker's Hand*

"*The Taken Ones* has Jess Lourey's trademark of suspense all the way. A damaged and brave heroine, an equally damaged evildoer, and missing girls from long ago all combine to keep the reader rushing through to the explosive ending."

—Charlaine Harris, *New York Times* bestselling author

"Along with an incredible cast of support characters, *The Taken Ones* will break your heart wide open and stay with you long after you've turned the final page. This is a 2023 must read."

—Danielle Girard, *USA Today* and Amazon #1 bestselling author of *Up Close*

PRAISE FOR *THE QUARRY GIRLS*

Winner of the 2023 Anthony Award for Best Paperback Original

Winner of the 2023 Minnesota Book Award for Genre Fiction

"Few authors can blend the genuine fear generated by a sordid tale of true crime with evocative, three-dimensional characters and mesmerizing prose like Jess Lourey. Her fictional stories feel rooted in a world we all know but also fear. *The Quarry Girls* is a story of secrets gone to seed, and Lourey gives readers her best novel yet—which is quite the accomplishment. Calling it: *The Quarry Girls* will be one of the best books of the year."

—Alex Segura, acclaimed author of *Secret Identity*, *Star Wars Poe Dameron: Free Fall*, and *Miami Midnight*

"Jess Lourey once more taps deep into her Midwest roots and childhood fears with *The Quarry Girls*, an absorbing, true crime–informed thriller narrated in the compelling voice of young drummer Heather Cash as she and her bandmates navigate the treacherous and confusing ground between girlhood and womanhood one simmering and deadly summer. Lourey conveys the edgy, hungry restlessness of teen girls with a touch of Megan Abbott while steadily intensifying the claustrophobic atmosphere of a small 1977 Minnesota town where darkness snakes below the surface."

—Loreth Anne White, *Washington Post* and Amazon Charts bestselling author of *The Patient's Secret*

"Jess Lourey is a master of the coming-of-age thriller, and *The Quarry Girls* may be her best yet—as dark, twisty, and full of secrets as the tunnels that lurk beneath Pantown's deceptively idyllic streets."

—Chris Holm, Anthony Award–winning author of *The Killing Kind*

PRAISE FOR *BLOODLINE*

Winner of the 2022 Anthony Award for Best Paperback Original

Winner of the 2022 ITW Thriller Award for Best Paperback Original

Short-listed for the 2021 Goodreads Choice Awards

"Fans of *Rosemary's Baby* will relish this."

—*Publishers Weekly*

"Based on a true story, this is a sinister, suspenseful thriller full of creeping horror."

—*Kirkus Reviews*

"Lourey ratchets up the fear in a novel that verges on horror."

—*Library Journal*

"In *Bloodline*, Jess Lourey blends elements of mystery, suspense, and horror to stunning effect."

—*BOLO Books*

"Inspired by a true story, it's a creepy page-turner that has me eager to read more of Ms. Lourey's works, especially if they're all as incisive as this thought-provoking novel."

—Criminal Element

"*Bloodline* by Jess Lourey is a psychological thriller that grabbed me from the beginning and didn't let go."

—*Mystery & Suspense Magazine*

"*Bloodline* blends page-turning storytelling with clever homages to such horror classics as *Rosemary's Baby*, *The Stepford Wives*, and *Harvest Home*."

—*Toronto Star*

"*Bloodline* is a terrific, creepy thriller, and Jess Lourey clearly knows how to get under your skin."

—Bookreporter

"[A] tightly coiled domestic thriller that slowly but persuasively builds the suspense."

—*South Florida Sun Sentinel*

"I should know better than to pick up a new Jess Lourey book thinking I'll just peek at the first few pages and then get back to the book I was reading. Six hours later, it's three in the morning and I'm racing through the last few chapters, unable to sleep until I know how it all ends. Set in an idyllic small town rooted in family history and horrific secrets, *Bloodline* is *Pleasantville* meets *Rosemary's Baby*. A deeply unsettling, darkly unnerving, and utterly compelling novel, this book chilled me to the core, and I loved every bit of it."

—Jennifer Hillier, author of *Little Secrets* and the award-winning *Jar of Hearts*

"Jess Lourey writes small-town Minnesota like Stephen King writes small-town Maine. *Bloodline* is a tremendous book with a heart and a hacksaw . . . and I loved every second of it."

—Rachel Howzell Hall, author of the critically acclaimed novels *And Now She's Gone* and *They All Fall Down*

PRAISE FOR *UNSPEAKABLE THINGS*

Winner of the 2021 Anthony Award for Best Paperback Original

Short-listed for the 2021 Edgar Awards and 2020 Goodreads Choice Awards

"The suspense never wavers in this page-turner."

—*Publishers Weekly*

"The atmospheric suspense novel is haunting because it's narrated from the point of view of a thirteen-year-old, an age that should be more innocent but often isn't. Even more chilling, it's based on real-life incidents. Lourey may be known for comic capers (*March of Crimes*), but this tense novel combines the best of a coming-of-age story with suspense and an unforgettable young narrator."

—*Library Journal* (starred review)

"Part suspense, part coming-of-age, Jess Lourey's *Unspeakable Things* is a story of creeping dread, about childhood when you know the monster under your bed is real. A novel that clings to you long after the last page."

—Lori Rader-Day, Edgar Award–nominated author of *Under a Dark Sky*

"A noose of a novel that tightens by inches. The squirming tension comes from every direction—including the ones that are supposed to be safe. I felt complicit as I read, as if at any moment I stopped I would be abandoning Cassie, alone, in the dark, straining to listen and fearing to hear."

—Marcus Sakey, bestselling author of *Brilliance*

"*Unspeakable Things* is an absolutely riveting novel about the poisonous secrets buried deep in towns and families. Jess Lourey has created a story that will chill you to the bone and a main character who will break your heart wide open."

—Lou Berney, Edgar Award–winning author of *November Road*

"Inspired by a true story, *Unspeakable Things* crackles with authenticity, humanity, and humor. The novel reminded me of *To Kill a Mockingbird* and *The Marsh King's Daughter*. Highly recommended."

—Mark Sullivan, bestselling author of *Beneath a Scarlet Sky*

"Jess Lourey does a masterful job building tension and dread, but her greatest asset in *Unspeakable Things* is Cassie—an arresting narrator you identify with, root for, and desperately want to protect. This is a book that will stick with you long after you've torn through it."
—Rob Hart, author of *The Warehouse*

"With *Unspeakable Things*, Jess Lourey has managed the near-impossible, crafting a mystery as harrowing as it is tender, as gut-wrenching as it is lyrical. There is real darkness here, a creeping, inescapable dread that more than once had me looking over my own shoulder. But at its heart beats the irrepressible—and irresistible—spirit of its . . . heroine, a young woman so bright and vital and brave she kept even the fiercest monsters at bay. This is a book that will stay with me for a long time."
—Elizabeth Little, *Los Angeles Times* bestselling author of *Dear Daughter* and *Pretty as a Picture*

PRAISE FOR *THE CATALAIN BOOK OF SECRETS*

"Life-affirming, thought-provoking, heartwarming, it's one of those books that—if you happen to read it exactly when you need to—will heal your wounds as you turn the pages."
—Catriona McPherson, Agatha, Anthony, Macavity, and Bruce Alexander Award–winning author

"Prolific mystery writer Lourey tells of a matriarchal clan of witches joining forces against age-old evil . . . The novel is tightly plotted, and Lourey shines when depicting relationships—romantic ones as well as tangled links between Catalains . . . Lourey emphasizes the ties that bind in spite of secrets and resentment."
—*Kirkus Reviews*

"Lourey expertly concocts a Gothic fusion of long-held secrets, melancholy, and resolve . . . Exquisitely written in naturally flowing, expressive language, the book delves into the special relationships between sisters, and mothers and daughters."

—*Publishers Weekly*

PRAISE FOR *SALEM'S CIPHER*

"A fast-paced, sometimes brutal thriller reminiscent of Dan Brown's *The Da Vinci Code*."

—*Booklist* (starred review)

"A hair-raising thrill ride."

—*Library Journal* (starred review)

"The fascinating historical information combined with a storyline ripped from the headlines will hook conspiracy theorists and action addicts alike."

—*Kirkus Reviews*

"Fans of *The Da Vinci Code* are going to love this book . . . One of my favorite reads of 2016."

—*Crimespree Magazine*

"This suspenseful tale has something for absolutely everyone to enjoy."

—*Suspense Magazine*

PRAISE FOR *MERCY'S CHASE*

"An immersive voice, an intriguing story, a wonderful character—highly recommended!"

—Lee Child, #1 *New York Times* bestselling author

"Both a sweeping adventure and race-against-time thriller, *Mercy's Chase* is fascinating, fierce, and brimming with heart—just like its heroine, Salem Wiley."

—Meg Gardiner, author of *Into the Black Nowhere*

"Action-packed, great writing taut with suspense, an appealing main character to root for—who could ask for anything more?"

—Buried Under Books

PRAISE FOR *REWRITE YOUR LIFE: DISCOVER YOUR TRUTH THROUGH THE HEALING POWER OF FICTION*

"Interweaving practical advice with stories and insights garnered in her own writing journey, Jessica Lourey offers a step-by-step guide for writers struggling to create fiction from their life experiences. But this book isn't just about writing. It's also about the power of stories to transform those who write them. I know of no other guide that delivers on its promise with such honesty, simplicity, and beauty."

—William Kent Krueger, *New York Times* bestselling author of the Cork O'Connor series and *Ordinary Grace*

AUGUST MOON

OTHER TITLES BY JESS LOUREY

MURDER BY MONTH MYSTERIES

May Day

June Bug

Knee High by the Fourth of July

August Moon

September Mourn

October Fest

November Hunt

December Dread

January Thaw

February Fever

March of Crimes

April Fools

STEINBECK AND REED THRILLERS

The Taken Ones

The Reaping

THRILLERS

The Quarry Girls

Litani

Bloodline

Unspeakable Things

SALEM'S CIPHER THRILLERS

Salem's Cipher

Mercy's Chase

GOTHIC SUSPENSE

The Catalain Book of Secrets

Seven Daughters

CHILDREN'S BOOKS

Leave My Book Alone! Starring Claudette, a Dragon with Control Issues

YOUNG ADULT

A Whisper of Poison

NONFICTION

Rewrite Your Life: Discover Your Truth Through the Healing Power of Fiction

AUGUST MOON

JESS LOUREY

THOMAS & MERCER

Published by Thomas & Mercer, Seattle

www.apub.com

Amazon, the Amazon logo, and Thomas & Mercer are trademarks of Amazon.com, Inc., or its affiliates.

ISBN-13: 9781662519284 (paperback)
ISBN-13: 9781662519291 (digital)

Cover design and illustration by Sarah Horgan

Printed in the United States of America

AUGUST MOON

Chapter 1

I brushed my hair for the seventh time, using my good arm because my other one was in a sling, and made a deal with myself. If Johnny knocked on my door tonight, I would open up to him like a lilac on a golden May morning. If he didn't show, I was swearing off men, packing it up, and moving back to Minneapolis to finish my grad program.

No one could claim I hadn't given Battle Lake a chance, not after what I'd been through the last three months. But oh, did I hope that Johnny would do right by me tonight.

While I waited, I tried reading an old issue of *Vanity Fair* I'd recycled from the library, but I didn't even have a sufficient attention span to follow Christopher Hitchens's latest rant. A *Frasier* rerun on my grainy TV was no more engaging. I settled on spending most of the early night beaming at my animals. Johnny Leeson was coming to my double-wide tonight!

My long dark hair was loose and natural. Except for the wisp of mascara around my gray eyes and the shiny, honey-flavored gloss on my lips, I was makeup-free. With me, what you saw was what you got, which might explain why there weren't a lot of men seeing and getting in my life.

Johnny had spent time with me at my worst, though, from inarticulate and dorky to bruised and battered, and he'd *still* asked to come over tonight. I hoped our transition from friends to lovers would be a smooth one. I'd tried that relationship conversion before and found it to be like that moment when you stroll onto the dance floor and shift from walker to groover—if you think about it too much, you mess it all up.

I peeked anxiously through the kitchen window, waiting for his headlights to appear down the driveway. When I saw nothing, I pushed open all the windows on the back of the house so I would hear his car. I breathed in the spicy woodsmoke-and-zinnias scent of Minnesota in July and listened to the clock tick a happy beat. Johnny Leeson was going to be with me tonight!

I moved from the couch to the kitchen table and then to the edge of my bed, where I tried reading a book. When the clock ticking began to sound a little too much like water torture, I looked for the best CD to slide into my stereo. I blipped through Sting, the Indigo Girls, and Gillian Welch before I figured Madeleine Peyroux would convey the desired attitude of suave aloofness and cool availability that I was after.

The moody jazz, however, soon became monotonous, and then taunting, as the minutes ticked off the clock and fell to the floor like gravestones. *Well*, I told myself, *we didn't agree on a specific time.*

I clung to my desperate optimism for nearly an hour before I moved on to worrying. Johnny was a decent guy. He would have called to cancel if he could have. By 11:00 p.m., however, I became darkly pissed.

I stabbed the stop button on my CD player and blew out the beeswax candles that'd been melting toward extinction. Apparently, Johnny had had second thoughts. Fine. That was fine. A romantic evening with him probably would have had a terrible ending anyhow, with me discovering that he was one of those guys who looked good on the surface, but when you started making out, you found out he was the type who liked to rub the area between your thigh and underwear line and breathily ask you if you were close.

That's what I was telling myself as I walked past my front door, angrily ripping off the cute rainbow T-shirt I'd chosen just for the occasion, the one that made me look like I had boobs. When, I wondered fiercely, would interactions with men stop being excruciating experiences I had to learn from, instead of nurturing relationships that I could grow in?

I rubbed at itchy tears, angry for even getting my hopes up. I should have known from the start. Relationships and me went together as well as dark chocolate and sauerkraut. A cloister loomed in my future, or maybe a job teaching English at a rural technical college.

That's when the first knock came. I jumped away from the door and yanked my T-shirt over my head as quickly as I could with only one good arm. I hadn't heard or seen a car. Then came a second knock, and my heart and loins took off like a rocket. The person on the other side of this door was going to decide whether I returned to Minneapolis to pursue a thrilling career in the English language arts or stayed in Battle Lake, wrapped in the loving arms of Mr. Jonathan Leeson.

Instead of waiting for the third knock, I ripped the door open, naked hope in my eyes. The hope quickly turned to shock, and then confusion. Actually, I shouldn't have been surprised at the person standing on my doorstep. This was Battle Lake, after all. Anything could happen here, and it usually did.

"Kennie?"

Chapter 2

At first I thought she'd gotten in a paintball fight, but then I realized she had been crying so hard that her bountiful makeup had run riot over her features.

"Yeah, it's me." She pushed past me, tripped over Luna, my now-growling dog, and didn't give my cat, Tiger Pop, a glance. If she'd checked out Tiger Pop, I'm pretty sure she would have seen she was smiling. My kitty likes drama. "What do you have to drink?"

Uh-oh. The only thing worse than Kennie without an accent was Kennie on a bender. I'd gotten to know the mayor of Battle Lake pretty well over the past few months. With her fake southern accent, tight clothes, cosmetics applied with a putty knife, crispy blonde hair, and a controlling streak that would make Martha Stewart blush, she was not your average central Minnesota woman. (The fake accent was what set her apart.) Rumor had it she was spooning Gary Wohnt, the local police chief, but I wasn't much for gossip. All I knew for sure was that Kennie was two clicks away from banana pants, and somehow she made it work.

"I think there's some vodka in the cupboard over the fridge." *Think, my ass.* I'd bought two liters of Absolut last week, after I'd lurched over my third dead body in as many months. I had managed to save half the second bottle, but only by supplementing it with wine.

When I'd relocated to Battle Lake last April by request of my good friend Sunny, who needed a house- and dog-sitter while she flitted off to Alaska with her mono-browed lover, my goal had been to take a life time-out—get sober, rest, reprioritize—and then launch myself back into the mix with both fists swinging. A small town was the perfect place to do that, right? Ha! Welcome to Battle Lake, Minnesota, where the women are churchgoers, the men like to hunt, and the body count is above average.

On the surface, Battle Lake was picturesque. You could reach it on a straight shot up Interstate 94 and a little jog north. The journey took three hours from Minneapolis, and you'd swear it was worth every minute when you crested that last hill and spotted the red-topped water tower, tree-lined Lake Street, and wide-open, smiling faces.

The town was packed with antique and knickknack shops, an art gallery, a full-service drugstore, and its very own accountant, health clinic, municipal liquor store, dentist, chiropractor, and law firm. In the summer, there was even a gingerbread shed right off the main drag where you could buy vegetables on the honor system. People in Battle Lake didn't lock their doors, and if you went in the ditch, you'd have someone pulling over to help before you even got out of the car.

The downside was that everyone in town would know you had slipped in the ditch just as quick.

Plus, you could tune in only two channels on your TV, and short of counting dead bodies and drinking, there wasn't much for a city gal to do. I had my gardening, of course, and two jobs, one as the librarian for the Battle Lake Public Library, open ten to five Monday through Saturday, and the other as the on-call reporter and regular columnist for the *Battle Lake Recall*, which now came out every Wednesday, thanks to a petition signed by the local churches, who felt the previous Monday publication day didn't give them enough time to get their Sunday happenings into the paper.

I was horribly unqualified to run a library, but a series of calamitous events in May had pushed me into a promotion. Mrs. Berns, a local bawdy old lady, helped me by shelving books and checking out patrons, and we limped along just fine.

I wrote two columns for the *Recall*. One was Battle Lake Bites, which featured a regional recipe each week. The other column, cleverly titled Mira's Musings, contained updates on local events. You wouldn't think that would be an edge-of-your-seat affair in a town of 797 people, but you would be wrong.

I had just composed a doozy of an article about the kidnapped Chief Wenonga and Big Ole statues, the former a twenty-three-foot fiberglass sex bomb who normally resided directly off the western shore of Battle Lake, and the latter a pasty, twenty-eight-foot fiberglass Norwegian "warrior" with a skirt, who was supposed to live in Alexandria, Minnesota, but who'd disappeared along with the Chief. Call it a run-of-the-mill July for this wacked-out pocket of the state.

However, despite the lethal mix of quirky locals and mischievous mayhem, I'd been eking out my place in town. People waved to me on the streets, I knew where to find a good cup of coffee and some killer Tater Tot hotdish, and both my jobs centered around reading and writing, the two consistent loves of my life.

And I'd been deliciously excited to make a little extra room for Johnny Leeson, local hottie. I didn't normally go for the Scandinavian type, but his dirty-blond hair was curly thick, his eyes so blue I swear I could see waves in them, and he had these tanned, muscular hands perfect for pulling you close for a brook-no-objections, Harlequin-romance-cover, marauding-pirate kiss.

Or so I'd imagined, during many a long shower.

Better than his looks, though, Johnny was smart. He had a BS in horticulture, and he was talking about applying to the University of Wisconsin–Madison's doctoral program in the same. He'd returned to Battle Lake when his dad was diagnosed with terminal stomach cancer. Johnny stayed around to help his mom take care of his dad and, after his father died, to help her adjust to her new reality. He was making the best of his current life—working at the nursery, teaching community-ed gardening classes, and playing around with a local band.

Oh, and making pants wet everywhere he went.

Johnny would be embarrassed if he knew how many chicks in Battle Lake dreamed about him. I'd sworn I wasn't going to be one of them. Nature had facilitated this by turning me into a sputtering dumdum in Johnny's presence. I'd been safe until we ended up working together last week to hunt down the Chief Wenonga statue.

Johnny's deep blues had stared hard into my core, his vibrating cell phone had thrummed between us, and his beautiful Cupid's bow of a mouth had asked if he could come over to my place. *Tonight.* And instead of consummating those plans, I was staring at the ass of a fortysomething woman digging into my panic-attack cupboard for the last bottle of vodka.

"Why are you wearing bike shorts?"

"I was exercising when I got the news." Kennie huffed as she pushed herself off my countertop, unscrewed the silver Absolut cap, and took a swig. She critically surveyed my green-and-white, prefabricated kitchen as she swallowed.

"I never liked these modular homes," she said. "One strong breeze and you're all of a sudden living in Douglas County." She fingered a hole in the sheetrock, left over from a party a few summers back. "The walls aren't even a quarter inch thick. Would you look at this?"

I was grateful for the distraction, as I'd been trying to look anywhere but at the giant moose knuckle spray-painted between her thighs, begging for attention. Some genius had decided that sewing padding into bike shorts would make for a more comfortable ride. Unfortunately, it also made Kennie look like she was smuggling a fast-rising loaf of bread in her shiny-tight pants.

"Maybe you want to sit down?" I asked, pulling out a chair.

She shrugged and plopped herself into the straight-backed wicker kitchen seat. I sat across from her, relieved to have a table between my eyes and her privates. Too bad the table was glass-topped. I slid the fruit bowl over to block my view of her down below and leaned over to snatch away the vodka, no pun intended.

"Let's start from the beginning," I said, putting the cap back on the liquor. "You were exercising when you got *what* news?"

"I don't want to talk about it."

I rubbed my forehead. "So why'd you come over?"

Her face screwed up. I thought she was going to burp, but then she started sobbing in loud, horsey snorts and seized the vodka bottle back. "It's Gary."

"Gary Wohnt? Is he OK?"

"Someone else," she said, between sobs. Her makeup shifted another level.

"Not Gary?"

"No! Gary's found *someone else*."

Ah. Police Chief Gary and Kennie *had* been dating. "Oh. I'm sorry."

Mostly, I was sorry that she was in my house. We weren't exactly girlfriends—due to our differing viewpoints on how to treat people, dress, speak, and think—and I took it as a depressing statement on her personal life that she had only me to turn to. *She must be one of those people who equates proximity with friendship.*

She certainly was a pitiful figure, snuffling and wiping her fist across her face to divert the cry-snot. Her hand trailed a little mascara mustache on her upper lip. "I have done everything for that man," she said. "And he has left me for another."

I didn't want to ask, but curiosity was driving. "Who?"

"Gary," she said, slowly, as if I were a ding-dong. "*Gary* has left me for another. Try to pay attention, Mira. I'm spilling my heart here."

It took all my self-control not to flick her on the forehead. "Who. Did. Gary. Leave. You. For?" I enunciated every word.

Kennie sighed dramatically. "God."

"I'm sure it must be tough." I waited for her to continue.

"No, *God*, you baboon. Gary left me for God. He's found the church, and he doesn't think it's proper for us to continue our 'unholy' relationship. That's what he called it."

For once, I agreed with Gary.

Chapter 3

I reached for the vodka and chugged, dismayed to find that it tasted salty. "What sparked his conversion?"

"Some new minister in town, a friend of a friend, Gary says." She shook her head miserably. "Rat bastard took my man."

I wasn't sure if the rat bastard in question was God or the minister, but I was all about trashing on the unfair sex right now. Gary'd chosen God over Kennie, and Johnny had chosen who-knows-what over me. "You can't rely on one single man in this town."

"Hallelujah," she said, sloppily high-fiving me. "Did you know that I just got done nursing that man after nose surgery?"

"Gary got a nose job?"

"No, he got his sinuses drilled." She shivered. "They scour out all the junk and then stick some cotton tubes up the nostrils to absorb the blood. He couldn't pull 'em out for days. I cleaned around them."

I threw up a little in my mouth. "You must have really liked him to do that."

"I did." She sniffled. "And who else am I supposed to date? I can't go out with strangers."

Ah, the *Little House on the Prairie* model of dating. Being originally from the tiny Minnesota town of Paynesville, I recognized this attitude. You could only go out with men you met at the Mercantile, or a friend of a friend you ran into on an occasional trip to Sleepy Eye for some poplin. Developing a relationship with someone no one in your circle knew, or, heaven forbid, seeking out new experiences, was out of the question.

I appreciated the benefits of sticking with the familiar, but the downside of this dating model was that even a Mr. Edwards or a Willie Oleson would start to look good after all the Almanzos were taken. Hence the plethora of smart local women living with seasonally employed mouth breathers.

"Maybe you could just be single for a while?" I asked.

She snorted and took a long pull off the vodka. "You got any more liquor?"

I did. It was for emergencies only, but if not now, then when?

I stood up and strode to the rear of the double-wide, fishing out the bottle of tequila from beneath the bathroom sink. I cracked it and shivered at the spicy kerosene smell. The bottle felt hot and heavy in my hand, and I recognized I was riding the buzz cusp, that point where you're sober enough to know you should go to bed right now and drunk enough not to care. I decided my arm didn't really hurt that bad, either, so I removed my sling, glided back to the kitchen, and mixed us both a tequila on ice with a squirt of lime juice.

"How long had you and Gary been dating?" I asked, handing Kennie her drink.

"I've known him since high school. He worshipped the ground I walked on."

The liquor I was drinking like Kool-Aid made me generous.

"Well, of course he does."

"Did. He *did*. Now he's all godly."

"Dink."

She clinked my glass. "I suppose you don't have to worry about any of this, being asexual."

I coughed, sending burning tequila through my nose. "Huh?"

"Oh, is it supposed to be a secret? Then you really should start wearing makeup, honey. And curling that field-worker hair of yours. Else, you might as well wear a sign that says you don't want a man."

I ran my fingers through my hair and self-consciously wound it into a bun at the nape of my neck. Holding my hands up that high made me feel dizzy. "I don't want a man, but not for the reason you think. They're unreliable. The whole lot of them."

Kennie nodded sympathetically. "Like your dad? The murderer?"

Christ on a cracker. No wonder Kennie didn't have any girlfriends. She didn't know how to *hang*.

For the record, my dad was guilty of manslaughter and not murder, but it had hurt everyone involved just the same. When he was alive, he tried drinking himself to death, and when that proved too slow, he'd drink and drive. One night, he crashed into another car, killing himself and the driver of the other vehicle. I was sixteen when it happened. People started calling me Manslaughter Mark's girl. Not to my face, of course, but I heard the whispers and sometimes thought I still did. Suddenly, the tequila tasted sour in my mouth, and my stomach felt oily.

"I'm tired, Kennie. I think I wanna go to bed."

"That's fine, sugar. I'll just crash on your couch." She made the "sh" on "crash" long and snaky.

"What?"

"Oh, don't mind me. I'll be as quiet as a dead man."

Oof. That hit too close to home. "Can't you sleep in your car?"

"No, ma'am. I biked here. I'm going to look so hot by the end of this month that Gary Wohnt will forget all about God."

I really didn't want to wake up to Kennie. "Biking home right now would be great exercise."

But she wasn't listening. She ping-ponged over to the sectional couch with the rust-colored, cabin-in-the-woods pattern, where she fell face down into the nappy cloth. She twitched and wriggled a little before she began snoring so vociferously that it came out her ears.

I sighed, stumbled over, and lifted her head to the side so she wouldn't suffocate. My hands were sticky blue with eye shadow when I pulled them away. I capped the tequila, returned it to its hiding place in the bathroom, and shoved the empty vodka bottle to the bottom of the garbage so it wouldn't judge me in the morning.

Without Kennie to distract me, I was left with my dark and slippery thoughts, which came surfing back on the tequila and vodka. Johnny hadn't shown up, and he wasn't ever going to. I had been a dope to get my hopes up, and I sure as hell wasn't going to make that mistake again.

It was long past time that I realized I wasn't going to find love here, or anywhere. *Fine by me.* I was an independent woman, à la Kate Jackson, circa *Charlie's Angels.* I didn't need anybody, and for sure nobody needed me in this lousy, dead-end, murder-drenched town. In that instant, my mind was made up.

I was going back to the Twin Cities as soon as I found a real librarian to take over my job.

Chapter 4

I woke up Saturday morning with a hangover so familiar I considered it a friend. Feeling a little sad, a little relieved, and a lot empty, I chewed four bitter aspirin and took a shower. I was surprised to find that my arm actually did feel better, so I decided I was done with the sling.

Once I was as ready as I was gonna get, I stepped out of my bedroom, quiet as a clam so as not to wake Kennie, who'd flipped herself over in the night. Her melted makeup had attracted some tufts of couch lint as well as a healthy dose of calico cat hair, thanks to Tiger Pop. She lay benevolently on Kennie's chest, a Cheshire grin on her pink kitty lips. Every now and again her tail would twitch over Kennie's nose, causing her to honk and sniffle in her sleep.

I set Tiger Pop on the floor, as much to save her from getting any more lipstick on her fur as to do Kennie a favor.

I grabbed an apple and a bottle of juice and opened the front door to herd out Luna and Tiger Pop. Outside, the sun's rays tattooed my hungover head, piercing my eyes like hot needles. The July morning was humid and pushing eighty degrees, even though it was not yet nine a.m. This summer had been tropical, and my vegetable garden looked like something from *Land of the Lost*, with monstrous green tomatoes dripping off the staked stems and orange squash blossoms as big as dinner plates opening to the sun.

I rinsed out Luna's and Tiger Pop's water bowls and filled them to the brim before tucking them in the shade under the house. Part of the apron had come off the double-wide, creating a cool retreat for my animals as well as a wayward skunk or two. I slid a couple bowls of food under there and promised them that I'd be home before dark.

"Stay out of Kennie's way," I warned them. Tiger Pop rolled her eyes at me, but Luna was eager to please, as usual. Dogs are such wonderful floozies.

Kennie's bike, an ancient no-speed with big black handlebars and a banana seat, lay flush on my blooming roses. I'd planted the peach and white climbers against a wooden trellis on the sunny south side of the house, and they'd been flourishing right up until the bike had flattened them. When I disentangled her two-wheeler, the salty-sweet smell of crushed roses drifted up. I rolled the bike to the front porch so Kennie would see it first thing and be on her way.

The last part of my morning ritual was feeding the birds. I'm not a fan of the winged population, and they don't exactly wait in line to beg for my autograph, either. I get pooped on at least three times a year, but I keep the birdbath and feeders full in hopes of an uneasy truce. They still enjoyed playing chicken with me, lunging at my head and then veering away after I made some embarrassing convulsive gesture to protect myself, but at least they didn't charge en masse.

I figured *that* was because of the food I put out every morning.

I curled into my two-door Toyota Corolla, slapped on the seat belt, and donned sunglasses against the bright, blazing ball rising behind me. It looked gorgeous reflecting its lavender and tangerine rays off Whiskey Lake outside my front door, but I wasn't in the mood for beauty. I was all business, intent on heading directly to the library to write a help-wanted ad. By the time I opened at 10:00 a.m., that ad would be in all the regional newspapers, at every college in the five-state area with a library sciences program, and on all the major internet job search sites.

I noticed my hands gripping the steering wheel tight enough to leave marks, and I forced myself to relax. Any life change was sure to create stress, I reasoned, and that's why I was so uptight about last night's decision to move. The thing about transitions was that at the outset, a good change felt as scary as a bad one. Sometimes you just needed to jump and hope you landed right.

That's what I was telling myself as I drove into Battle Lake, already bustling as tourists hauled their boats and RVs into town. I nodded at Harold Penderly, the owner of the Hardware Hank, out front washing his windows, and pulled into the library parking lot, cruising into the spot marked "Reserved for Librarian." I stared at the yellow brick building that I'd come to love and shook my head to clear out any sentimentality.

The phone greeted me shrilly as I unlocked the front door. I jogged over to it, my keys jingling in my hand. "Hello?"

"Mira! I was hoping I'd get you."

My heart leaped and then dropped like a bag of rocks. "Johnny?"

"Yeah! How are you? I just called your house, but you weren't home. Did you know Kennie Rogers is there?"

Anger, disappointment, and a third, unrecognizable emotion fought for my attention. "Yeah. What can I do for you?"

He sighed. "You sound mad. I don't blame you. I should have called last night, and I'm sorry I didn't. You know when I left you to go check in with my mom? When I got to her place, there was a call from the University of Wisconsin. At Madison." There was a pause as he waited for me to respond. "Mira? Are you there?"

"Yup."

"It's amazing, but it was one of my old professors! She said she has a six-week project she needs a research assistant for, and it might lead to a full ride for fall semester, if I want to start grad school. She said she needed me out here immediately."

"'Here'? You mean you're in Madison right now?" My old friend, the hangover, suddenly felt like an iron maiden.

"Yeah!"

"I thought you were taking a year off to help your mom." It was a spiteful thing to say, and I immediately regretted it after I heard the guilt in Johnny's voice.

"I was, but she said she's fine and would never forgive herself if I didn't go."

"Well, I guess there's nothing holding you back." My heartbeat thudded in my ears. "Good luck."

He was quiet on the other end of the line, so quiet that I almost apologized for my chirpy, dismissive words. "I'll be visiting a lot," he finally said. "There are some people in Battle Lake who I care about."

"Yeah, there's some nice people here." I squished my eyes shut. I hated being a crybaby.

"I mean *you*, Mira. I think we have something."

"I guess we'll never know, huh?" My voice came out hot. "You're in Madison, and I'm moving back to the Cities."

"What?"

"Yeah, there's not much for me in Battle Lake, you know?" I liked myself a little less with every word that cracked out of my mouth, but I couldn't stop. "You're a good friend, and we should keep it that way. Hey, maybe we can be pen pals!"

A pause. "That's what you want?"

My blood thudding grew so loud I could hardly hear myself, and my injured arm had begun to throb as well. "It is. I'll be sure to check in on your mom for you when you're gone, OK? Until I move, that is."

"OK. Fine. Bye."

"Bye, Jeff!" The name of my murdered ex-lover dangled heavy in the air between us, and I couldn't for the life of me decide if I had thrown it out there on purpose.

"What?"

"Johnny, I meant! Sorry. I was just putting away a book by some Jeff guy. It's still early, for me. Bye, *Johnny*."

He hung up without another word. I stumbled into the back room to splash water on my face. On the way, I gathered all my feelings around me like a billowing parachute, carefully folding and tucking until they fit into a neat knapsack, which I put off to the side.

It was the last time in my life I'd be able to compartmentalize so easily.

Chapter 5

August lumbered in, the weather grew impossibly hotter, and farmers muttered about a drought as their crops turned crispy and their irrigation systems taxed the water supply.

The tourists loved the hot, clear weather, though. The beaches and local shops were packed like seeds in a pomegranate. The out-of-towners seemed not to notice the lawns turning brown or the watering bans and happily packed themselves into Stub's every night to enjoy live music and juicy butter-knife steaks. In this way, the dance between the needs of an agricultural community and the requirements of a tourist-based economy played out as it had since rich East Coasters discovered the beauty, solitude, and plentiful fish in Battle Lake back in the early 1900s.

As the résumés for the Battle Lake head librarian position began trickling in, I studied each one, reminding myself it was a ticket out of here, away from memories of Johnny, and Jeff, and strange people too numerous to count. I was too far into feeling sorry for myself to even be embarrassed by how wildly unqualified for this job the incoming applicants proved me to be.

When a little downtime in the library presented itself, I created a banned books display to feed my low-burning but constant anger. The display featured some of my favorite books of all time. *Of Mice and Men*, *The Catcher in the Rye*, *I Know Why the Caged Bird Sings*, *A Wrinkle in Time*, *The Color Purple*, pretty much anything by Judy Blume and

Stephen King, and *The Handmaid's Tale*. I took grim pleasure in the fact that books flew off the display so quickly that I needed to continually dig for more censored literature to add.

I also sent Sunny a postcard to let her know I was moving. It would have been braver to call, but her hours were unpredictable, I reasoned, so mail would be the best way to let her know that in a couple weeks, a very nice couple from town would be moving from their apartment to Sunny's vast and beautiful farm to care for her house and dog until her return. My heart would break leaving Luna, but I needed to move on.

Before I knew it, it was time to interview the crop of hopefuls to find my replacement. Mrs. Berns had agreed to come in early to get the library spick and span before the interviews. Not surprisingly, I found myself alone outside the yellow brick building at 8:00 a.m. on this scorched but cloudy day.

The weather, a colicky mix of heat and shade, set my teeth on edge as I unlocked the library door and went inside. The air had a hint of smoke despite the burning ban, which created a mental image of the prairies surrounding us going up like a Kleenex. There'd be no white knight to save me, I thought petulantly, missing Johnny so much in that moment that my skin felt swollen. I hadn't heard from him since our unpleasant July phone conversation. When a rap came on the door behind me and pulled me out of my self-pity, I was grateful.

Mrs. Berns, I figured. *Now I'll have someone around to be mad at.*

I turned and was surprised to see a young and pretty woman instead of a geriatric and libidinous one. For a moment I thought it was Lucy, the peppy high school girl who'd been helping me out on the busy shifts, but when the young woman tented her hands around her face so she could peer in the door, I saw she was a stranger.

I made the universal point-at-your-watch-and-shake-your-head gesture for "we're closed, come back later," but she shrugged and smiled like she didn't understand.

I pulled the door open. "The library doesn't open up until ten o'clock. You'll have to come back."

"Oh no! I've got a superlong shift, and I don't have a thing to read. I was supposed to be at work five minutes ago, but I can't bear the thought of another day without any books!" She made a little pouting face. "I'm Alicia, by the way." She held out her manicured hand.

I sighed. I knew Alicia, or at least her type. It was her brunette-Barbie beauty, youthful arrogance, and overfamiliar *you'll give me whatever I want, won't you?* smile that tipped me off. She was *that* girl, the one who, in middle school, convinced the desperate follower girls to wear their Guess jeans and turtlenecks on Monday because everyone would be doing it, and then showed up in a completely different outfit herself.

On Tuesday, she'd coach those same hopeful girls to be mean to a randomly chosen chick in their group. When Wednesday rolled around, she'd make them all drink some nasty concoction to demonstrate their loyalty to her, then ignore them when the popular kids strolled past. And so it went, until no girl in Alicia's orbit knew who she could trust and either got smart and started hanging out with the nerds or morphed into a miniature, poorly dressed Alicia.

Be sure and ask me how I know so much about what the hopeful, lonely follower girls went through in public school.

Yes, I knew Alicia's type—the ones who were pretty, popular, confident, and entitled in elementary, middle, and high school—and thought they could coast on that for the rest of their life. Too bad no one bothered to tell them you could cash those checks only until you were eighteen. After that, the playing field evened out.

A little.

"Sorry," I said. "You'll have to come back later. Maybe over your lunch break?"

"Is that a mouse behind you?"

I turned toward where she was pointing. "I don't see anything."

She squinted. "I swear I just saw something run under that desk over there. Maybe it was a rat. I'm gonna go peek, and we can herd it outside together." Alicia sailed past me, flashing a conspiratorial grin on the way. We were going to hunt rodents together. No scaredy-cats, us.

She crouched on all fours. "Mind turning on the lights?"

I flipped the switch and went to fire up the front computer. There was no mouse. She wanted to play Power Ball, but I wasn't in the mood. That was more telling than any other sad-sack thing I had done in the four weeks since Johnny had ditched town and me. If I wasn't willing to outwit an obvious control freak in my own territory, I was seriously depressed. "You might as well grab a book or two, since you're in here already."

She smiled innocently. "You sure you don't want me to get the mouse?"

Crafty, that one. She was an inch or two taller than my five foot six, maybe ten pounds lighter but two cup sizes larger, and her long brown hair was curled and sprayed into place. She wore a fair amount of makeup, but it was expertly applied to look natural.

"We both know there's no mouse. You need a library card, too?"

She appeared ready to argue and then smiled. "If you don't mind."

I slid the form toward her. "Fill this out."

Alicia attempted to catch my eye and make nice, but I kept my gaze fixed on my computer screen. When she grabbed a pencil out of the cup in front of me and filled out the form, though, her necklace caught my eye. It was a delicate golden cross hugged around her neck tight as a choker, and splayed on the cross was a tiny crucified Jesus in all his scrawny glory.

She caught me staring. "It was a gift from my mom."

"Hmm," I said by way of a response. "Where'd you say you work?"

"I didn't." She slid the card back toward me. Alicia Mealy, and an address in Clitherall, the two-bars-and-a-post-office town just up the road from Battle Lake. Ms. Mealy looked like she had neither done an honest day's work in her life nor eaten venison, pheasant, or snapping turtle, which would make her stand out like a purple pig in that town.

"You're new around here?"

"Not exactly." She shrugged. "We've been in the area a few months. Anyhow, I better be going, or my boss is going to get crazy angry. It took longer to get a card than I thought it would. Maybe I'll come back over my lunch hour?"

Took longer than she'd thought? I'd folded in less than five minutes. "We're open until five o'clock."

"Great! This is an awesome library." She trailed her fingers over the front counter as she left, pausing at the banned-book display on her way out. "Unbelievable!" She laughed. "You've got a display of naughty books! Too cool for school. Aren't you worried you're going to get in trouble?"

I warmed to her a hair. A microscopic split end of a hair. Could be she was a misplanted chick, just like me. "In Battle Lake, you don't get in trouble. It gets in you. Besides, they're just books."

"You're a little bit of a rebel, Mira James."

Chapter 6

The door dinged as Alicia Mealy let herself out, and I searched for anywhere my name would appear. I didn't wear a name tag or announce it anywhere on the front desk, and I didn't post newsletters around town. For someone I'd never met before, she knew a little too much for my comfort.

Or maybe my melancholy was making me paranoid.

It didn't much matter. If all went well today, I'd be gone in two weeks, and Alicia Mealy could turn Battle Lake into a hemp-harvesting, pyramid-worshipping, electrolysis-mandating commune, for all I cared. I shelved the books that'd been dropped off after closing last night, dusted and vacuumed, and had all the résumés arranged by time of interview when Mrs. Berns showed up with Lucy in tow.

"You're both late."

"I'm so sorry, Mira." Lucy looked ready to cry, her wide brown eyes extra glossy and her dusting of freckles disappearing beneath a blush. She was a salt-of-the-earth teenager who somehow managed to find time to volunteer at the nursing home between earning straight As and cheerleading. Her smile lit up a room, and I'd never seen her without a bright-pink ribbon in her hair. Lucy and I met last May, when she offered to work at the library for minimum wage. She'd been a junior in high school at the time and said she loved books more than anything. There wasn't enough money to hire her on regularly, but her earnestness had convinced me to let her help out on an as-needed basis.

"Mrs. Berns called and asked me to pick her up, and when I went to get her, well, it took a little longer than I thought." Lucy glanced uncomfortably from Mrs. Berns to me, then dashed to the back room to grab dusting and watering supplies, her hair ribbon flashing as she hurried away.

"What'd you do to her?" I asked Mrs. Berns, who—I was happy to note—looked exactly like you'd think a little old lady should: tight-curled apricot hair, penciled-in eyebrows, big saggy nose shading a pair of salmon-pink lips, a red Sedona T-shirt one of her grandkids had given her, a pair of white shorts, a huge purple purse, and white bootie socks with flat white tennies. If not for the pair of sharpshooters tucked into her gun belt, you'd want to hug her and call her grandma.

She smiled at me. "We were gettin' jiggy wit it."

I cocked my head. "Have you been watching MTV again?"

"Gotta be a ray of light."

I pursed my lips. "You're just repeating popular song titles back to me."

"Guess you're still not a player," she said, shaking her head. "You should do the evolution. Lucy over there was just helping me out."

More song titles. How much time was she spending in front of the TV? Because no up-north-Minnesota radio station was playing Will Smith, Madonna, Big Pun, *and* Pearl Jam. "How?"

Mrs. Berns yanked a Polaroid out of her pocket. "We pimped my ride."

I held the photo of Mrs. Berns's never-used walker and had to admire the flames on the tennis balls stuck to the bottom of it, as well as the skull-and-crossbones stickers up and down the metal sides. The black plastic streamers coming out the handles were particularly arresting. "Very nice."

She snatched the picture back. "Thought so."

"You ready to work?"

She set her purse on the counter. "I'm here, aren't I?"

I blew air out my mouth and settled in. The plan was for her to run the library as I conducted the interviews, but to check in on all the candidates surreptitiously. That was funny because Mrs. Berns was subtle like an arterial bleed. I figured, though, since she was going to work with whomever I hired, she had a right to weigh in on them.

"How many applicants you got?"

"Four interviews." I indicated the belt she wore. "What's up with those pistols, anyhow?"

"These?" She tugged them out of their holsters and fired a couple rounds toward the ceiling. The smell of sulfur filled the air as the caps popped off. Delicate smoke curled out of each plastic barrel. Lucy, to her credit, didn't jump as she shelved books. "I had such a hoot with them and Randy after the Fourth of July parade that I figured I'd just hang on to them. They make a good conversation piece. Now tell me again why you're leaving town, chickenshit."

"If you promise to stop calling me 'chickenshit.'" It was how she'd been addressing me since I'd told her I was quitting.

She holstered her guns and pretended not to hear me, one of the luxuries of the golden years. I answered her question anyway. "I'm leaving town because there isn't anything here for me. I'm not qualified to be a librarian, I don't get paid enough to be a columnist, and this town is full of wackadoos and murderers."

"Pah, pah, pah, and pah. This town was just fine until Mr. Johnny Leeson ditched you like a deer carcass. Don't you know you're not ever supposed to do anything just because of a man? Don't *stay* for a man; don't *leave* for a man. You make your decisions for yourself. Chickenshit."

I sighed. The door opened, saving me from a chickenshit reply. In walked a woman whose attitude was certainly in its fifties if she was not. Her hair was noosed back in a severe bun, her scraggly eyebrows erupted above her horn-rimmed, bechained glasses, and her nose spread out in an effort to slow its descent into the colorless razor-cut where her lips should have been. Her blouse was gray, as were the sweater tied over her shoulders, the shapeless pencil skirt covering her bony lower body, and her support hose. The only flashes of color were her black orthopedic shoes. She apparently had not gotten the memo that librarians were cool.

"You hire her, girl," Mrs. Berns whispered sharply, "and I'll make her life a living hell."

I believed Mrs. Berns, and I believed it when she said it before, during, and after the next two interviews, one with a statuesque former ballerina who could no longer dance due to a toe injury and the other with a shiny-faced boy fresh out of grad school. The spitballs she lobbed at them along with the fake cat turd she pretended to slip on while I interviewed each ("Ouch, my hip!") cemented their lack of interest in the job.

When the fourth woman strode in at noon, I was frazzled, frustrated, and not optimistic. This candidate resembled a brown-haired Shelley Long, circa *Cheers*, with good posture and a bad perm. She appeared to be in her early forties. She struck me as one of those women who was so pleasant and average as to be almost invisible. According to her résumé, her name was Sarah Ruth O'Hanlon, and she had ten years' experience as an assistant librarian in the Saint Cloud regional library system.

When she shook my hand, her grip was firm and dry.

"Welcome to our library," I said, furtively scanning the room for Mrs. Berns. She'd gone AWOL when she saw Sarah Ruth enter, and I didn't want to imagine the fresh hell she had planned for the latest candidate. I saw only Lucy behind the front desk checking out books and wearing a happy smile.

"Thank you," Sarah Ruth said. "It's lovely, as is this town. I appreciate your time."

When Mrs. Berns leaped up from behind the giant green dinosaur in the kids' reading section and popped a couple caps with her fake gun, followed by a hoot, a holler, and a fart so powerful that I swear it used consonants, Sarah Ruth didn't flinch.

"You're hired," I said.

She appeared confused. "What?"

"Your résumé looks impeccable, and the job starts immediately. Are you interested?"

"Well, I, ah, I guess." She smiled at me, a little frown line appearing between her eyes. "Are you sure you don't want to call my references?"

"Do you think you'd be OK living in Battle Lake?"

"I imagine so. I grew up in a small town, and I have family here." She nodded, convincing herself as she spoke. "I think I'd love it."

"That's all the reference I need." I smiled on the outside. "Can you start training on Monday? I'll stay around for two weeks to show you the ropes, and then you'd take over."

"What will you do after the two weeks are up?" she asked pleasantly.

I blinked, one eye closing sooner than the other. "I'm moving back to the Cities. I just came here to house-sit for a friend for a couple months, and I think my time is up. I'm getting someone else to take over her house, so I can pick up my life where I left off." *Alone, living in a dreary apartment on a depressing street, drinking too much, and cutting classes.*

My nose started to run, so I stood and held out my hand. "See you Monday?"

Sarah Ruth gripped my proffered hand warmly, and rested her free one over it. "I'm excited to start, but sad that it means you'll be leaving. I think you and I would get along great, Ms. James."

I became aware of a tiny silver crucifix on her neck, a miniature version of the one Alicia Mealy had been wearing this morning. Crosses were not unusual, but crucifixes were rarely worn as jewelry in these parts.

"That's an interesting necklace. Do you mind if I ask you where you got it?"

Her hands dropped and moved self-consciously to her throat. "It's a little macabre, don't you think? My niece bought it for me in Mexico, and I wear it out of loyalty. It wouldn't be my first choice in jewelry, given my druthers."

Mrs. Berns, who'd holstered her pistols and army-crawled to the open spot in the middle of the library where I was conducting interviews, saved me from a reply. "Shit or get off the pot," she said.

Sarah Ruth released her necklace. "Excuse me?"

"Either start working, start reading, or get out of the library. This isn't a halfway house."

I helped Mrs. Berns off the floor. "This might be a good time to introduce you two. Mrs. Berns, this is Sarah Ruth. She's going to run the library when I leave."

"You ain't leaving."

I sighed. This was an argument I couldn't win. "Sarah Ruth, Mrs. Berns. Mrs. Berns, Sarah Ruth."

Sarah Ruth chuckled. "It was nice to meet you, Mrs. Berns. I look forward to working with you on Monday."

"If I come." She sniffed. "My social calendar fills pretty quick, you know."

With that, Mrs. Berns went back to shelving books. No more farts, fake cat feces, or gunshots. I took that to mean she liked her new boss. I introduced Lucy to Sarah Ruth, then walked her out into the blazing heat of the early afternoon, wondering at the squishiness of the molten pavement.

"It's a good summer to own a lake home," I offered.

"Yes, I love it."

I smiled politely. My comment had been general, but her response had been specific. When Sarah Ruth slid into her car, waving as she drove away, I returned to the air-conditioned coolness of the library and breathed deeply. I tracked down Mrs. Berns in the reference section, where she was looking up "thespian."

"Huh. Guess Ida wins that bet." She snapped closed the dictionary.

"Sarah Ruth seems nice," I tossed out.

"Humph. If you like those gangly, pear-shaped women with pizzly home perms. Mostly, that type's just good for childbearing, but if you think she can be a librarian, then what do I know?"

I smiled. "You might end up liking her."

Mrs. Berns appeared doubtful. "What's in it for me?"

Lucy appeared from behind the Pla–Sca aisle, a sweet smile on her face. "I thought she was very nice."

I nodded. Lucy looked for the good in everyone and always found it. It wasn't a particularly useful quality in my eyes, but it hung nicely on her. I turned to the back room. "I'm going to get our new shipment cataloged. You know where to find me if anyone needs me."

I'm pretty sure I heard a muttered "chickenshit" as I strode to the back, but it was too quiet to be certain. It could have just been my conscience.

Chapter 7

When Monday scorched around, I hadn't yet screwed up the courage to give Ron Sims, owner, editor, publisher, and adman for the *Battle Lake Recall*, my two weeks' notice. I figured I'd send it in an email today with my two deadlined columns, one on the upcoming August Moon Festival and the other featuring a gnarly recipe for Battle Lake Bites. To that end, I'd risen before the sun and gone into town to fire up the library computer.

I was actually looking forward to the August Moon Festival, my first and last in Battle Lake. Based on my research, the agricultural celebration had a primitive, pagan feel, and I loved any excuse to get back to the dirt. It appealed to my inner gardener. I gathered my notes around me and began a draft of the article in the quiet, predawn library.

August Moon Festival Celebrates the Harvest

Saturday, August 21, marks the 55th annual August Moon Festival in Battle Lake. The festival can be traced back to the mid-1950s, a time of challenges and privation for agricultural west-central Minnesota. In the fourth year of a drought that had ravaged the region, local farmers became desperate. Those who were WWII vets had heard about a Chinese tradition called the August Moon Festival, when families celebrated the harvest with a feast to honor nature's bounty and encourage it to return the next year. The farmers decided they had nothing to lose, and the Minnesota version of the August Moon Festival was born.

Chinese tradition holds that the midautumn festival should be celebrated the 15th day of the eighth lunar month. That worked for local farmers who decided to hold their festival in mid-August to coincide with the wheat and oat harvest. The celebration originally included a community potluck in the streets of Battle Lake, along with dancing and an annual drag race.

The August Moon Festival has since evolved to a potluck masquerade ball held at Hershod's Corn Maze on Highway 210, between Battle Lake and Clitherall. The festival begins at 5:00 p.m. this Saturday and ends at midnight. It is open to the public, and there is no entrance fee if you bring a dish to share; otherwise it's $5 a person. Costumes are optional but encouraged. The band Not with My Horse will be playing from 9:00 p.m. until midnight.

Incidentally, the drought ended shortly after the initial August Moon Festival, and Battle Lake has had green harvests ever since, until this year. It has been nearly four weeks since the last recorded rainfall in Otter Tail County. Hopefully, the celebration this year will once again work its magic.

I winced when I typed the name of the band. The lead singer of Not with My Horse was my ex-boyfriend, who I now referred to as Bad Brad. Brad and I had dated in the Cities, right up until I caught him making skin-flute music with my neighbor's niece. I moved to Battle Lake shortly after.

When Bad Brad's band showed up in July to play a gig at the Battle Lake street dance, he fell in love with the place and took up shop. He was now odd-jobbing during the day and bartending at Stub's and playing with his band at night. Other than one close bikini-wax run-in with Bad Brad and Kennie last month, I had successfully avoided him since he'd moved to town. I was hoping I could maintain my perfect record at the August Moon Festival this Saturday.

I proofed the festival article and put it aside until noon. That was my deadline and would give me enough time to look over the piece with fresh eyes before I zipped it off to Ron. Next on my list was the recipe search. My personal crusade was to find unique recipes that were representative of the oddness, flavor, and overall feel of Battle Lake. I eyeballed the wall clock, too old-fashioned to check the one on my computer, and saw I had an hour before Sarah Ruth showed up for her first day.

I fired up my search engine and typed "Food I'd Never Eat" into the search bar. I came up with worm, lizard, and moose-testicle recipes, but nothing that screamed Battle Lake. I changed my search to "Weird Minnesota Food" and mostly pulled up dishes that were thinly disguised vehicles for Cream of Mushroom soup. I revised my search to "Moving Food," with the thought that I would soon be relocating. I think the computer thought I meant food that moved one's bowels, because I clicked on a whole slew of strange edibles.

I skipped over "Spam Shake" and "Kitty Litter Cake" (complete with Tootsie Rolls as garnish—yum!) as too obvious. I wanted to go out with a bang, with something really wild and memorable. That's when I tripped across it: turdeasant—a turkey stuffed with a duck, stuffed with a pheasant, stuffed with dressing. How grody-toad meaty was that? Three dead birds in one. People'd be eating it long after I'd moved.

The recipe was deceptively simple. You brine all three birds overnight in one cup of salt, one cup brown sugar, and one gallon water.

The next day you heat the roaster to 500°F and shove some Stove Top stuffing into the turkey. Not too much, though, because you've got two more birds moving in. Next, you nestle the duck inside the turkey cavity on its fluffy stuffing bed, and then you grab on to something for leverage and shove that pheasant as deep into the duck as you can. Don't forget to surgically insert the leftover stuffing into any hint of an orifice.

Then comes the final step, the turdeasant coup de grâce. You truss the turkey cavity (read: sew the birdhole) by inserting a metal skewer about one-half inch from the edge of the skin and up through the other side. Next, run butcher's twine between the skin and the skewer and tighten it until you've drawn both sides together. Once that's done, tie together the turkey legs so your hybrid creature resembles a standard turkey. No ducks and pheasants hiding in here, says Dr. Frankenstein!

Finally, you sprinkle paprika on the turkey and roast the turdeasant long enough to brown. After about fifteen minutes, turn the oven down to 325°F and bake for approximately three hours. Remove the turdeasant from the roaster once the innermost bird, the pheasant, is at 170°F. Let it sit for twenty minutes and think about what it's done, and then serve to your ever-lovin', ravenous, knife-wielding family.

I was onto something here. Maybe we could start a pigoosken- or deerlamalina-roasting tradition. Why eat just one animal when you could scarf down a threefer? Sigh. I was going to miss Battle Lake, a little bit. I changed the roasting time on the recipe from three hours to five—I didn't want to get sued for giving someone salmonella—saved the recipe on my computer, and cruised to unlock the front door in anticipation of Sarah Ruth's arrival, as she didn't yet have a key.

At the door, I spotted an oddly dressed family of three making their way down the street. The man was clad in a lightweight black coat and slacks and a preacher's collar, one of the women was in a wheelchair and a turtleneck on this sultry August day, and the younger woman pushing the wheelchair wore a modest dress.

The way she carried herself struck a familiar chord, but I couldn't see her face well under the rolls of dark hair. They must be heading to the apothecary for some odds and ends, I thought, retreating to the library's cool interior.

I grabbed the books out of the after-hours drop bin, relishing their solid feel and the clean, comforting smell of ink on paper. There were five nonfiction (*Jesus: Then and Now, Don't Stand Too Close to a Naked Man, Just Say Yes, Men Are from Mars, Women Are from Venus,* and *Cod: A Biography of the Fish That Changed the World*) and three mysteries. I was on my way to the front computer to enter them into the system as returned when the front door let out its chirpy, muted ding. I turned, expecting to see Sarah Ruth, and instead was greeted by the sight of the somber family I'd just witnessed on the street.

"I'm sorry, but we don't open until ten o'clock. Another twenty minutes or so."

The man smiled widely and offered me his hand. "I'm Pastor Mealy. We're making our way through town and introducing ourselves to the businesspeople."

I darted a glance at the dark-haired woman, the one who had seemed familiar on the street. *Mealy.* Alicia Mealy, the assertive young lady who had stopped by the library on Friday and left without a book. Her transformation from then to now was shocking. She'd gone from pretty and outgoing woman in her early twenties to matronly Christian girl still in high school, makeup-free in her shapeless flowered dress.

The only carryover was the golden crucifix at her neck.

Chapter 8

Alicia Mealy caught my look and gave me a devilish wink, like we shared a secret, and my original take on her was reaffirmed. She was the human equivalent of a Twin Bing candy bar, sweet on the outside and weird and nasty on the inside. Problem was, a lot of people liked Twin Bings, and I bet a lot of people fell for Alicia, too.

I shook the pastor's hand. "I'm Mira James, the librarian. Well, at least for another two weeks, I am."

He nodded distractedly, as if I'd interrupted his chain of thought, and pushed up his old-fashioned, gigantic, rectangular-framed glasses, the kind that only shop teachers and lumber salesmen wore. "This is my wife, Naomi, and our daughter, Alicia."

Naomi held up a bony, beringed hand from her seat in the wheelchair. I shook it, gently, and ignored Alicia's outstretched paw. She dropped it when I returned my attention to her father.

"You're new in town?"

He glanced sharply at Alicia before continuing, and I wondered what he made of the body language between us. "No. We've been here for several months, building up a congregation at the New Millennium Bible Camp, south of Clitherall. Are you familiar with it?"

"I've driven by it on the way to Inspiration Peak."

"Ah, yes. Beautiful area over there. We're very pleased to be part of the community. Tell me, Ms. James, are you a believer?"

The Monkees song—"I'm a believer!"—thrummed irreverently through my head, and it was all I could do not to sing it back to Mr. Mealy. But I resisted, just, fighting down sarcasm, my natural antidote to arrogance in others. "I don't go to church."

I could see him taking stock of me, and my price was dropping. Before he could respond, his wife interjected. "Our faith is the most important thing we have. 'Now faith is assurance of *things* hoped for, a conviction of things not seen'—Hebrews 11:1."

Mr. Mealy looked approvingly at his wife. "Very apt."

"You are the head, Robert. Through God's grace, I am only the neck."

I shivered. Could this be the new minister and his family that Kennie had talked about, the ones who'd slipped inside Gary Wohnt's skull? "You seem like a very close family." My joke was lost on them.

"And we'd like to invite you to be part of our family, Mira. Is it OK if I call you Mira?"

I nodded at Robert Mealy, and he continued. "Although participation in the Bible camp is open to only those who can commit to a week of faith, fun, and fellowship, we've opened the church at the camp to the public for one service Wednesday nights and two services on Sunday. We hope you'll join us."

"Thank you for the invitation, but I'm not really a faith-and-fellowship kind of gal."

"But we're having an open house this Thursday!" Alicia said, handing over a flyer. "You should at least come to see what we have to offer. I'm sure you wouldn't object to having us leave these on the counter, right?"

The flyer was well done, with a lot of white space and not too much distracting information. It listed the name, date, and location of the event, along with the facts that it was open to the public; there would be food, drink, and games; and guests were invited to view the Creation Science Fair put on by local youth.

My question leaked out before I could stem it. "Creation Science Fair? Isn't that an unlikely pairing?" I swear I couldn't help myself. Religious pressure was the worst kind because proponents weren't just bargaining with your social standing; they were holding your very soul at stake.

Pastor Robert's eyes narrowed. "You'll distribute the flyer?"

"I'm afraid I can't. As a state-funded agency, I'm not allowed to promote any religious activity." I was 98 percent sure I was lying, but it sounded better than "I'm afraid you are brain-eating zombies, and if I give you an inch, you will remove my free will and coax me into driving a minivan, staying in the kitchen to cook while the men watch sports in the den, and nervously shushing people when they want to talk about sex, drinking, or public education."

"Ah. I see. I see *clearly*." The pastor snatched the flyer out of my hand and walked past me to the banned-book display. "The state doesn't support religious freedom, but it sponsors blasphemous literature?"

I felt momentarily shamed by the display, like it'd been childish to exhibit banned books and maybe I was about to land in big trouble. Then my shame turned to anger, as it's wont to do. "Those are books. This is a library. In this country, people are allowed to read and to write what they want."

Pastor Robert turned, his eyes unreadable. "Maybe it's not the government that does or doesn't want these things. Maybe it's *you*." He looked down his nose at me. "I won't leave the flyers here, though I know I can. It is my hope you find your way to us in a manner that is comfortable to you. Come, Naomi, Alicia. We have many more friends to make."

Cripes, I hated it when someone took the higher road than me. It rankled to lose at the rock, paper, scissors games that, strung together, made up our lives. I thought about thanking them for coming, decided that would be insincere, and instead made up my mind to avoid them for the next two weeks. Then I would be outta here.

The jangle of the phone startled me, coinciding as it did with the ding of the door as the pastor and his family exited. "Battle Lake Public Library."

"It's Ron Sims at the *Recall.*"

As if there were any other. "Hi, Ron."

"We've got a new family in town." My stomach dropped. It wasn't possible. "The Mealys, over in Clitherall. They're having an open house at New Millennium Bible Camp on Thursday, and you're covering it for the paper."

"I'm leaving, Ron," I spat out. "I'm moving back to the Cities in two weeks."

I hadn't meant to tell him like that. Ron and I had developed a comfortable relationship over the last few months. I ignored the fact that he lacked social skills and was addicted to making out with his wife in public, and he ignored the fact that I couldn't stay out of trouble and regularly disregarded deadlines. I liked him, and I felt like a louse for leaving him with a position to fill.

"You better hurry with that article, then."

"I'll miss you, too."

Click.

I was left with the phone in my hand and a quiet smile on my lips. Ron was nothing if not consistent. I sighed and squared my shoulders. I'd cover the open house, but I wouldn't like it.

I went back to the books I had been about to enter in the computer when the Mealys had shown up. When the door donged again, I turned, clenched, to see who else this morning was going to deliver up.

Chapter 9

"I'm so sorry I'm late! The first day on the job and I'm not on time. I feel like an ass." Sarah Ruth's long, kinky hair was coming loose from her ponytail, and she tried to stuff it back up as she spoke. Problem was, her hands were covered in black, which she was transferring to her hair.

I took it all in from behind the front desk. "What happened to you?"

"Flat tire. Thank God it happened over by Koep's gas station in Clitherall. I never did learn how to change one of those by myself."

My eyes dropped to her greasy hands. "Someone changed it for you?"

She nodded. "Yes, an attendant at the station."

"Then what's all that black stuff?" I asked, pointing.

Sarah Ruth held her hands palm up and chuckled. "I held the nuts for him. They must have been covered in oil. I can be such a ding-dong. I bet I got it all over my hair, didn't I?"

I smiled. "Yeah. You can use the bathroom in back to wash up. You didn't miss much, by the way. We're not quite open yet."

"Oh, good." Some of the stress melted off her face. "I'll be right back."

I proofed and then emailed the two articles to Ron, and when Sarah Ruth returned, I showed her the library opening processes, went over the book sections, and talked about our more colorful clientele. When it was time for Monday Madness, the moniker I'd affectionately given to the kids' reading hour, she helped to keep the wilder ones interested as I narrated *The Monster at the End of This Book* (I did a mean Grover).

Reading to kids was the part of this job I would miss the most. They were so sweet, not a cynical one in the bunch, and when they started laughing at the stories, the hilarity passed through the whole group like a happy flu until everyone was doubled over. Some Mondays it sounded like a calliope of giggles in the kids' corner, and all it took was a book with a talking monkey. At first it threw me that some of them liked to sit on my lap as I read, playing with my hair or turning the pages for me, and then I began to look forward to their wiggling warmth.

Sarah Ruth seemed to enjoy the toddlers and preschoolers as much as I did, which gave me a comfortable liquid feeling rare this past month. She was pleasant, smart, and a quick learner, and I was amazed to see that it was one in the afternoon. "Jeez. I've been working you like a dog. Why don't you take your lunch break?"

She glanced at the clock. "I've got a better idea. How about I get us some grilled cheese and french fries from the Shoreline, and we can have a picnic in back? I hate to leave you for an hour when it's this busy."

"Deal," I said, smiling. "Bring lots of ketchup."

As closing time on Sarah Ruth's first day rolled near, I dare say I was in a sunny mood. I was leaving the library in good hands, and that made me satisfied, if not happy. When Tina Mathison strolled in, a basket of Nut Goodies in hand, I amped it up another notch.

Tina, along with her husband, owned the business four doors down from the library—Tom and Tina's Taxidermy and Trinkets, which everyone called 4Ts. Tom stuffed animal cadavers and gave them marble eyes in the back room while Tina sold reasonably priced high-quality silver and pewter jewelry in the front. We didn't know one another socially, but Tina was a frequent library patron, and I made a point of stopping by her store to buy up some of her great Bali earrings and bracelets.

I waved her over. "Come by to give our new librarian a welcome basket?"

"Actually, Mira, it's for you." For the first time, I noticed Tina's normally bright face was sagging. In her late fifties, she told anyone who'd ask she'd escaped most of the calling cards of age by staying out of the sun and eating right. She normally had pleasant wrinkles around her eyes and lips, but otherwise appeared youthful. Today, though, her mouth was pulled down in a rare frown, and grayish bags puffed up her eyes.

"Are you OK?"

She forced a smile, but it didn't make it to her blue eyes. "Not really. I need your help, and I've come with a shameless bribe."

"And you know my weak spot. There's enough Nut Goodies here to get me through a month!" I swallowed the bonus saliva produced at the sight of so many vividly red-and-green wrappers. Inside each was a little bit of heaven created by the geniuses at Pearson's, a Minnesota candy company. They made salted nut rolls, too, which were good, but they weren't *nut* good, if you know what I mean. I had a true addiction to the chocolate- and peanut-covered maple candies. I'd lately been using the treat like methadone to wean me off my returning liquor habit, but based on the contents of this basket, I was past due for a little hedonism.

"There's more than candy in there," Tina said.

I swiveled the basket and jumped when I saw two beady black eyes staring back at me. "What is it?"

"A ferret. It died of natural causes, and the owner never came back for it after Tom stuffed it." She shrugged. "I figured you could put it in your living room. I also got you a pile of those beaded elastic bracelets you like so much."

Talk about a mixed bag. I flipped it back around so I could see only the Nut Goodies and not the dead creature fraternizing with them. "Thanks, but I'm sure I don't need all this. I'd be happy to help out, if I can."

Tina glanced at Sarah Ruth, who took the cue and headed to the rear of the library to shelve books. "This is uncomfortable," Tina began, her voice low and her eyes flicking toward the front door, "but I don't know who else to turn to. I can't go to the police because it'll look like I can't run my business. Besides, I don't want any of my girls to go to jail. I just want to talk to them, give them a second chance."

Her nervousness was contagious. "Back up a little. Go to jail for what?"

"I think one of my clerks is embezzling from the store. Money is missing from the till at least twice a week, but it's not specific to anyone's shift." Two red circles bloomed on her cheeks. "Tom or I are there all the time, but I go on short buying trips most weeks and that leaves him working in the back room. He can't keep an eye on the store every second."

"You've talked to Tom about this?"

"Yes." Her head bobbed. "He's upset, but I made him promise to give me a chance to figure out what was going on before we tried the police. You know Annika, the new girl I hired? The embezzling started around the same time she did."

I thought through who'd been behind the counter last time I stopped by. "She's the one from Henning, the tall blonde?"

"Yes. She just graduated from high school last year and is working part-time for me before she starts at the tech school in Alexandria come fall."

"Have you thought about just confronting her?"

Tina wrung her hands. "But what if I'm wrong? That would be a terrible way to treat her if she's innocent. But if she's guilty, I want to lend a hand, not arrest her. Can you help?"

I grimaced. "I'm not sure how."

"Just stop by and check things out. You're so good at figuring out these little local mysteries! See if you can, you know, pick up any clues. You can talk to each of the girls and fill me in on what your intuition tells you." She clasped her hands in a begging gesture. "I'd be forever grateful."

I didn't know how good I was at solving mysteries. I had a natural curiosity, certainly, and more than my share of nosiness, but it seemed like mostly I was just in the wrong place at the wrong time. In fact, I could go my whole life without finding another dead body, killer, or fiberglass statue. I wanted to turn this down, but Tina's long face made up my mind. "Well, for a basket of Nut Goodies, how can I resist?"

"Thank you! You've got a good heart."

"I think I just have a sweet tooth," I said, smiling. "I can't promise anything, though, and I won't spread rumors. Unless I see clear evidence of stealing, I won't have anything to report."

"Fine. Can you start today? Here's the girls' schedules. Two of them are working until eight o'clock tonight, Kaitlyn and Annika. They're both working tomorrow. Wednesday it's Jennifer and Annika."

"Annika is working all three days?"

"Just this week. We're doubling our shifts to cover the extra crowds in town for the August Moon Festival."

I wrote down the schedule, and after Tina left, I named the ferret Nut Goodie and stashed it in the window near the kids' section. I figured I could work it into a story or two and give the children some cheap thrills. I tucked the bracelets in my prize box. I liked to reward the kids for meeting their reading goals and had collected various curios the last few months. The actual Nut Goodies, I saved for myself.

Once an addict, always an addict.

A voice broke into my musing. "You really like this job, don't you?"

"Huh?" I was so into organizing the new treasures that I hadn't heard Sarah Ruth return.

"You were smiling just now while you were working."

I scowled. "Was not."

She chuckled softly. "I love being a librarian, too. We get to be the ultimate teachers, only with no papers to grade. Connect someone with a book, and they get to travel to exotic places, learn how to build a greenhouse, or reach out to their children by reading to them. It's exhilarating."

"That's a Happy Hannah way of looking at it, I suppose."

"You suppose," she said, shaking her head kindly. "Well, you're good at your job, Mira, and people appreciate it. You know everyone who's walked through that door by name."

"It's a small town," I grumbled. I wasn't a fan of having sunshine blown up my skirt.

"It's a small town, and you're their librarian. They're going to miss you, and miss the courage it takes to do something like a banned-books display."

I needed to nip this in the bud. "Why don't we go over the closing routine? I've made a list of the procedures, though you can certainly change any of them if you find something that works better."

Why was it so hard to hear nice things about myself?

Chapter 10

We worked quietly, me to recover from the ill-fitting praise and her because she was taking notes as I showed her where to dump the garbage, where the vacuum cleaner was stored, the book-check rotation so all the shelves were reviewed at least once a month to make sure everything was Dewey decimalized, and all the other small tasks that were undertaken between four and six p.m.

When we locked up and parted ways, I steered myself toward 4Ts. My plan was to observe Annika and Kaitlyn and see if I could pick up anything suspicious. I wasn't hopeful, but I owed Tina that much. Plus, I'd be right across from the Turtle Stew and could grab something for supper.

The night was shimmery with heat, and everything had that too-bright, post-camera-flash look of drought. The bits of remaining grass on Lake Street's boulevard were as brown and sharp as hay, and the heavily watered municipal planters with their pansies, vivid and cheerful gerbera daisies, alyssum, and devil's ivy seemed frivolous. Granny's Pantry, the local candy store and ice cream parlor, was so full that people were lined up outside. Those who had their double-dip waffle cones in hand were in a hopeless race to lick the rapidly melting ice cream before it ran past the tiny marshmallow sealing the cone bottom. This weather was bad for farmers and good for business, I thought, turning into 4Ts.

The store was packed, jammed with sunburned tourists just off the lake and looking for distraction and relief from the heat. The small, crowded front room that made up the Tina portion of the shop smelled of coconut sunscreen and pine-scented mosquito repellent. I wove my way over to the ring display at the back of the store near the till, hundreds of handcrafted silver circles displayed in black velvet. They were plain, or had semiprecious stones like amethyst and garnet cleverly worked into them, or held intricate designs. It was a wonder *everyone* didn't steal from Tina, what with all this glittery splendor within easy reach.

Behind the counter, two young women, Annika and presumably Kaitlyn, smiled as they answered questions and rang up sales. They were both comfortable with their jobs, reaching smoothly around one another to grab gift wrapping, a calculator, a ring sizer. Kaitlyn was a typical Battle Lake high school graduate—fresh, blue-eyed, and blonde. She was curvy and wore a royal-blue sundress that showed off her strong shoulders.

Annika was also blonde, but her height set her apart from the crowd. She was at least six feet tall, maybe a little more. She dressed boldly for a tall woman, wearing a hot-pink tank top over an acid-green and yellow skirt. I remembered those colors from my high school years in the '80s. They didn't look good then, but it might have been because they couldn't compete with the big hair with claw bangs, *Dynasty* eye makeup, and pinned jeans we all wore with them. On Annika, the colors appeared electric. They almost distracted from the very expensive-looking jewelry dripping from her wrists, fingers, neck, and ears.

I grabbed from the display box a tiny yin-yang ring that I could give away to one of the kids next Monday and made my way to the till. Kaitlyn was free, but my target, Annika, was busy, so I pretended to dig through the basket of elastic toe rings at the front counter. When a woman as pink and skinny as a newborn pig asked Kaitlyn for help clasping a necklace, I pounced on my prey.

"Hi! Can I buy this ring?"

"You sure can. Those are very popular this week."

"I guess, with the festival coming up on Saturday. Say, aren't you from Henning?"

She studied me curiously before removing the price string from my purchase. "Born and raised. Are you from there?"

"No, I live in Battle Lake. I've seen you around, though. I work at the library."

"Oh, sure. You're Mira, right?"

"Right. Oh jeez, that's gorgeous," I said, pointing to her tennis bracelet of tiny green jewels. "Did you get that here?"

She smiled. "No. We've got nice stuff here, but it's more for the tourist crowd, you know?"

"Sure." On her other wrist she wore four bangles that appeared to be real gold. She also had matching earrings and a necklace, each with a larger teardrop version of the green gem. Her fingers sparkled as well.

For all I knew, she could be wearing $19.95 worth of cubic zirconia or $1,995 worth of emeralds. Either way, Tina must certainly have noticed the extravagance, so I didn't have anything new to report. Besides, the fact that Annika owned nice-looking jewelry didn't prove a thing. "You guys get much shoplifting here?"

"We've got mirrors," she said, nodding over my shoulder. "We try to keep a good eye on things, but sometimes people get a five-finger discount. It's mostly ladies in their fifties, if you can believe that." She took my money, made change, and handed the package to me.

"Thank you," I said.

I glanced at Kaitlyn on my way out. She was the picture of youthful innocence, and I didn't want to ask her questions in front of Annika. They would be sure to talk about it after I left, and if one of them was the embezzler, she'd be on her guard. I'd come back on a day when only Kaitlyn was working, or Kaitlyn and the other girl, to see if they'd offer anything about Annika. Of course, since the stealing wasn't shift-specific, two of them could be in cahoots, but that seemed unlikely. Stealing from a till seemed like an activity best done alone.

I strolled over to the Turtle Stew and relished the familiar sight of the red Naugahyde booths, bustling waitstaff, and tables crammed with hungry, happy people. It smelled like fresh-baked bread and slow-cooked meats, with an undercurrent of sauerkraut or some other exotic German fare. The Stew was a full-service restaurant with a setup bar, which meant that if you wanted hard liquor, you had to bring it yourself. The locals were usually four to a table, a pair of couples who would play 500 or Solo after supper, a big bottle of Canadian Club in a hand-crafted carry case between them. Out-of-towners sipped wine or 3.2 beer, which you could buy on-site.

When it was my turn to order, I picked one of my favorites, my tummy feeling warm at the thought of the comfort food. "Tuna casserole, green beans, and a salad with french dressing on the side. Can I get sunflower seeds on that? And it's to go."

I read the community board as I waited, my food-anticipation high dulled by the thought that this might be the last time I'd buy takeout from the Stew.

Oh well. I can always visit.

In less than twelve hours, I'd gladly have given a kidney to return to the normalcy of this moment.

Chapter 11

I woke early on Tuesday morning, feeling so organized that I managed to take Luna for a forty-five-minute walkjog before I headed off to work. It was hot as an orange stovetop ring outside, but I was in too good a mood to complain.

I'd found a fantastic librarian to take my place and do a much better job than I ever could, Ron Sims knew I was leaving and hadn't been mad, and I had my whole future ahead of me. Starting over was hard, I acknowledged, but I was brave for trying. I wasn't a quitter—I was a *leader*. I'd missed the deadline to accept a past professor's offer of being his research assistant, but when I called him up, he said he might have something winter quarter. In the meanwhile, I could get settled in Minneapolis and force some direction back in my life.

That's what I told myself as I steered the Toyota along snaky Whiskey Road, one bare foot with blue-painted toenails resting on the driver's side window, the other on the gas pedal. I was heading to work three hours early to scour the library from top to bottom and get it ready for its new boss. I reached over to crank up the Tom Petty song leaking out my stereo and riding the acrid air, wondering about the high whine in the song, almost like a siren. I'd never noticed it before. Maybe my ears were getting more refined.

That's when I spied the cherries in my rearview mirror.

"Curse words!" I yanked my leg down. It wasn't illegal to drive with one foot up, was it?

I slowed the car, my heart racing, and pulled off on a flat spot. I squinched my eyes shut and tried to hide in my shoulders, hope hope *hoping* it wasn't Gary Wohnt. We didn't get along so well when he was a regular guy. Now that he had Jesus in his life, I was sure he was going to be that much crabbier.

When the Battle Lake police car raced past, scaring up dust on the shoulder as it swerved around me, my head shot up like a turtle. I hadn't been the target! I peeled out after the royal-blue vehicle without thinking. A police car in a full rush at seven a.m. meant something terrible had happened, probably an accident or a fire. What if it was Mrs. Berns hurt, or Johnny Leeson's poor mom, or even, I supposed, Kennie Rogers? I was better off being at the scene to help rather than growing gray hairs at work, worrying about my friends.

The cop car had a good lead on me, but I could hear its sirens to the south as I hit Larry's Grocery, so I turned right toward 210. I spotted it zooming toward Clitherall, tractors, pickups, and minivans pulling off the road to let it through. I knew everyone who saw it race by had a freezy grip on their heart like mine, wondering if it was their neighbor, their husband or wife, their child that the police were speeding to save.

I was cruising seventy-five miles an hour, but as I crested the hill where I could turn left to enter Clitherall or right to go to Koep's Korner, it became chillingly obvious there wasn't anyone available to write me a ticket. A half a mile ahead of me, all three local police cars were turning north.

I rode the brakes, recognizing the back road they were veering onto. Clitherall Car Wash, the locals called it, because it took a sharp turn that no one was ever prepared for, particularly a person leaving Bonnie & Clyde's. To the east of the razor curve was a large swamp, complete with cattails and sludge, that had christened many a vehicle full of drunk teenagers, tipsy housewives, and beer-chugging farmers.

As I turned down the Clitherall Car Wash road, a heavy, salty-bitter taste formed in the back of my throat. Somebody was seriously in trouble and potentially very hurt, and I was about to find out who.

I flashed back to the night the police had called my mom and me in to identify my dad's car. His body had been burned too severely for a visual identification, but it's hard to significantly alter the appearance of a 1973 Cordoba. It had been bent like a Coke can under a giant's fist, the stench of cooked flesh still strong on it.

Somehow, by the next fall, the Paynesville driver's ed instructor had gotten his hands on the wrecked vehicle and set it up as a permanent "don't drink and drive" display, one that I was forced to walk past to get to school my senior year. Even though the interior had been power-washed, I still imagined that smell, was embarrassed by it, was certain all my classmates could also smell my dad roasting next to an open bottle of vodka.

I never wanted to witness something like that again, but I couldn't help myself. I was convinced someone I knew had been hurt. I numbly noted the orange-trimmed fishing shack to the left, contrasting with the bright-green swamp grass of the shoulder against wheat-brown cattails to the right. Then I registered a group of people standing in the ditch at a low point in the road, at the spot just before it shrieked left toward Bonnie & Clyde's.

I parked a hundred feet away from the gathering. I slid out of my car, the sound of the door clicking shut behind me muffled in the oppressive air. I floated toward the police cars, hearing but not understanding the shrill buzz of a woman, weeping. No one noticed me as I rounded the police car closest to the group and walked down through the sand-sprayed grass.

I smelled it before I saw it, that metallic, gory smell of violent death, playing through the fresh country air. A cluster of police surrounded the weeping woman to my left, and straight ahead two more officers crouched around a female shape face down on the ground.

It was her hand I noticed first, unwrinkled, taut, spread out on the ground like she was jumping off a barn beam into a pile of hay and hadn't yet landed. She was no farther away from me than a clerk at a drive-through, but I felt like years and miles obscured her. Around me, people buzzed and moved, but I felt invisible.

I followed the arm up past the bracelet, noting the dark-green cloth covering it. Her hair was long, dark, and messy, splayed over her head like a fright wig where it wasn't matted with blood, a bedraggled pink ribbon still tangled in it. My eyes skimmed over the dip in her back, about the size of a baby's fist, couldn't process that detail, and traveled over to where her other arm should be. I couldn't see it.

It must be twisted under her.

She was wearing a skirt, short, pleated, and trimmed in white. Her legs were bare, firm and strong, and on her feet were white socks and sneakers. One shoe was untied, and the leg it was on was twisted gruesomely around so her toes were almost pointing up at the bright, unforgiving sky. I glanced back at the depression in her torso, relatively clean and round at the entrance point, though it looked like it had been made with an elephant gun.

The dead girl was a cheerleader, and she'd been shot in the back.

"What are you doing here?"

I couldn't pull my eyes away. They were stuck on that murky hole and the missing flesh that should have protected her heart. I fancied I could see the bright grass underneath her through the wound, but then realized it was mucky bones, shattered, sharpened, and reflecting sunlight.

"I said, what are you doing here?"

A hand grabbed me, roughly, and I caught a glimpse of Gary Wohnt before I wobbled to the other side of the road and threw up. Between retches, I scoured the ditch for more dead bodies, or body parts, but the grossest thing on this side of the street was coming out of my mouth. When my stomach settled, so did my ears. I heard the woman who'd found the cheerleader describe how she was staying at a local resort and had been jogging when she came across the body. The tourist was near hysterical and had nothing to offer.

I spit and wiped my mouth with the back of my hand. I felt empty, but far from cleansed. My nose and throat burned, and I needed a shower.

I knew that dead girl.

Chapter 12

I lurched into my house like brain-eating zombies really had attacked me. Tiger Pop and Luna followed. When I tumbled onto my couch, Luna snuffled my hand and Tiger Pop lay across my lap. My head was empty except for the picture of the ragged wound in Lucy's back—Lucy, who loved books more than anything and always looked for the best in people.

I wondered if her parents knew yet, if they were just puttering around their house, waiting for her to get home from summer cheerleading practice, if Gary Wohnt was about to knock on their door and ruin their lives. Lucy's parents were dairy farmers, the old-fashioned kind who believed in hard work and good manners. They were also the ones who'd given Lucy the lovely gold charm bracelet with red dangling hearts on it that I had seen on her cold gray wrist as she lay sprawled in the ditch. Because of that, I would have recognized her even if she hadn't been wearing the pink ribbon.

Dark thoughts chased each other in my head like wild animals, their claws ripping and slashing until I had a bleeding muscle of a headache. I don't know if I passed out or fell asleep, but when I next looked at the clock, I'd lost an hour. It was nine a.m., and I was soaked in sweat.

I concentrated on the blinking numbers on my VCR, orienting myself to the room, the house, the town, the planet. None of it felt right. All I knew for sure was that I was in Battle Lake, and sweet young Lucy—the girl who was going to Saint Cloud State after her senior year to major in elementary education, who liked to party with her friends but always showed up for work early and with a smile on her face—had been shot in the back. I stumbled off the couch and stepped out into the oppressively hot day.

A cow lowed in the distance, and I could hear families already splashing in the lake near the Shangri-La Resort. My sweet garden stretched out in front of me like a black, freshly dug grave. I strolled over to it, walking lightly, and bent down to rub my cheek against the soft and spicy tomato leaves. For the whole month of June, I'd eaten fresh lettuce, radishes, and peas. As those crops waned, cherry, pear, and beefsteak tomatoes, baby potatoes, kale and chard, and onions replaced them.

All the plants were robust and tall, and it was easy to separate the week's growth of weeds from them. I plucked and pulled for several minutes, moving back and forth to put weeds on the same pile. I tasted salt and dirt as I worked, the combination of steamy air and dusty soil making for a fine layer of black earth clinging to my moist skin.

My weed pile was not impressive, but then again I was meticulous about my garden. Here was my order and structure. It was the one place in this whole world where I could feel safe and necessary. I could nurture without being seen and without fear of criticism, permanent loss, or shame. I gathered up the weeds and tucked them around the base of my three cabbages, each of them nestled in a bottom- and topless giant tomato can, shoved deep into the earth to keep grubs from destroying the roots. The weeds would keep the moisture in and deter new weeds from taking root.

My brief bout of gardening finished, I stood up and heard both knees creak. The sprinkler lay next to the plot, where it had been earning its keep and then some for the last four weeks. I centered the oscillating waterer and cranked the faucet on the side of the house, watching the cool water spurt into the air before it got sucked greedily into the bone-dry earth. The sprinkles were a soothing, soft rain feeding my hungry plants.

Without any concrete plan, I stripped off my clothes and lay down next to the sprinkler, between the potatoes and peppers. The oaks and lilacs were thick around my yard, creating a natural barrier to any wandering eyes, but it wouldn't have mattered, because at the moment, I didn't feel connected to this world's rules.

As the water washed over my naked body, making tiny clean spots on my dirty skin and reflective pools in my tender parts, I became aware of my own roots leaking into the ground, looking for purchase. Water began to puddle, seeking out the powdery dirt still protected under my back. I thought I heard the plants sigh.

I got up, turned off the water, and went inside to get ready for work all over again.

Chapter 13

I opened the library a half an hour late, seeing Lucy's million-dollar smile in the books, the plants, the furniture. I even thought I heard her giggle once, but when I went to the stacks where I thought it had come from, no one was there. The library was a lonely place to be on this day, and I was grateful when the door opened, even if it was Kennie who walked through it. We hadn't seen each other since she'd melted on my couch in July.

"I see you've pissed off God," she said.

"What?"

The question was as much directed at her outfit as at her declaration. She was dressed in head-to-toe leather, from the animal-skin headband holding back her brittle platinum hair to the bedazzled vest to the chaps over tight leather pants that would make Cher feel exposed. I looked over her shoulder at the shimmering heat rising off the paved parking lot and back at her tightly sealed body. All I could think was, *Mushroom farm.*

She thrust a stapled sheaf of papers at me. "See for yourself."

Her outrageously orange lipstick curled in a smile, nearly colliding with her Anna Nicole–esque fake eyelashes. The sheaf was a petition, and the cause being supported was succinctly and clearly stated at the top: "Ban the Battle Lake Public Library until decency returns. Sign below if you support removal of the GODLESS literature currently being promoted." Alicia Mealy's signature was the first, followed by 112 others, including Gary Wohnt, Elvis Aron Presley, and Ima Pigglicker.

"Jesus. Where'd you get this?"

"I'm the mayor of this town, and I got my finger on the pulse," she said indignantly. "You're lucky we're friends, so I can look out for you. I'm passing this on as a heads-up, but it's just one of three going around town. People can't sign it fast enough."

My hands shook in anger laced with fear, both emotions amplified by this morning's tragedy. How *dare* the Mealys try to tell people what books they could and couldn't read, and turn librarians into censors! But even more troubling, could they force me to take down the banned-books display? Was I about to get the library in big trouble? Well-stocked libraries with decent hours were an endangered species in today's political climate.

"Can I keep this?" I asked.

She brushed a crispy lock of hair back from her face. "It's all yours, darlin'."

I folded the petition carefully, squeezing my fingers tightly along the creases. My voice cracked as I asked my next question. I knew it was Lucy in that ditch, but I couldn't bear to say her name out loud. "What do you know about the dead girl in Clitherall?"

Kennie drew up tall, making a *squeak-woof* sound that I prayed was only leather on leather. "How do you know about that?"

"A little birdie told me." I don't know why I said that. I hated that phrase.

"Since Gary has found God, it takes a little longer for me to get my information, but you're gonna find out soon enough. She was that girl you had working here part-time. A real sweetheart, by all accounts, about to start her senior year. Lucy Lebowski. She'd been missing since cheerleading camp the night before. A jogger found her shot in the back."

My legs started shivering. I reached out to the counter for support. "Do they know who killed her?"

"They're interviewing her coach, the girls who saw her last, but they don't have anything solid right now. Why? You gonna solve another murder?"

I was suddenly reluctant to tell Kennie I was moving and so wouldn't be around long enough. "Not if I can help it."

She was studying me closely, her eyes glittering. "Be sure to stop by my house later. I have a new business proposition for you."

I nodded absently. When she left, I went online, feeling jittery and insignificant. I needed to erase the picture of Lucy's corpse from my mind, and I wanted to distract myself from the dangerous and irrational anger I was feeling toward the Mealys' petition. Sure, it sucked that they were organizing meanness toward books, but I knew if it weren't for the stress of Lucy's murder, I would be able to put it in perspective.

To get my mind off things I couldn't change, I settled for researching a passive-aggressive anti-church recipe for the column the week after next. I landed on "Devil's Food Cupcakes with Sinfully Rich Frosting." I typed up the recipe and sent it off to Ron, who would probably pop a zipper when he realized I was turning something in before deadline.

As I clicked the "Send" button, I thought about my teen years, something I'd been doing a lot this month. My last up-close and personal encounter with organized religion had happened in high school. My mom had turned to the church, as many women in abusive relationships do, and been advised to stick it out for the betterment of her family. I was certain that if her minister hadn't told her that her marriage was a test of her strength and faith, she would have left my dad.

Probably he still would've died a stupid death, but Mom and I wouldn't have had to have front-row seats. I wouldn't have been forced to walk past that stinking car every school day for a year, wouldn't have needed to wonder what people were whispering about when I walked by. But my mom was urged to keep her family intact—told, in fact, that that was what God wanted.

A worse plan I've never seen executed.

That was enough religion for a lifetime for this girl.

I was relieved when the front door opened. I looked up, hoping to see Sarah Ruth coming in to help. I could tell her about Lucy and maybe share the burden, and come up with a battle plan to deal with the petition.

Instead, in walked a man wearing a cape.

Chapter 14

In this life, there are some things you can be sure of. One of them is that a man wearing a cape in Minnesota in August wants you to ask him some questions. I wasn't in the mood.

"Hello!" He walked toward me, his hand outstretched.

Except for the slick black cape—which was more of a capelet, I amended—he was average-looking. Tall, maybe six four, with the awkward body of a man whose bones grew faster than his muscles. His dark hair was mussed and hanging over tiny, round John Lennon glasses. He grinned at me lopsidedly, making his unremarkable nose tug up over the left nostril.

"I'm Weston Lippmann," he said.

We appeared to be about the same age, so I dropped the formalities. "Hi, Weston. I'm Mira. New in town?"

"Pleased to meet you, and I sure am." I thought I detected a soft southern accent, a natural one Kennie would kill for. "But I'm not going to be here for very long. I'm a researcher around for a few weeks, and I was hoping you could point me in the right direction."

I couldn't help it. My curiosity was piqued. "What're you researching?"

"Wood ticks. I'm the curator of the United States National Tick Collection, which is currently housed at Georgia Southern University."

Aaaannnnnddd curiosity deflated. "The collection travels?"

"Yes! Just like wood ticks." He smiled apologetically.

"Mind if I ask what's up with the cape?"

His cheeks reddened. "A personal eccentricity. I'm not fond of birds. They have a bothersome habit of, um, dropping on me. If I'm going to spend a lot of time outdoors, it makes more sense to wear this so I can wipe off any leavings."

"No way!" All my judgment of him immediately melted away. It's embarrassingly relieving when you find you share a neurosis with another person. "Birds don't like me, either."

"Really?" He wasn't sure if I was teasing him.

I nodded. "I think it's because I accidentally killed one when I was a little girl. I found a nest, transplanted it to my sock drawer, and forgot about it. Ever since then, birds lunge at and generally harass me. People think I'm weird."

His eyes glowed as we bonded over our shared peculiarities, two lone geeks at the prom comparing pocket protectors. "Me too."

There was an awkward silence, which I struggled to fill. "So, you ran outta ticks in Georgia to study?"

He made a funny throat-clearing noise. "Right now we've got more than 123,000 ticks in our museum, but I had some vacation time coming up, so I figured I'd head north. I'm looking for information on a new breed of deer tick reported in west-central Minnesota."

"That's a vacation?"

"Well, I don't normally do fieldwork. Not anymore. But I love it, and I have some family not far from here, so I thought I'd combine work and pleasure."

"Hmm. Well, good luck with that." He and I had very different ideas of what constituted pleasure. "What do you want to find here? In the library, I mean."

"Do you have any locally published history? Farmers' journals, business ledgers, and the like?"

I mentally scanned my holdings. "Most of that you can find at the Otter Tail County Historical Society in Fergus Falls, about twenty miles up 210. I do have a copy of *After the Battle*, though. It's a pretty interesting history of Battle Lake, put together by the Centennial Committee when the town turned a hundred."

"Perfect!"

I directed him to the spiral-bound book in the reference section in the rear of the library and was startled to find Sarah Ruth settled behind the front counter when I returned. "I didn't even hear the front door open!" I said.

She smiled sadly, looking a little ashen. "All librarians are quiet. Who've you got in back?"

"Just a guy in a cape. Pay him no mind."

"Whatever you say." Her acceptance of the eccentricities this town threw at her amazed me. She twisted her crucifix necklace around her finger, and her mood darkened. "Did you hear about poor Lucy? Shot and left for dead in a ditch in Clitherall this morning."

My stomach bucked. "She wasn't shot in the ditch."

"What?"

I didn't realize I'd said it out loud, or that I had even been conscious of that detail, until I heard my own voice. "She was lying in a ditch, but there was no blood spatter near her." The deep ache returned as I thought of Lucy's last moments. "I don't know a lot about guns, but I do know you can't shoot someone in the back without leaving a pretty mess. Whoever murdered her did it before they tossed her into that ditch."

Sarah Ruth hurried over and threw an arm around me. "You poor thing! You actually saw that horrible scene?"

Weston reappeared. "Oh! I'm sorry." He pushed his glasses up his nose with his index finger and glanced from Sarah Ruth to me, obviously uncomfortable. "I didn't mean to interrupt. I . . . It's just that, is there any chance I can check this out?" He held up a red, white, and blue copy of *After the Battle*.

I stepped away from Sarah Ruth and sucked a deep breath, all business. "No, but the newspaper sells them. I think they're twenty dollars a copy."

"The *Battle Lake Recall*, right? Where's their office?"

"Right next to the post office. Go left out of here on Lake Street and you can't miss it—right across the street from the Village Apothecary."

"Would they also have information on any sort of community gatherings, sports events in the summer, that sort of thing?"

"I suppose."

He flicked his cape at me and smiled shyly. "Thanks, Mira. I hope to see you again."

He went back to return *After the Battle*. As he passed me on the way out, I said, "Watch out for the flying lizards."

He gave me a double thumbs-up. "You know it."

With him gone, I didn't know what to say to Sarah Ruth. Her hug had thrown me off, so I returned to familiar territory—righteous anger. The banned-books petition reasserted itself at the forefront of my mind. "Do you know about the ministry over at the New Millennium Bible Camp in Clitherall?"

She smiled distantly. "Yes. I went to services there last week. It's right up the road from where I'm staying."

"Really?" I wanted her to be as upset as I was. I was pretty sure she hadn't recently been stood up and ditched across state lines by a very hot landscaper, gotten skunk drunk with a zaftig woman in bike shorts, or seen a young and sweet, tragically murdered cheerleader, but I knew there was one knob I could twist to get her tweaked. "Did you know those zealots are sending a petition around town to shut us down?"

Her eyebrows met over her nose. "Shut down the library?"

"Well, at least shut down our banned-book display." She still wasn't getting on my anger train. I tried again. "Who are they to say which books people can and can't read?"

"Are you sure you have that right? The Mealys seem like nice people, very supportive when I told them I was a librarian."

I grimaced. "Next time you're at one of their services, would you mind letting it drop that we're not the enemy here?"

"Of course."

I wish that I could have left it at that, but patience was not a virtue I possessed. That's when I had a wild thought: it was time to crank up the Pat Benatar, dig out the glitter eye shadow, and come out swinging.

I had just the plan to restore a little justice to the world, and tomorrow afternoon would be the perfect time to put it into play.

Chapter 15

The next day at the library couldn't pass fast enough. When I wasn't able to stand it any longer, I gave Sarah Ruth the keys and asked if she would mind closing up.

I had one final obligation to fulfill before I could slip undercover. I'd promised Tina I'd stop by her store and see what I could discover about Jennifer, the employee I hadn't yet met. It'd also give me a chance to see if I could find out any more about Annika, the suspicious worker. I would much rather be putting my excellent plan into play, but I'd given Tina my word.

When I stepped out of the library, the hazy, hot air was as heavy as a hand pushing down. Everyone around me was wilting and hugging the sparse shade beneath business awnings. Across the street, a gaggle of children held rapidly melting Popsicles, grape and orange sticky-juice running down their arms. If we didn't get relief from this weather soon, the lakes were going to be full of boiled fish.

I spotted Annika before I entered 4Ts. She was in the front display window rearranging some walleye, wood ducks, and beaded earrings. I waved as I entered. "Nice day to get in from the heat!" I said.

She smiled. "Can you hold this bird for me for a minute? I need to dust these bracelets up front, and I can't get to them with his plume in my way."

She held out the stuffed duck, its glass eyes sparkling.

If I accepted it, the living birds would certainly smell their dead comrade on me and seek revenge as soon as I left the store. If it weren't for Tina, I would have spit once on the ground for good luck and run. Instead, I said, "Sure," grabbing it with a cringe.

I held the bread-loaf-size corpse gingerly, surprised at the silky softness of the feathers and how little it weighed. It had a strange airiness, a cold dead husk of a thing, and it emitted a faintly rotten chemical odor. "Ever think it's weird to have jewelry and stuffed animals together in one store?"

She shrugged. "It works. Speaking of, how do you like that yin-yang ring?"

"You've got a good memory."

"Just for jewelry. I love it. See this aquamarine pendant?" She leaned forward so I could get a view of the big blue sparkler around her neck. "Just got it. It's rare to find an aquamarine this size."

"They must pay you well." I tried to make my smile easy, but I was a terrible actor, and the bird carcass in my arms made it that much more difficult to feign cheerfulness. Her eyes turned hard, and she snatched the duck out of my hands and turned away.

"I'm good with money," she said, her back to me.

I'd bet she was. In that moment, I had my first hunch that Tina was right and Annika was supplementing her income on the sly. A hunch was just gossip all dressed up and ready to go out, though, and I'd told Tina I wouldn't report anything that wasn't concrete. I decided to fish in a different pond. "You know that Lebowski girl? The one who was murdered?"

That brought immediate camaraderie, as death does. Annika turned to me, her eyes wide. "Isn't it awful? She worked at the library with you, didn't she?"

I nodded, my lips pursed.

"That must suck." Her eyes fell. "My friend Sally's boyfriend, Rick, had just seen her at a party the night before."

I wasn't surprised. Like most teenagers in a small town, Lucy liked to drink with her friends. There wasn't much else to do at night, and given the number of bars in each town, teens certainly saw the behavior modeled often enough. I had nothing to lose by leading Annika along, however. "Yeah? Did she go to a lot of parties?"

"For sure. She was a total Frito-Lay."

"Huh?"

"Easy. She was easy. And she liked to whoop it up on the weekends."

I withheld judgment. If being a partier were a capital crime, there'd be no cheerleaders left in rural Minnesota. Come to think of it, there wouldn't be much of anyone left. Just the kids and people in full-body casts. Plus, I knew firsthand Lucy was a sweet person, and what she did in her off time didn't change that. "More than the usual?"

"Depends on who you ask." Annika tensed a little, maybe sensing I wasn't jumping on board the "blame the dead girl" train quickly enough. "Why're you asking?"

"She was my friend, and someone's killed her." My voice came out hoarse.

"Well, you know what they say—live hard, die young, and leave a hot corpse." She shrugged.

I felt a burst of anger, but it quickly dissipated. She'd clearly led a sheltered life, and I couldn't begrudge her that. In fact, I hoped she never had to learn the pain of losing someone to a violent death.

"Anyhow," Annika continued, "Jennifer's the one you want to ask about Lucy. They were both on the cheerleading squad."

She returned to rearranging the recently departed fauna and gold-plated jewelry, and I considered this piece of information. I was here to help Tina, but would it hurt if I also gathered some information about Lucy's last night on earth? As her friend and employer, I owed her that much.

I moved to the rear of the store, hoping to catch Jennifer when she emerged from the "employees only" door. Two couples entered the front and browsed the racks. I inched closer to the back and knelt to sift through a basket of bangles. That's where I picked up on some tense whispering coming from the back room. As I stopped messing with the clangy jewelry, I could make out words.

". . . to steal from us!" It was a woman's voice.

"If you thought someone was stealing, you should have gone to the police like I told you. But you *know* no one's stealing. Maybe you should lay off the blonde juice a little and learn to count the till better." This, a man's voice, condescending and dismissive.

My hackles rose.

"I'm not stupid, Tom." As I inched closer to the door and pretended to study the elastic toe rings on a shelf next to it, I recognized Tina's voice. "I know how to count a till. Will you please listen to me?"

He mimicked her in a singsong voice. "'Will you please listen to me? Will you please listen to me?' God! You sound like a spoiled brat. You're just as bad as those pea-brain girls you hire."

"I'm sorry, Tom. I didn't mean to make you mad."

"'I didn't mean to make you mad.' Maybe you should try a little thing called *thinking* before you open your piehole, then."

I clenched. I didn't know Tom Mathison well. He spent most of his time in the back room or working in his shop at home, but when I bumped into him in town, he was always friendly, a broad grin on his ruddy face. He was short and meaty, with hands like baseball mitts, and a habit of slapping you on the shoulder when you talked. I wondered if he also enjoyed slapping his wife as she talked.

Tina sighed, and it was heartbreaking for its timidity. "I'm sorry."

"Yeah, you are." A statement of fact. "Are we done with this?"

"I won't bring it up again."

When Tina appeared a split second later, it was so abrupt that I didn't have time to pretend I hadn't been eavesdropping. "Hi."

She flushed and studied her shoes. "Sorry if you had to hear that. Things are a little tense around here since the . . . well, lately."

I wanted to make her comfortable but didn't have much left in my toolbox. "Must be the weather. It has everyone on edge," I said lamely. "Is Jennifer here?"

"She called in sick." Tina's face drooped. "She was one of the cheer-leaders at camp with poor Lucy Lebowski, you know. She's too dis-traught to come to work." She looked over her shoulder, toward the back room where Tom still was. "Anyhow, I guess I don't need you to help anymore. It maybe wasn't a problem like I thought."

I glanced toward the front door opening and was momentarily blinded by the sun reflecting off Annika's pendant. I wanted to help Tina win back some of her confidence. She was a nice woman who seemed to be in a bad marriage, a terribly common situation I'd wit-nessed firsthand growing up. I lowered my voice. "I don't mind. It'll just be between you and me. When do you think Jennifer will be back?"

Tina considered my words, cast a furtive glance at the rear room, and whispered, "She said she'd keep her shift tomorrow, working with Kaitlyn. You better go."

"OK." I raised my voice to its normal volume. "That would be great, if you could order me that Celtic puzzle ring. Fantastic! I'll be by tomorrow to see if it's in."

Before she could answer, I was out the door and into the dragon's mouth. I stretched my arms over my head, shaking off the dirty feeling of hearing Tom abuse Tina. His wife had been giving him good com-mon sense—it was entirely possible Annika was stealing from right under their noses—and he'd ridiculed her. Verbal put-downs like that didn't spring up overnight, and it saddened me to think that she had been enduring this behavior for years. It must have taken a lot of cour-age for her to come to me with the embezzling problem.

I'd done my duty by Tina, and I would follow through tomorrow as promised. I couldn't pry her out of an icky relationship, but maybe, if I was lucky, I could finger whoever was stealing from her. In the mean-time, it was time to spy on some of God's blessed flock.

If they were going to fling dirt, I'd best be armed.

Chapter 16

It was a Wednesday night, so the New Millennium Bible Camp services would be open to the public. I could attend wearing my regular clothes, blend in somewhere on the expansive grounds that would be full of kids and parents on this roasting summer evening, and avoid the Mealys.

My plan was to find out what sort of people these Mealys were and get some dirt on them. Once I had more information, I'd have leverage when dealing with the banned-book petition as well as future conflicts with the Mealys that were sure to crop up now that the gauntlet had been thrown.

At the very least, it would be good to know my enemies. That's what I was telling myself as I turned right on County Road 8 and followed it south, straight across the Clitherall prairie, a little curve past Glendalough Lake, and then straight again. The New Millennium Bible Camp sign on my right was hand-painted wood, leaning dangerously. I'd never taken notice of it before, so I wasn't sure if it was suffering from neglect or abuse.

I followed the arrow on the sign and was relieved to see that there were dozens of cars parked along the side of the road and, when I reached the end of the two-mile driveway, that the parking lot by the church was also nearly full. If my car had been any larger, I wouldn't have been able to squeeze between a Chevy Blazer and a Ford extended-cab pickup. As it was, I was forced to crawl out through my window.

Everyone was piling into the church, which indicated the service was about to start. That made it a safe bet that all three Mealys were inside, leaving me to explore the grounds unattended. I strode to the nearest rise to get a lay of the land.

To the east was the church, a simple white structure with red, gold, and green stained-glass windows. Straight north and nearest the lake were six cabins, as tidy as hospital beds, and east of them was a partially submerged circle of benches and a pulpit. The furniture was in five inches of swampy water, as if God had sent the flood prematurely and washed his flock away midworship. To the west was the main hall, where they likely held assembly, meals, and public affairs. Farther up the hill, between the main hall and the cabins, was a house that I presumed was the Mealys' residence.

"It's as fine as frog's hair, isn't it?"

The voice startled me, and I turned to see a woman in her midthirties wearing a beatific smile. "What is?" I asked suspiciously.

"The Bible camp," she said, spreading her arms to indicate everything in view. "It was closed for three years before Pastor Mealy brought it back to life last fall, bless him. He put all his own money into painting it and getting wheelchair ramps for his wife set up. He is a beacon of faith and fellowship."

I studied her more closely. "You live around here?"

She offered her hand. "I'm so sorry! I should have introduced myself. My name is Christina Sahlberg. I live right over on Spitzer Lake. Are you here for the service?"

"I am. I'm new. Could you direct me to the church?"

"Silly, it's right over there." She pointed at the building at the bottom of the hill. The line of her finger led directly to the back of a man entering the church, and he appeared to be wearing a cape. It could only be Weston Lippmann, tick curator and fellow bird-fearer. Hmmm. I wouldn't have pegged him for a churchgoer.

"Of course. Well, thank you."

"I am but a humble shepherd." She floated off toward the main hall. Once she was out of sight, I sneaked around to the cabins to peek into the windows. All six of them were set up like typical resort cabins, with one main room housing the kitchen, living, and dining spaces, and three bedrooms off the central room, each with two bunk beds.

I passed the sunken log circle to the east, noticing the hand-hewn logs in a horseshoe shape around the humble pulpit. My movements made the sunning turtles plop into the water. Something about the space was eerie. Maybe it was the wetness in this time of drought, as if it had intentionally been built underwater. Or maybe it was because up close, it looked lascivious, like the wet smile of a dirty and prune-faced old man.

I marched back across the gravel road winding through the camp and straight west to the main hall, away from the church. I could hear singing coming from inside, and wondered if there was a junior service going on for the kids attending camp.

No one appeared to be watching me, but I chose caution and darted around to the back of the building before peeking in, scaring up dust as I scuttled. I slid along the side of the building and peered in an open window, settling my fingers on the splintered wood of the sill. Body heat and rhythmic singing poured out.

At first, I couldn't make sense of what I saw. There were at least fifty children inside, ranging in age from about five to their late teens, and they were all wearing camouflage pants or shorts and army-green T-shirts. The group was mostly male, and they were in various stages of prostration, ripping their clothes, bowing, and throwing their hands in the air.

Through the cracked window, I could smell sweat and incense, and the organic tang of hardworking farmers' kids.

"Are you a warrior for Jesus?"

The rhetorical question came from a female voice in the front, and by hugging the rough outer wall, I saw it was Alicia Mealy. She looked different from my last sighting of her, her face intense and luminous, even with her eyes closed in rapture. The crowd of kids raised their hands and swayed—some moaning, others spouting rapid gibberish.

"I said, are you a warrior for Jesus!"

This earned a rallying cry, and I noticed a young boy, about six, hitting the side of his head with his right fist as he stared, rapt, at Alicia. "I will fight for Jesus!" he yelled. Forty-plus voices agreed with him.

"Are you ready to do as Jesus asks?" Alicia's eyes opened, her smile euphoric.

"We are!"

She raised both hands in the air. "And you will lead the way for the righteous, and shoot down the unbelievers who block your path?"

"So sayeth the Lord!"

She nodded gleefully. "Then you are always welcome in Christ's Church of the Apocryphal Revelation!"

Christ's Church of the Apocryphal Revelation? I'd never heard of them, but I was pretty sure they weren't Lutheran. I scoured the large room for any familiar faces, maybe a regular from my story hour at the library, but didn't see anyone I knew.

The whole scene felt about as agreeable as a high-speed enema.

"I thought you were looking for the church?"

I spun around, my heart gyrating like a go-go dancer on payday. "Hi, uh, Christina. I guess I got a little lost."

Her eyes gleamed, sharp and hot. "Let me walk you to the church. And I didn't catch your name."

I made to follow her, but she stood her ground until I led the way. She felt dangerous at my back, but I didn't see as I had a choice. "I'm just visiting," I offered. "Getting a feel for the grounds. You know, trying to choose a church."

"Your name?"

"Mary Catherine Gallagher," I lied.

Her voice was sharp behind me. "Are you a believer?"

"I certainly am." It wasn't a lie. I did believe in something, just probably not the same thing as her. "You really have a lovely camp here, but I guess I better get going. Home, not to the service. So many churches, so little time."

I turned to see her arms crossed at her waist, her eyes shooting fire. "I hope to see you back again, Mary Catherine," she said tightly. "God watches over us all."

"Thank you, Christina." I backed away until I was beyond pouncing distance, and then I turned and beat cheeks, feeling her eyes burn an X across my back. It took every shred of willpower not to run to my car.

The Ford pickup had left, and so I could open my door. When I crawled in, I risked a peek back, and there she was, standing like a scarecrow, her arms still crossed at her waist, watching me. I felt a fly buzzing around my neck and swatted at it. Then I felt another near my hairline and smacked my forehead. My hand came away empty.

Heart hammering, I cranked my car, not-so-stealthily rolled up the windows, locked the doors, and squealed out.

Well, it was a 1985 Toyota hatchback. I *whined* out.

I considered stopping at Bonnie & Clyde's to cleanse my scarred soul but decided it'd be cheaper to drink at home. In fact, getting deeply drunk tonight in front of the TV, and then every night until I moved away from this freakish coil of a town, sounded like a brilliant plan. Let Sarah Ruth deal with the petition and the police deal with Lucy's murder.

When I pulled into my driveway, an unfamiliar car was parked in the shade of the gigantic lilacs in the center of the turnaround. My stomach tumbled. I was not in the mood for dealing with anyone.

Luna ran out and snuffled my hand.

"Who's here, girl? Who is it?"

My dog smiled at me, and I returned the look, until I saw the dark-haired woman come around the corner of the house, her expression indecipherable.

Chapter 17

"Mom?"

She held out her hands. "Mira."

I stood my ground. My mom and I had talked on the phone in June but hadn't seen each other in more than a year. She'd never visited me in Battle Lake. I felt territorial, off-balance.

"What are you doing here?" I asked.

Her hands hovered in the air like two premature greeters at a surprise party before dropping to her side. We had the same eyes, gray and serious. We were also the same height and build, but her dress and hair were conservative, particularly against my tank top and Indian skirt. "I'm sorry. I wanted to see you. I should have called. Is this the dog you're sitting for, Luna?"

I wasn't letting her off the hook. "Why'd you want to see me?"

"I don't know, Miranda, because you're my daughter?" She shook her head, sounding exasperated. "Because you call me in June and tell me you've been beaten up and haven't called since? Because you've been here since April, living not even a hundred miles from me, and I don't know what your house looks like?"

Luna whimpered between us. My mom and I also had the same voice. "You might as well come on in, then," I said. "I have plans tonight, though, so you can't stay long."

I strode past her, and she quietly followed me inside. I gestured, encompassing the interior space. "This is the living room, over there is the kitchen, my bedroom and bathroom are off this door, and the spare bedroom and office are over there."

"Tiger Pop!" Mom held out her hands to my kitty, and the traitor ate it up. Mom hugged her, scratching her eternal ear itch. "I can't believe how healthy she looks! How old is this cat?"

"Thirteen." I glared at her.

"And your house looks really beautiful. Clean. You must love it out here."

I didn't want to tell her I was moving. I didn't want her to be here. It felt too close, too unexpected, and besides, she always brought the specter of my dad. We'd pushed through some barriers over the phone, but having her in my house was too much, too soon.

"It's fine," I said.

"Can I see your gardens?" She set Tiger Pop down and headed out before I could object.

"It's been dry," I said defensively, following as she went straight to my vegetables.

"Oh, Mira! They're gorgeous! Look at the size of your tomatoes. And you have fresh dill. Are you going to can this year? You could come home. We could process veggies together."

"I *am* home."

"Of course." Her smile faltered, and she twisted one hand with the other.

"Mom, why are you here?" This week had already thrown a lot at me. "Why today?"

Her smile fled. I witnessed her fifty-four years grind down on her with all their weight, and she laid it out between us like rotten food. "I have breast cancer, Miranda. I found out last week. I didn't want to tell you over the phone."

The earth grew papery underfoot.

I'd ditched Paynesville as soon as I graduated, deliberately leaving behind as many memories as I could, determined to craft my own life from that point on. Suddenly, though, long-forgotten mental pictures were bursting out. My mom pushing me on our tire swing when I was five, or staying up to read to me when I had chicken pox in eighth grade, or driving me to my first dance, the one where the boys stood on one side of the gym and girls on the other. With those memories came a glimpse of my dad before his drinking got bad, bringing home a calico kitten for me, laughing as it pounced at the air. "How bad?"

"They caught it early." She smiled, almost apologetically, and brushed her hair back from her face in a gesture I recognized from my childhood. "I start chemo in three weeks, and the prognosis is good. I should be fine, Mir, with God's grace. I just thought you deserved to know. Face to face."

Tears and angry words fought for escape, one climbing on the back of the other to reach my mouth. The angry words won. "What am I supposed to say to that?"

She came over and held me while I stood rigid. "You don't need to say anything. I came by to let you know, that's all, and to say I love you. You have a home whenever you need it."

I nodded stiffly. "I know." It was petty, horribly petty, but I couldn't tell her I loved her. Not right then.

"Mira, look at me." She held my chin and then tucked my hair behind my ears. "I'm going to be fine. This is just a wake-up call, that's all. Life's short. I'd like to see you more. What do I need to do to make that happen?"

Suddenly, the whole outdoors were too big, and I could feel myself disconnect and spray out. It was terrifying. "I need time."

"How much?"

"I don't know." I was trembling. "I have to process this. I'll call you in a few days, OK?"

Her smile was small, but it had a flash of hope at its corners. "OK. Call me next week." She waved at the pets. "Bye, Luna! Bye, Tiger Pop! You take care of each other. Love you, Mira. You're a good person." She wiped my cheek, got in her car, fastened her seat belt, and drove away.

I walked into the house, straight to the bathroom, and yanked out the bottle of tequila. It was suppertime, and I was going for liquid nourishment. I took two big swigs and held the bottle up. "Here's to you, Mom and Dad."

I kept the bottle in my hand, ripped the *Tank Girl* CD out of my rack, and cranked it to full volume. Between the liquor and the music, I was going to drown out the raw truth: that I'd realized I missed my mom terribly at the same moment I discovered she wasn't going to live forever. I supposed that possibility was part of what I'd been running from since I moved to the Twin Cities after graduation. Now, it'd hunted me down all the way in Battle Lake.

It was frightening.

By the time the sun was taking its unrelenting heat to another part of the world, I was toast.

"Luna? Tiger Pop? You wanna help me garden?" They weren't in the mood to enable, so I tripped outside, fighting the tilting earth. "You're a pretty big weed," I said, reaching for the base of my tallest tomato plant. It took three tries before I had it out of the ground, ripe fruit busting around my feet like bloody bombs.

"And you. You've never been anything but trouble." Up came the brussels sprouts, followed by a broccoli, two cabbages, and a whole row of onions, their green stems turned to brown as they were getting ready to set up for winter. When my arms were too tired to rip, I stomped, feeling vegetables go flat and dead underfoot.

"And thanks for all the help planting, Johnny. You've really been a big, stand-up, follow-through kind of guy."

I leaped in the air and came down on a watermelon. It was hard, and I bounced off, landing with a painful thud. I dragged myself to my feet, nodded at my double-vision gardening, and went inside.

I made it as far as the couch before blacking out.

Chapter 18

"Luna? Huh? Luna?"

The licking wouldn't stop, and when I rolled over to push her away, my skin felt tight and sticky. I raised myself up on shaky arms and the room shifted beneath me. My heart was tripping oddly, and I could have woken up in Marrakech for all that I recognized my surroundings.

I blinked. The room was hot and close, the sun already two clicks off the horizon. It must have been near eight a.m. Luna continued to lick me patiently, bringing me back to myself.

I finally recognized the couch, and the house, and when I pulled myself up and lurched outside, the front lawn. My stomach twisted, and I had to swallow hard to keep everything down.

"I must have tied one hell of one on," I said to Luna, who was still by my side. She glanced at me sadly. I returned the look, and that's when I spotted the white bumps on my arms. Tomato seeds? How'd they get there? I squinted at my garden. I sensed it, a fiend lurking in the back of my brain, some horrible news about to break through and burn my life down. I stumbled down to my hand-tended plot, the center of my summer universe, my one saving grace, my garden.

It was destroyed.

It looked like an elephant had rolled in it, grazed in it, danced on it. There were a few spindly vegetables still in the ground tilting precariously, but they were so denuded it was impossible to tell what sort of plants they'd been. Whole onions lay scattered like dirty pearls, and green leaves were stomped into pulp.

I fell to the ground and wept at what I'd done, and then cried harder when I remembered that my mom had breast cancer. I cried so hard that I got hiccups. It wasn't until my throat was hoarse and my body was as dry as the air around me that I went into the house and gathered up all the liquor. I even pulled my secret stash of whiskey from the desk drawer in the office.

I crashed the bottles into the burning barrel and lit them up into a whooshing blaze. Mrs. Berns's words—"don't do nothing for a man"— whispered to me, and I listened to them. I was done with drinking. It'd killed my father and wormed its way into my life, but his problem wasn't going to be mine. I had been here before, but I wasn't ever coming back.

When the flames burned themselves out, I turned to my pillaged, heartbroken, betrayed garden, my head thick and raw. I picked what whole vegetables I could find and gathered enough to fill two bags. I made a pile of the plants I'd killed and burned them also.

When it was all said and done, I was left with two live tomato plants, the carrots and potatoes, and one helluva hard watermelon.

A clean start.

That's all I wanted.

A clean start.

Chapter 19

Mrs. Berns and Sarah Ruth sensed my strange, impenetrable mood and left me alone for the morning shift. I worked robotically, grieving what I'd done. The worst thing about hurting the earth was that there was no one to forgive me.

"You should go get some lunch."

"I'm not hungry, Mrs. Berns."

"I am," she said sunnily. "Will you please get me a bagel?"

"You hate bagels."

"Not as much as I hate mopey, pain-in-the-ass, black-mood girls. I don't know what put you in this funk, but Sarah Ruth and I need a break from it. Take a walk."

"Fine." The coffee shop was as good a place as any to hate myself.

I grabbed my grocery bag of peppers, onions, and tomatoes and shuffled over to the Fortune Café. I figured I could donate my abused vegetables to Sid and Nancy, the café's owners. They'd been in business in Battle Lake for five years, but they'd been a couple at least two decades.

The café's front room was a coffee shop, and their back room was a combination library, computer room, and visiting space. I'd played many a Scrabble game with Sid in the back, her vocabulary a fair match for mine. The three of us were solid friends, though I was closer to Sid than to Nancy, and I felt my shame sink even deeper as I stepped into their store, the inviting smell of cinnamon and coffee washing over me.

"Hey, Mira!" Sid smiled from behind the counter she was washing. The lunch rush had already come and gone, and except for a three-seat table of tourists near the front window, the place was empty. I normally felt comforted by the surroundings—forest-green-and-white tiled floor, blond wood tables, and white walls hung with watercolors of flowers and country schoolhouses. Now, the familiarity somehow increased my guilt.

"Hi."

"Jeez," she said, her expression concerned, "you look rough. Catch a summer cold?"

"Maybe."

She stopped washing the counter and crossed her arms in front of her. "*Maybe?* There something you want to talk about?"

I couldn't meet her eyes. "You ever do something so bad that you could never fix it?"

Sid studied all the vegetables I'd placed on her counter, then looked at me with a glimmer of understanding under her graying eyebrows. "This is an awful lot of vegetables all at once, some of them not ripe. You get a storm out there?"

"Of sorts."

Sid sighed. "No, I never did anything so bad I couldn't fix it, and if you're still alive, neither have you."

I snuffled. "What if it was *really* bad?"

"Like attacking your own garden?"

I couldn't meet her gaze. "Yeah," I said miserably.

"Then you apologize to your spot of earth, you replant what you can, and you figure out what made you so unbalanced."

"I already know."

She nodded. "I figured you did. Anything you can do something about?"

I thought about my dad, my mom, Lucy, Johnny with his sweet blue eyes and strong hands. "I don't know."

She hollered toward the kitchen, "Nance, can you watch the front? I'll be right back." Then she wiped her hands on her apron decisively and grabbed my hand. "Come here. I have something to show you."

She led me upstairs, to her and Nancy's living quarters. I'd spent plenty of time with her in the lower half of the building but had never been to the second level. This section of the house was as neat as the downstairs, with a separate kitchen, bathroom, living room, and bedroom. The country-fancy look of the café was not duplicated on this level. Everything up here was clean lines, hardwood floors, and pale denim-colored walls. The smell of baking bread wafted up through the cracks, but it wasn't as strong, and a clean soap scent up here cut through it.

Sid led me into the bedroom and opened the dark oak chest at the foot of the bed. She riffled through the deep container, smiling fondly as she brought up a box of pictures.

"Have a seat," she said, indicating the white, yellow, and blue patchwork quilt on the bed. "I'm going to show you something that I've never shown anyone but Nancy."

I took a weak stab at a joke. "Your senior photo?"

"Worse." She handed over a Polaroid of a burned building, its supporting beams sticking up like blackened bones. I held it close, sniffing for charcoal.

"What is it?"

"My parents' garage."

"Oh my god! Was anyone hurt?"

"No." She chuckled. "My mom and dad were on vacation. That's why I chose that day to set fire to it."

My eyes widened. "You burned down your parents' garage *on purpose?*"

"To the ground," she said, nodding. "In the process, I destroyed their minivan, all the pictures they had in storage in the garage attic, and all their gardening tools."

I glanced from the photo to her face. "Why?"

She sat heavily on the floor with a mix of sadness and humor on her face. "I was pissed off. I was a teenager, and I'd been trying to come out to them for years. They wouldn't hear me, and so I thought I would do something they couldn't ignore. Pretty stupid, huh?"

I turned the photo so it faced her. "Did they listen after this?"

She studied the image, her expression momentarily twisting. "No. And they still haven't. They prefer to think of me and Nancy as 'roommates.' They also didn't press charges against me for torching the garage, they didn't claim any insurance, and they paid the fire station's bills. We all just acted like nothing happened." She sighed. "They probably thought they were doing me a favor, but it was the worst possible response."

I chewed on that for a second. "Did you tell them you were sorry?"

"Eventually, after many, many years of feeling horrible for burning their memories." She rubbed her face. "It wasn't until after I figured out I didn't need their approval that I could finally apologize and mean it." She looked up at me, her eyes clear. "Even better, I forgave *them*. And I saved a picture so I'd never forget where I'd been and how far I've come, and so I never go back."

She stood, brushing off her bottom, and took the photo from me. "We make mistakes, Mira. We learn, we change what we can, and we forgive ourselves, as hard as it is. That's life."

I felt an interior weight shift. It didn't go away, but it didn't feel so heavy anymore. "You're a wise woman."

"You're not so bad yourself." She treated me to a smile like balm and packed up the picture. On the way back downstairs, she also offered some juicy gossip. "By the way, you know the family at New Millennium Bible? The Holier Thanthous?"

"The Mealys?"

She nodded. "That's them. You'll never guess what happened this morning. Their daughter, Alicia, the one who looks like a young Lynda Carter?"

"I wouldn't go that far, but yeah."

"She came to the coffee shop today. Nancy caught her stealing a bag of biscotti. Can you believe that!"

Nancy met us at the bottom of the stairs at the mention of her name, wiping her hands on her apron. "Yeah, caught her red-handed. And do you know what she said to me? She said she was just putting it into her purse so it'd be easier to carry to the counter."

I raised an eyebrow. "You didn't believe her?"

"That's like the lion telling the antelope it's just going to clean its hind end. I told her I was going to call the police, and she threatened me with the Liberty Law School. Said it was started by Jerry Falwell and was turning out lawyers only too happy to deal with people like me."

I smiled for the first time that day. "Coffee shop owners?"

"I guess." Nancy chuckled, but then grew serious again. "That one's wicked."

That about summed it up, as far as I could tell. "So what'd you do?"

"Let her go. We don't need the trouble." Nancy straightened her apron, squeezed Sid's hand, and headed back to the kitchen. On her way, she hollered over her shoulder at Sid, "Did you ask her yet?"

"Ask me what?"

"A favor," Sid said, apologetically. "I know you're busy with two jobs, but we're hoping you can open up the café tomorrow. Nancy's sister is having surgery in Fargo later today, and we want to stay overnight so she isn't alone."

"Anything serious?"

Sid shook her head. "Not too bad. Just gallstones. She doesn't have any other family close by, though, so we want to be there."

My dearth of family felt sharp for a moment, but the pang was replaced by my bounty of friends. "Of course I'll open up. I can't promise to do any baking, though."

"Thanks," Sid said gratefully. "We'll have it all stocked up, plus a sign saying that the fancy coffees will need to wait. We're planning on being back by ten, so you'll be able to skedaddle to the library before Mrs. Berns turns it into a house of ill repute."

"Perfect."

Chapter 20

As I collected keys and opening instructions, I warmed inside. Action felt good, as did helping my friends. Sid was right. I needed to fix what I could, starting with finding that dirt on the Mealys I had yet to uncover. It was bad enough they were messing with the library; I wasn't going to let Alicia mess with my friends, too. I'd promised Ron I would head out to New Millennium Bible Camp this afternoon to check out the Creation Science Fair, and my very innocent reporting for the *Battle Lake Recall* would be a perfect cover for some earnest snooping. Once I evened that playing field, I could work on repairing my garden.

Sid gave me an overview of the till before sending me on my way with a free sun-dried tomato and Greek olive cream cheese bagel and some parting words.

"Hey, you know why Lutherans hate premarital sex?" she asked.

"Why?"

She winked. "They're afraid it'll lead to dancing."

I left ten pounds lighter. I decided to take further advantage of my lunch hour to visit 4Ts and place another check in my "good deeds" column. I worked on the chewy bagel as I trudged through the kiln-like air, sweat beads gathering at my hairline and separating to race down my neck. I pulled my V-necked T-shirt from my chest and peered down at the rivulet forming between my A-cups.

"I wouldn't hold my breath, darlin'. If they haven't grown yet, it doesn't do any good to water 'em."

I spun around. "Hi, Kennie."

"And didn't I tell you to stop by my house?" She was dressed surprisingly low-key, wearing a sequined tank top, jean shorts, and hot-pink espadrilles. "I have a business deal that I know you're going to want to get in on."

I thought back to our conversation in the library and realized she had in fact invited me to her house, but I'd been too distracted by the petition to react properly. Visions of topless octogenarians, pre-assembled penis-enlargement devices, and a walkie-talkie-sex service scuttled through my brain, and all the apprehension I should have felt the first time she mentioned a "business deal" came at me like a swarm of mosquitoes.

I shoved my bagel back into its bag and glanced around. There were plenty of witnesses on the street should this go south. "Why don't you just tell me what it is right now? I've got a minute."

"Nope." She put her hands on her hips. "You've gotta see the demo model at my house."

Fudge cakes. It *was* the penis-enlargement device. I was sure of it. "I'm not much of an entrepreneur."

She shook her head. "You've got it all wrong. I just want to know if I can display one in the library. Once you see it, you'll want one for yourself, and who knows?" She shrugged. "You might decide to invest. I tell you, it's gonna be big."

What a great motto for a penis enlarger. And if I could blow off Kennie just a couple more times, I'd be able to make it out of Battle Lake without ever seeing her latest "business proposition."

"I'll come over tomorrow morning, 'kay?" I said. "I have to open up the Fortune for Sid and Nancy, and then I'll stop by before I open the library." There wouldn't be time, but she didn't need to know that.

"You won't be sorry, darlin'!" She wiggled her fingers at me and marched off in the other direction, the spangles on her sequins catching the sun and turning her into a strolling disco ball. The brightness was probably for the best, as her blinding shirt made it nearly impossible to see her Daisy Dukes, or, on Kennie, ill-fitting denim underwear.

I entered the cool interior of 4Ts and navigated through the milling shoppers. I recognized Kaitlyn from my first visit, near the front window. The short, bubble-nosed brunette behind the counter must be Jennifer. I made my way over and prepared to tell a little white lie.

"Hi, are you Jennifer?"

She smiled. Her eyeteeth were unusually skinny, giving her mouth a quirky, friendly appearance despite the haunted look in her eyes. "Yup. Can I help you?"

"I'm Mira James. Lucy worked for me at the library. I wanted to say I was sorry about her death. I heard you two were good friends."

Her upper lip quivered. "Yeah."

"Did she make it to cheerleading practice the day before, um, before she was found?"

"Yeah." Jennifer rubbed her arms. "She was there. Like I told the police, it was the same as any other practice."

"Did she seem in a strange mood, or leave with anyone you hadn't seen before?"

Jennifer shook her head, tossing brown hair into her eyes. "She was happy Lucy, just like usual. And she left on her own, no strangers picking her up. Everyone else there was part of the squad. People *used* to come watch us practice, until the coach made them stop." Big warm tears were collecting at the corners of her eyes. "Do you think they'll find out who killed her?"

"I hope so." I thought of the terror Lucy must have felt before she was shot. Who had taken her? Why? I changed the subject before I started to cry myself. "I'm looking for Annika. Is she here?" I knew she wouldn't be, but it seemed the most natural way to bring her into the conversation.

"No, it's her day off." Jennifer dabbed at her eyes. "She should be here tomorrow, though."

I ran my fingers over a display of worry stones. "Does she ever stop in when she's not on the schedule?"

Jennifer nodded. "Totally! She's the best. Sometimes, when I'm the only one on, she'll watch the store for me so I can go and grab lunch or run some errands. On her day *off*! Can you believe it?"

I could. And that would explain why the money missing from the till wasn't shift-specific. "She sounds like a real pal."

"Absolutely." She nodded agreeably. "Do you want me to give her a message for you?"

I smiled at Jennifer. Her sweetness was infectious, even if it was soaked in sadness. "No thanks. I'll just stop back."

"OK. Let me know if you need anything else." She smiled and moved off to help a customer near the front window, and I filed this situation away as "mystery solved." Annika was dripping with expensive jewelry she couldn't possibly afford on this job, and she routinely volunteered to watch the till for her coworkers, the same till that was regularly short on cash. The problem was, I had only assumptions, and like I'd told Tina, that wasn't enough. I decided to suggest that she be clearer about the rules to her employees—only one clerk using the till per shift—and install a camera in the front. I was sure that would put an end to the stealing without getting anyone in trouble, which had been her goal from the start.

I stepped out of the store and walked back to the library, still feeling good about helping. I'd finish a few hours of paperwork, then ask Mrs. Berns and Sarah Ruth to close so I could return to the Bible camp.

Of course, when had things ever gone as planned for me?

Chapter 21

"I'm back!" I said, strolling into the library.

Mrs. Berns peered up at me. She was on all fours, looking under the table on which the banned-book display rested. "I thought you were just going for a bagel. Did you get laid between here and there? Or maybe a lobotomy?"

"Huh?"

Mrs. Berns grunted. "I sent you away because you were Crabby Cathy, and now you come back Suzy Sunshine. What happened?"

"I ran into some good advice," I said, rubbing the back of my neck. "What are you doing on the floor?"

"Dropped a pencil under here."

"Let me help you." I crouched next to Mrs. Berns and reached my hand underneath the table. I came up with two pencils, a magazine insert, and Nut Goodie, the ferret.

"What's he doing down here?" I asked, dragging out the mangy creature.

"Gives me the creeps," Mrs. Berns said matter-of-factly. "It's a long-dead rat. I tried sticking it in the trash, but it kept reappearing behind the counter, so I gave it a time-out down here. Probably that angelic Sarah Ruth is the one who kept digging it out."

"What's that crack mean? 'Angelic'?"

Mrs. Berns shrugged. "Just that she can never do anything wrong."

I looked at Mrs. Berns, who was still sporting six-shooters strapped to her waist. She had also rounded up a pair of Fleet Farm cowboy boots and was wearing a snap-front Western shirt undone halfway down her droopy chest. This was a woman who could do *a lot* wrong, and I loved her for it.

"Sarah Ruth's just being on her best behavior because she's new," I offered. "She'll mess up soon enough, I'm sure. Where is she, anyhow?"

Mrs. Berns gestured over her shoulder as she pushed herself off the ground. "In the back room. She rushed there when you left for lunch, and I haven't seen her since."

"Thanks."

I strolled into the storage room. We had boxes of books accumulated back here, as well as holiday decorations, stuffed animals we rotated through the kids' section, a bathroom, and next to it, a tiny office whose door was currently shut. The office had room enough for a desk, two file cabinets, and not much else. It wouldn't be unusual for Sarah Ruth to be in there getting a handle on the paperwork, but it would be odd for her to do it with the door closed. The library rule was to keep it open in case you were needed on the floor.

I grabbed the cool doorknob in my hands and twisted, half expecting to find the office empty. Instead, I found Sarah Ruth on the old black circle-dial phone, which she shoved down guiltily when I peeped my head in.

"Sorry! Did I interrupt a conversation?"

Sarah Ruth patted her brown hair nervously and shook her head. "Wrong number."

I smiled. "But I didn't hear the phone ring."

"Oh, I mean I dialed the wrong number. I was trying to call the *Recall* office, but I got someone's home number. I know it's so rude to hang up, but I get too embarrassed to stay on the line once I realize it's a mistaken call."

I felt a familiar buzzing along my hairline. Sarah Ruth was lying, but I didn't know why. "I can give you the *Recall* number if you need it. Or maybe there's something I can help you with? I still work there, you know." I tried another polite grin.

"Nothing that can't wait," she said, talking too fast. "I wanted to find out advertising costs. I thought maybe we could run some contest, like having an all-town read or something. No biggie." She stood abruptly and brushed past me on her way out.

I didn't see anything out of place in the office, so I turned and followed, raising my voice to speak to her back. "Would you mind closing up this afternoon, along with Mrs. Berns? I have to do some research for an article."

She slowed her pace and seemed visibly relieved that I was no longer asking her about her phone call. "I think we can handle it just fine. Your library will be in good hands with us."

Out of the corner of my eye, I saw Mrs. Berns slitting a hole in one of the beanbag chairs in the kids' section. She slid Nut Goodie, the ferret, into it, and then began to sew it shut with a heavy-duty needle and thread. I chose to ignore it.

"I have no doubt," I told Sarah Ruth.

"When are you leaving?" she asked.

My hairline tingled again. "Not for a couple hours. I need to finish paying some bills, and I wanted to follow up on a grant I wrote for the library. I figured I'd head out to the New Millennium around three."

"The Bible camp? What could you possibly want there?" Her voice carried a sense of urgency before she dialed it down. "I mean, you don't really go to church, do you?"

"No, I really don't." What the hell was up with Sarah Ruth? "But I told Ron Sims at the newspaper that I'd cover the Creation Science Fair this afternoon. Should be a quick in and out."

She smoothed her plain brown skirt and pulled down her matching button-front shirt. The woman was always a vision of brownness, and I noticed the humidity turning her brown perm curls into kinky waves. "Be careful, Mira. I know how you like to make fun of people, but they're good folks out at New Millennium."

I cocked my head. "Then why would I need to be careful?"

"It's just that disrespecting people can get you into trouble, and I know there is no love lost between you and the Mealys." She rested her hand on my shoulder. "I just worry about you, that's all. And there's still a murderer out there."

I scowled. "If he's after cheerleaders, I'm not his type."

Sarah Ruth nodded absently. "If the killer's even a 'he.' These days, you can never be sure."

Chapter 22

I carried Sarah Ruth's disturbing comment in my head all afternoon, handling it like poorly packaged dynamite. I'd done my best to not think about the murderer, to leave that investigation to the police, but when the image of Lucy Lebowski's shattered corpse made its way into my brain, I'd always assumed it was a man who had killed her. I now had to face facts—a woman could hold a gun and shoot someone in the back just as well as any man.

As I cruised out to New Millennium Bible Camp, my windows down and my radio up, I promised myself I'd keep a good eye on all the ladies, starting with Alicia Mealy, two-faced stealer of biscotti, leader of weird paramilitary sessions, and signer of book-banning petitions.

First, though, I'd need to find parking. Cars were stacked end to end all the way up the gravel road to the Bible camp, and the parking lot was as full as a baby's diaper in the morning. I couldn't even turn my car around and so had to drive in reverse all the way out to the blacktop, visions of dinging doors and clipping people blurring my focus. I've never been particularly skillful at reversing course.

I parked the Toyota on County Road 8, grabbed my notebook and digital camera, and hoofed it back to the Bible camp's main hall, the building where I'd spied on Jesus's youngest warriors prepping for battle only yesterday.

I had no idea what a Christ's Church of the Apocryphal Revelation Creation Science Fair would look like, but I did have a plan. I was going to eyeball the participants' goofy projects long enough to bluff my way through a short article, and once I was sure the key players—namely, the Mealys—were all accounted for, I'd slip into their house for a little private revelation time. If I was busted, I'd just say I was lost.

What's the worst they could do to me?

I licked my lips, tasting the salt of a hot day, and strode through the central area, the church on my right and the main hall to my left. The grounds were packed, with folks walking in and out of the cabins and sitting on the submerged benches in the watery pulpit. People around me felt celebratory, on their way to faith and fraternity, but there was something odd that I couldn't immediately put my finger on.

When a smiling gentleman next to me removed his hat, I finally realized what it was: everyone was dressed for a different era—the men in fedoras, button-down shirts, and pleated khakis, the women in frocks that fell below their knees.

It was as if I had stepped back in time to the Eisenhower years.

I felt conspicuous in my purple sundress, what with my naked knees and elbows, but I did my best to blend in. At the front doors of the assembly hall, I accepted a flyer from two clean-scrubbed preteens wearing starched shirts and pants. They smiled as sweat beaded on their foreheads, giving them a fevered look.

The flyer was the same one Robert Mealy had tried to leave at the library, and so I set it on a table and got a feel for the place.

It looked like your average grade school cafeteria and smelled like tempera paints and baked french fries. Twelve round tables had been set up, six to a row, and each one featured the hallmark of a science project—trifold tagboard with uneven writing.

The room was not air-conditioned, and many of the people packed in were fanning themselves with flyers. I yanked a notepad and pen out of the small India-fabric purse I'd looped across my chest and strolled up to the first table. A teenage boy, his acne pulsing and his eyes bright, was explaining the inner workings of his discovery using wildly animated hand gestures. A group of elderly folks, some of whom I recognized from the Senior Sunset home, nodded along.

I skirted them and checked out his tagboard: How Noah Used Vertical Integration to Get the Ark Ready in Time. Only "vertical" was spelled with two *l*s and no *a*.

The next table over featured a creation-science project named My Great-Great-Great-Grandpa Was a Christian, Not a Monkey. I leaned in to examine photos of gorillas glued alongside a daguerreotype photo of an old guy, bubble dialogue pointing out the differences: "Gorilla: hairy face. Great-Great-Great-Grandpa Matthew: no hair on his face." Several other differences were pointed out. The last fold in the tagboard ended with "Therefore, Evolution Is False."

People were buzzing about that one.

The third table featured a display of rainbows, hearts, and pictures of babies. I didn't want to read the title, but my eyes betrayed me. Biology Proves Women Designed for Housework. The pictographs showed a smiling woman, her "lower than male" center of gravity pointed out with a two-inch red arrow at each hip, a mop in one hand and a baby in the other.

My stomach turned. Was I in Stepford?

I scurried to the table devoted to the claim that Thermodynamic Readouts Confirm Satan Is More Active Than Ever, then quickly moved to a display featuring an anatomically incorrect sculpture of Adam and Eve made out of Popsicle sticks and macaroni. I edged over to the teenage girl standing proudly next to it. "This yours?"

She smiled. "Yes. It took me three weeks to make."

I tried not to stare at the large wet spots under each of her armpits. "Wow. That's a commitment."

She crossed her hands at her waist. "I am a believer."

"Say, about that." I held up my notepad and pen. "I'm a reporter for the *Battle Lake Recall*, and I'm doing an article on this Creation Science Fair."

She stood up tall then and pushed her hair behind her ears. "That's great! Are you taking any pictures?"

"Maybe." I wore the digital camera around my neck. "What I think the readers will want to know, though, is what exactly is Christ's Church of the Apocryphal Revelation?"

She stared at me like I'd just asked her what that thing on the middle of her face with the two holes was. "You're at it."

"Of course. I'm just looking for a quote from someone participating in the fair. I'll use your name."

"It's Betsy Zimmer."

"Great." I wrote it down. "And in your words, what sets Christ's Church of the Apocryphal Revelation apart from other churches?"

"That's easy." She put on her best lecture voice, obviously repeating a litany she'd heard many times. "The Apocrypha were vehicles for God's word, but they were too profound and too sacred for just anyone to hear. It wasn't until Pastor Mealy got his hands on them—and shared them with us—that regular people could learn them. Now that we've heard the word of God through the Apocrypha, it's our duty to share it with others."

I was pretending to write this all down. "You folks use a regular Bible?"

"Totally." She nodded like a Muppet. "That's God's instructions to us. But we also have the Apocrypha. It's like an appendix that Pastor Mealy typed up? He's the only one who has the original."

I paused my pretend writing. "Have you seen the original?"

She gasped. Clearly, my suggestion had been blasphemous.

"No. No one has." She shook her head vigorously. "The original Apocrypha are for Pastor Mealy's eyes only."

If I hadn't already planned on some serious snooping at the Creation Science Fair, I'd be clearing my calendar for a big helping of down-and-dirty Nancy-Drewing about now. I was willing to bet a basket of Nut Goodies that that "original" Apocrypha might be just the Mealys' undoing that I'd been searching for. "Thanks for the quote, Betsy! You've been a great help."

"Not at all." She smiled primly despite the rivers of sweat coursing down her hairline, then turned away to talk to a couple admiring her display.

I moved on to check out the next row of displays. "Using the Lord's Prayer to Microevolve Bacteria" was diagrammed at the nearest stall. I shook my head, appalled at the lack of curiosity here, all these bright kids closing their minds to other ways of seeing the world and the people in it. This Apocryphal Revelation was quite the religion, made up of people trying only to prove concepts dreamed up hundreds of years ago by men who had neither the cleverness to envision dinosaurs nor the creativity to imagine airplanes.

"Quite a turnout, wouldn't you say?"

I whipped around and discovered Pastor Mealy standing behind me, appearing more gaunt than I remembered. His lips curved in a smile as warm as a leech.

Chapter 23

"Lots of people, that's for sure," I said, swallowing.

"I take my greatest pleasure in days like today, where I can touch the faithful by teaching children to recognize the Truth of the Word of the Lord, and to see His hand on every aspect of their life." He leaned toward me, and I caught a whiff of something sausagey. "Tell me, Mira, are you considering joining our church?"

An Emily Dickinson poem, one of the few I remembered from college, spilled past my lips. "Some keep the Sabbath going to church, but I keep it staying at home, with a bobolink for a chorister, and an orchard for a dome." I smiled. Turned out my entire English degree had come down to this, a $12,833 comeback.

Pastor Mealy clearly didn't think it'd been worth the time or money. His eyes hooded, like he was about to slip underwater, and his lips drew down. I was sure he would have begun exorcising me if not for the commotion at the far corner.

He glanced over his shoulder and then back at me. "That's Naomi. You remember my wife? She conducts prayer circles for the needy. Possibly she can help you?"

I knew when I was being dismissed and strolled gladly out of Robert Mealy's presence toward the noise and away from the rows of displays and crowds of people dressed for the sock hop. Naomi was indeed at the center of a circle of women. She was dressed plainly except for the bright rings she wore on her left hand, and she was seated in her wheelchair, a quilt across her lap on this sweltering day. She appeared relatively young, in her late thirties or early forties, and I wondered what had put her in the wheelchair.

Her eyes were closed, and she spoke rapidly in a guttural voice. I couldn't make out her words, but the tone reminded me of the horking sound Luna made just before she threw up. Only Naomi was horking rapidly, and there was an unsettling familiarity to the syntax of her speech. It brought to mind a Pink Floyd album played backward, something an old college friend of mine liked to do when he got high.

"She speaks in tongues."

I turned to see Christina Sahlberg, the woman who had escorted me off the grounds the day before, staring reverently at Naomi.

"Can you understand her?" I asked.

She tapped her chest. "Listen not with your ears, but with your heart."

Both organs heard only horking sounds. "What does *your* heart hear?"

"According to the apostle Paul, anyone who speaks in tongues does not speak to men but to God. Indeed, no one understands him; he utters mysteries with his spirit."

Yup, just what I thought. She couldn't understand what Naomi was saying, either. Fortunately for those of us with just the one tongue, Naomi was winding down. Her speedy grunting was becoming sparse, and her eyes were fluttering. She swooned a little, blinked, and stared right at me.

"Have I been speaking with the Lord?"

"I guess," I said.

The women around me started applauding quietly. Naomi's face grew stern. "He has told me that we are not being proper women. 'Wives, submit yourselves unto your own husbands, as it is fit in the Lord. Neither was the man created for the woman, but the woman for the man.'"

Boy, would Mrs. Berns have a field day with that. "Mrs. Mealy?" I interrupted, my heart hammering. I didn't like to make a scene, but my bullshit bucket was about full up. "I think we all have a right to be here, even without a man."

She studied me, her eyes on fire. She wasn't used to being questioned. "Here in this room, or in God's house?"

"Anywhere," I said, holding out my hands. "All of us have value."

The women around me were whispering, but Naomi commanded their attention. "Of course. All of us have value. And if you ever feel lonely, you can turn to God."

I shrugged. As someone who'd as recently as last month turned to a fiberglass statue when I felt lonely, I was not in a position to judge. I merged back into the group of women circling Naomi as she started on another mini sermon. I found myself standing next to a stranger, a mousy woman hovering near Naomi's wheelchair.

She had kinky permed hair that was a drab brown, no makeup, and a shapeless dress covering her sturdy body. She looked to be in her early forties, and she had terrible posture. Except for her feverishly bright eyes, she struck me as the human equivalent of a paper bag, unassuming, waiting to be filled. What caught my attention was the ferocious intensity with which she stared at the back of Naomi's head, like she was drowning and Naomi was the sharp end of a sword held out to pull her in.

"Hi," I whispered. "My name's Mira."

The paper-bag woman slid her eyes at me and blushed before returning her gaze, passionate and hungry, to the back of Naomi's head.

"Do you go to the church here?"

No response.

"Do you live in Clitherall?"

Still no response, but I caught a glare from one of the other women in the circle and took the hint. This was going to be one hell of an article, I tell you. Stepford meets *Hee Haw*.

I was beginning to write it in my head while searching for an exit when I ran into my third Mealy of the day. Alicia stood in my path wearing a proper cotton dress that covered her from shins to wrists. Her hair was held back in a tortoiseshell band, and she was makeup-free. Surprisingly, she wasn't sweating.

"Mira! I can't believe you made it! That is so awesome!"

I eyeballed her, my short supply of patience long ago sapped by this alien atmosphere. "Cut the shit, Alicia. I don't like you, you don't like me, and nobody wants me to be here."

She stepped out of her good cheer like it was an ill-fitting sweater. "Suit yourself." She studied her thumbnail. "Do unto others what you would want them to get for you."

"I think that's 'Do unto others as you would have them do unto you.'"

Alicia scowled. "You might work at a library, but that doesn't mean you know The Book. Don't correct me."

"Hm." I felt my fight reflex stand taller. "How about I lend you some money?"

She appeared genuinely confused. "What for?"

"So you don't have to steal anymore."

Alicia's face twisted into an ugly mask. "Did those bitches at that jewelry store say I was stealing? I'll be on their asses so quick."

Stealing from the jewelry store? She was a piece of work. "Actually, I wasn't referring to the jewelry store, though I guess that means you tried to rip them off, too." I spoke out of the corner of my mouth like I was sharing a secret. "I don't think Jesus likes thieves."

She puffed herself up and jammed her pointer finger into my shoulder. "You know what Jesus doesn't like? He doesn't like Bible-bashing, bad-book-reading false witnesses like you. My dad is going to shut you down, you know? He's going to bring lawyers from Liberty Law School to the library, and they're going to bring so much media with them that you won't even be able to get to the front door. Everyone is going to know what sort of filth you buy and promote with their tax dollars.

Everyone." Her face was turning an unattractive purple, and I felt my own mug darken to match hers.

I pushed her hand away and leaned in close. "I'm not doing anything wrong. It's a library, and they're books."

She smirked. "Then why are you shaking?"

I clenched my fists to still my hands. I was angry, but I was scared, too. Had I really gotten the library in trouble? "I guess I'm just overcome with God's love," I said through gritted teeth. "Thanks *so much* for showing me the way."

I turned on my heel and marched out, but my tail wasn't between my legs. It was checking the wind, and when I saw it was clear, I scurried over to the Mealys' house behind the assembly hall. I was either going to uncover something to shed a true light on this fanatic family or I was going to poop under their sink.

My heart pattered around my rib cage as I strode toward the tiny white house and up the wheelchair ramp like I knew what I was doing. My ears were extra large and set on rotate, scanning for that first "Hey you! You can't go in there!"

But I heard no such warnings, which I took as tacit permission to enter.

I yanked open the screen door and strolled into the combination kitchen and dining room. Not surprisingly, it was spick and span. No subpar wives here.

Off the kitchen was a living room featuring a threadbare sectional couch with a mismatched recliner. There was one bookshelf sagging with religious texts next to a modest-size television. Three doors and a stairway led off the living room. The first doorway opened to a bathroom, the second to a bedroom. A quick glance indicated it was Alicia's. The bedspread was orange with pink flowers, there was a romance novel with a florid cover on the nightstand, and the clothes neatly hung in the closet appeared to be Alicia's size.

I riffled through the two storage boxes in the closet, sure I could hear a giant stopwatch in the sky ticking off the moments until I was caught. I wasn't going to stop, though, not until I found something. Unfortunately, the boxes were no help. They both contained ribbons from track and home economics, high school yearbooks, and dolls. At the bottom of the larger box was a tidy collection of clothes that were definitely *not* from the Eisenhower era—spandex tank tops, miniskirts, and heels. I wasn't surprised at this evidence of Alicia's double life. I'd seen both sides of her already.

I hurried through the dresser drawers, starting with the small one. All women hide the good stuff in their underwear drawer, and Alicia was no exception.

"Bingo," I whispered, pulling out a dime bag of weed. I thought for a moment what I could do with this information. I'd get personal satisfaction from telling her dad or the cops, but how would I explain that I knew she had pot in her dresser drawer? I settled for spritzing her feminine deodorant spray all over the grass. It probably wouldn't kill her, but it'd give her one mother of a headache when she smoked it.

I never claimed to be a taker of the high road.

I cruised into the last room on this floor—the primary bedroom on the north side of the house. I bypassed the bed, which was watched over by a sad-faced Jesus on the wall, and made straight for the mission-style dresser. The top was covered with photos of a cute baby girl with thick black hair and brown eyes, and she was about nine months old in all of them.

A framed birth certificate stood at the center with Alicia Marie Mealy's name stamped on it in cursive letters. I studied the birth certificate, surprised to discover that Alicia was in fact twenty-four years old, a good four or five years older than I would have guessed. I studied the pictures of the brown-eyed baby, recalling that the Alicia Mealy I had just spoken to had cornflower-blue eyes, the light kind you can't get with colored contact lenses.

Who was the baby in these photos?

I snapped a shot of one of the baby pictures and the birth certificate with my digital camera.

I was reaching for the smallest drawer in the dresser when I heard voices right outside the open window. My heart stopped, and then galumphed forward. I crouched, but the voices didn't move on, so I crawled out of the bedroom and toward the front door. Straining, I could still hear the rhythm and tones of a man and a woman talking outside the Mealys' bedroom window on the far side of the house, and it sounded like they were fighting. Was it the pastor and his wife?

At this point, I had two choices. I could try to sneak out and hope they didn't come around and see me, or I could stand up and walk out proudly like I was supposed to be here. I voted for the latter, and before I could talk sense into myself, I popped up, pulled open the screen door, and ran straight into Battle Lake police chief Gary Wohnt.

Chapter 24

"Oof."

That was the sound he made as I barreled into his side, bounced off, and fell onto my bumper.

"Oh, jeez," I said. "I'm totally sorry. I didn't see you there."

Gary stared at me through his mirrored glasses and offered me his hand. It was strange to see him out of uniform. He seemed smaller in his white T-shirt and khaki shorts, but he was still a solid man, and he appeared angry as a bear. His lips were pulled tight, reflecting sunlight off their Carmexed surface, and his black hair was slicked back with gel.

"What'd you hear?" he growled.

I wasn't sure I'd caught that right. "What am I doing here?" I asked.

My question threw him off, and as he darted a glance over my shoulder, toward the back of the house, I realized it must have been him I'd heard arguing outside the Mealys' window. Me running into him had been an unhappy accident, and I moved from defense to offense. "Who were you talking to?"

Gary squeezed his hands into fists, and he grew a little taller. "What were you doing inside the Mealys'?"

Uh-oh. "I asked first."

"I wasn't breaking the law," he grunted. Given that I'd been trespassing, his jab was a less-than-subtle trump card.

"I was looking for a bathroom," I said, trying the lie on for size.

"In someone's house?"

My story picked up a couple decorations. "The one in the assembly hall was full, and I didn't want to miss any of the inspiring exchanges going on inside. I thought this was one of the cabins. Certainly, the pastor and his wife can spare a little toilet paper."

He crossed his arms. "So you knew this was their house you were breaking into and entering?"

Ooh, he was good. "I wasn't positive until you just told me. Like I said, it looks like one of the cabins. Besides, there was no breaking going on, just entering. No harm, no foul."

I tried to brush past, but Gary caught my arm in a grip as tight as a handcuff. "You were at the murder scene in Clitherall."

My stomach clenched. "I was."

"How'd you end up there?"

I decided to tell him the straight truth, that I followed a police car thinking it had been a friend of mine who had been hurt. It was hard to tell whether he bought it, his red-brown face seeming impassive behind the sunglasses. Not for the first time, I wondered what frivolous, fickle Kennie and he had ever talked about, and what sort of sex life they could possibly have had. Did he take off his sunglasses in bed? Did he whisper in her ear?

Not anymore—at least I knew that much for sure.

"That's it?" he asked. "You don't know anything more about Lucy Lebowski?"

I shook my head. "She's worked at the library for a couple months. She was a sweet kid, and I can't believe anyone who knew her would hurt her." I sized him up. "Got any leads?"

He snorted, but for a millisecond, it'd looked like he was going to let something spill. Unfortunately, Sarah Ruth chose that moment to appear.

"Mira! I was hoping I'd run into you here."

"Hey." Her sudden appearance discombobulated me. "How'd the library closing go?"

"Just fine. No problems at all." She tossed Gary a quizzical expression. He did his best impression of a statue.

"Sarah Ruth, this is Gary Wohnt. He's the Battle Lake chief of police. Gary, this is Sarah Ruth. She's going to be running the library soon." This was probably the first that Gary had heard I was moving, but he didn't act surprised. In fact, he didn't seem to be breathing.

Sarah nodded at him. "We've met. We both attend services here." She fidgeted and turned her attention to me, but not before I picked up on a silent communication passing between them, some shift in the air and the tilt of their heads. "Have you gotten a chance to visit the science fair?"

Gary took that as a cue to leave, striding toward the assembly hall. "I didn't see much science," I said, watching him go, "but I did take a gander at the projects inside." Once he was out of sight, I returned my focus to her. "Can I ask you something? You work at a library, and you read a wide variety of books. As an educated person, how can you support a church that would host a Creation Science Fair?"

Sarah Ruth draped her arm over my shoulder and steered me toward the assembly hall. "I take some of it, like the faith and fellowship, and leave the rest, like the talking in tongues and good wives / bad wives stuff. The important thing is that I feel like I'm part of a community."

I snorted. "A community that thinks women should be in the home and evolution is a joke?"

"Come on, even you don't know how evolution got started," she said softly. "Who's to say that it wasn't part of God's master plan?"

I pulled away. "You know, I think I've had enough religion for one day. You go on without me."

She frowned. "You sure?"

"I'm sure. See you at work tomorrow?"

"Sounds good."

I couldn't miss the easing of her expression as I walked toward my car, and it made me sad. I liked Sarah Ruth, and I wanted her to be a freethinker. I supposed there was a lot I didn't know about her. One thing was for sure, though: I had lied when I told her I'd had enough religion for the day. My next stop was going to be Nordland Lutheran Church in downtown Battle Lake. I didn't know Pastor Harvey Winter personally, but Sid and Nancy, regular congregants, said he was a stand-up guy. I wanted to get his perspective on this new Bible camp, and maybe shed some light on the warriors-for-Jesus tableau I'd witnessed the other day.

I wasn't sure if pastors kept regular business hours, but was happy to find the church unlocked. I had long admired the building—compact, constructed of old-fashioned brick, and shaped like a one-room schoolhouse until the large addition had been tacked on to the back. The church was on Lake Street, the main drag in Battle Lake, and its location promised standing room only on summer Sundays. It had originally housed a Baptist congregation and in the early 1900s had been the only church that offered services in English. That congregation had moved on, and now the church was Lutheran.

When I pulled open the door, I was soothed by the rush of cool air and smell of fresh flowers and lemon furniture polish. The original building was 125 years old, and it had that serene, solid feeling of lasting architecture and gathering people. The foyer bulletin board was covered with flyers, but it held no furniture except for a worn bench. I walked forward, reluctant to enter the churchy part, when I heard the echo of a distant conversation coming up the stairs to my right.

I followed the voices down the cement stairs, into the musty basement, past a cafeteria and kids' playroom, and to a wooden door with a large smoked-glass pane in the top center. Pastor Winter was written on the glass in two-inch black, scrolly-font letters.

"I advise you to think twice before you follow that idea. I simply cannot endorse it."

"Y'all haven't even seen it!"

Kennie. And she was talking to Pastor Winter! I held up my hand to knock on the glass.

". . . coffins outside of the church or a funeral home is . . ."

I paused my hand. I'd missed Pastor Winter's main point, and my curiosity was killing me. I was pretty sure the two of them were *not* talking about penis-enlargement devices, though.

"Well, I didn't come for your blessing, Pastor Winter. I came to seek your advice on Gary, and I guess I've gotten that. Good day to you."

A huffy Kennie yanked open the door before I had a chance to rearrange my snooping face.

Chapter 25

"Hi, Kennie."

She was dressed in a leather motorcycle hat and Sturgis T-shirt with the bottom yanked up over the front, through the collar, and back down to the bottom, turning it into a makeshift halter top. Her belly button winked at me above her denim skirt, and she wore silver-bell anklets on each foot. It was actually an outfit I'd wear, which made me grab the wall for support.

"You were listening in?" she asked, her face tight.

"I just showed up. I didn't hear anything. Didn't you see my hand, ready to knock?"

She pursed her lips but let me off the hook on that front. "You still coming over tomorrow morning?"

"You betcha," I lied.

"Good." With that, she turned and jangled out of the basement, which left me staring at a tiny man who'd just stood up from behind an enormous wooden desk. He reminded me of a friendly mole, with a twitchy nose and kind brown eyes peering from behind reading glasses. He wore a white cotton shirt and blue jeans, and the informality of his dress caught me off guard.

"Hi, Pastor Winter? I'm Mira James."

He smiled and offered me a hand. "Of course. The librarian. Sidney and Nancy talk about you often. It's my good pleasure to welcome you to our church."

"Thank you." I entered his office, shook his hand, and relaxed a notch. "Do you have a couple minutes? I have a dilemma I'm hoping you can help me with."

"I'm meeting with a couple for wedding counseling in twenty, but I'd be happy to talk with you until then. How can I help?"

I had a hunch that Pastor Winter wouldn't talk smack about religion, even if he were the gossipy type, which he clearly wasn't. He radiated quiet confidence, and Santa Claus didn't have better smile wrinkles. I considered lying and pretending I was putting together an article on local churches, but if I was going to lie in front of Jesus, it was going to be about something important. I dived straight to the truth. "I have concerns about the new Bible camp, the one over by Clitherall?"

Pastor Winter's face darkened, but he didn't interrupt.

"It's run by the Mealy family, and they've been stepping on some toes. They've started a petition to censor what books I can display at the library, and I think they're dangerous."

He spoke over steepled fingers. "Do you have any evidence of that?"

I thought of Alicia's likely homophobic comment to Nancy. I couldn't remember her exact wording, and even if I could, it would be secondhand. Still, I felt defensive. It's hard to justify your instincts to strangers. "No, but I did see something really disturbing out there a couple days ago. In the assembly hall, there were a bunch of kids who seemed like they were in a trance, and they were chanting about being warriors for Jesus."

Pastor Winter nodded. "Christ's Church of the Apocryphal Revelation is, in many ways, a religion unto itself. They are very evangelical, charismatic, and conservative. You haven't told me anything that's out of line with their tenets."

My defensiveness grew. "You don't think it's weird, turning little kids into warriors? Who are they fighting?"

Pastor Winter raised an eyebrow. "Possibly those who are judging and censoring their beliefs?"

I sighed. "Judging someone who's attacking me seems like a perfectly sensible reaction. They have no right to say what the library can and can't carry, or what sort of people God loves and hates."

"God loves us all, Mira, and I would encourage you to practice greater tolerance."

I eyed him suspiciously. "Does Nordland have Apocryphal Revelation leanings?"

He chuckled, and ten years fell off his face. "No, this church belongs to ELCA, the Evangelical Lutheran Church in America. We consider ourselves the progressive arm of the Lutheran church, but there's room for all those in service of God."

I kept pushing. "So you don't think the Mealys' behavior is worrisome at all?"

"If by 'worrisome,' you mean out of character for charismatic believers, no, I don't think it's unusual. And while I support the library's right to offer a wide variety of literature, I also support any person's right to question that selection."

That's when I realized that I'd come here to validate my hypothesis that the Mealys were dangerous aliens from outer space, and to get Pastor Winter's support in purging them from this town. That support wasn't forthcoming, but I was no quitter. I tried a different tack. "Have you met the Mealys?"

He hesitated. "They introduced themselves to me when they first moved to town several months ago."

"What'd you think of them?"

"I thought they were devoted in their faith and transparent in their intentions."

Not good enough. "Did you like them, or did they make you want to check for your wallet?"

He brushed his hand over his mouth, like he was trying to erase a smile. "I'm sure you understand that I can't comment on other people's personalities." He adjusted his glasses. "This church is a haven for all, and all have a place here."

I wouldn't give up. "Did you know they had a Creation Science Fair today?" I asked.

"I did. Science and faith are compatible."

"Compatible, maybe; interchangeable, no." I sighed. "You're not going to give me anything, are you?"

His smile lines crinkled. "I understand your discomfort. Encountering those different from us can be difficult, and I'm glad you felt able to talk with me about it." He stood. "I encourage you to attend services here at Nordland this Sunday so you can get a feel for a different type of worship than what you encountered at New Millennium. I'm afraid I have to be going now, though."

I shook his offered hand, disappointed and weirdly relieved that he hadn't joined in on bashing the Bible camp. "I appreciate your time."

"Not at all. Please let me know if I can help you with anything else."

As I turned to leave, I had a fleeting picture of the meek, mousy woman who'd been watching Naomi so intently. It was a long shot, but I had nothing to lose. "There might be one more thing. There was this woman at the Creation Science Fair today, and she looked so out of place and couldn't peel her eyes off of Naomi Mealy. Since you know most locals, I'm wondering if you know her?"

"What was her name?"

"I'm afraid I didn't catch it. She was a couple inches taller than me, pear-shaped, with sort of frizzy brown hair. She was overall sort of brown. I'd guess she was in her forties."

He nodded. "That could be Mrs. Mealy's sister. If it was, she lives over on Hancock Lake, a couple miles from the Bible camp. On Golden Pond Road, I believe, right next door to the Krausses' pink house. The Krausses are congregants here at Nordland."

That she could so quickly acquire a lake home surprised me. "Did she move here with the Mealys?"

"No, she's lived here for many years."

The mystery deepened. "I wonder why I've never met her."

"She has a job toward Saint Cloud, I believe."

"That's one heck of a commute."

I could tell he was losing patience, but he kept his voice neutral. "Many Battle Lake residents drive to jobs many miles away. They consider it a small price to pay to live in such a beautiful area. Back to your mystery woman. We can't be sure she is the sister I am describing. Is there a reason you're asking?"

"Not really." I sighed. "I just can't get her out of my head. She looked so lonely and angry."

His forehead puckered. "Sorry I couldn't be of more help."

"No, no. You've been very helpful. If nothing else, you've shown me that not all pastors are loopy." I offered him a grin, but he didn't take it. He nodded at me once, a bemused expression on his face, and I left the way I came.

As I walked into the sun, I felt a crawling under my skin, like it was shifting over my muscles, and looked to see red welts growing on my arms.

Stress hives.

I needed to get out of this town.

Chapter 26

Guided by Sid's words, I spent the rest of Thursday evening making amends to my vegetable garden. I bought lettuce and radish seeds and three overgrown tomato plants on my way home, though it made me sad that Johnny wasn't the one selling them to me. Had he started a window garden in Madison? Was he making new friends? Did he ever think about me and what could have been? I tossed my head. There was no point in hauling those thoughts around.

Under Luna's watchful eyes, I planted the quick-growing vegetables and the gnarly, overgrown potted tomatoes in the garden's empty patches. I'd be long gone by the time my repairs came to fruition, but it felt good to be down on my hands and knees in the dirt, visibly making amends. When I was done, my garden didn't look great, but it looked better, and when I watered the plot early the next morning, I whispered an apology.

I wasn't used to gardening before dawn, and I was amazed at the freshness of the day. The sun wasn't yet pinking the horizon, and nature had set aside her August cotton mouth to sparkle the grass with dew. After I watered my vegetable and flower gardens and fed and watered my kitty and dog, I stretched. I would bike to town today. The three-mile trip was hilly, but I didn't want to interrupt the blanketing stillness of dawn by cranking up my car.

As I cruised the gravel on my ten-speed mountain bike, rocks crunching like cornflakes under my tires, I mulled over the people I'd be leaving Battle Lake to. The Mealys were religious fanatics and had a daughter with questionable ethics. Pastor Winter seemed like a stand-up guy, though he was a little too generous in his judgments for my taste.

Sarah Ruth fit well in the library and the town. Tina at 4Ts was going through a bad patch, but I could help her deal with her embezzler, if not her husband. Weston, the tick curator, was just passing through, but that was one thing about Battle Lake that I'd really miss—how it attracted all types from all corners. Between the odd tourists and the odder locals, like Mrs. Berns and Kennie, I could honestly say I'd never been bored in this town.

My plan was to start packing tonight after opening the Fortune Café for Sid and Nancy and putting in my shift at the library. I could get a couple rooms bundled up and still have time to run out to Naomi Mealy's sister's house on Hancock Lake to see if she really was the chick I had seen at the Creation Science Fair. Something about the intensity in her eyes drew me, and I figured the more activities I did away from home, the easier it'd be to avoid drinking.

Nothing like spying on strangers to keep a gal distracted.

I coasted down the last big hill on Whiskey Road before I hit Battle Lake. My hair flew behind me like wings, and I closed my eyes. Only for a millisecond, though. I had terrible balance. As I cruised into town, I was soothed by how quiet it was. I felt like I could walk into any house and grab something out of the refrigerator without the sleeping owners being any the wiser. You feel invincible in the early morning, when everyone else is so vulnerable. Getting up early might be part of my new regimen when I moved back to the Cities.

My bike glided down Lake Avenue to the Fortune Café. I smelled West Battle Lake half a mile away and imagined I could see the giant statue of Chief Wenonga around the corner, six-pack abs rippling in the morning sun, fierce eyes ever watchful over the lake. I was glad to have him back in town. He was the man I was going to miss the most when I moved, even if he was fiberglass.

"Morning," I whispered in his general direction.

No point in being desperate. Hot statues preferred subtlety from their admirers.

I slapped out my kickstand and dug around my jean shorts pocket for the Fortune key, admiring the café. It had originally been a cool Victorian house, full of windows and small rooms, around since the early 1900s. When Sid and Nancy bought it, they slapped on a coat of sage-green paint with white trim and renovated the inside to turn the downstairs into the café/bakery and the upstairs into the apartment.

I strode up the front lawn. The marigolds and lavender lining the sidewalk looked a little crusty, and I made a note to water them before I left. I didn't see a hose on the front of the house, but there were the double tracks of a wagon in the lawn. I could fill up buckets with water and haul them out here.

A strong whoosh of bakery-goods odors gusted toward me on a breeze, and I smiled. I couldn't wait to get inside and be surrounded by that heavenly cinnamon smell. As I drew in another deep breath, my hackles tapped my shoulder. The smell of baked goods should *not* be this strong, ten feet from the front door. Had it been left open?

My heartbeat did a little giddy-up kick.

The deathly quiet of the town was all of a sudden not so benign. I glanced left, right, and spotted nothing out of place. I continued to the door and found it firmly locked. Shoulders still tense, I unlocked it and stuck my head in.

"Hello? Anyone here?"

The fresh-goody smell was even stronger inside, and rightly so. The front room was washed in shadows with the uneven rays of the rising sun peeking through the curtained windows. I stepped toward the only light switch I was sure of, the one behind the front counter that I looked at every time I ordered food.

I minced through the dark, toward the light, feeling better with my decision. Once the room was fully illuminated, I could shake the paranoid feeling.

My hope proved to be premature, however. Three strides to the counter, and I was on my knees. I'd tripped over something, and sharp glass ground into my knees and palms. I pushed off, feeling my skin pierced in thirty different spots, but I couldn't make out what I'd landed on. Panicking, I bolted toward the light switch.

I flicked it on.

Washed in light, the main room was a mess.

Chapter 27

The window facing the West Battle Lake side of the house was a gaping, jagged hole, and the floor was covered in hundreds of glass shards. I gingerly brushed them from my hands and blood-pricked knees and eyeballed the large rock I'd tripped over. It was gray, about the size of a cooking pumpkin, and it had white paper strapped to it with twine.

The paper crinkled as I tugged it out. It was a standard 8.5-by-11-inch white printer sheet, and some unoriginal genius had cut out letters from a magazine to spell GOD MADE ADAM AND EVE, NOT ADAM AND STEVE. GO BACK TO SODDOM, IMMORAL HEATHENS.

Blood from my nicked palms melted into the paper, creating a gruesome frame, and I realized I was holding my breath.

"Those fucking *fuckers.*"

And I knew who I meant.

Somebody from that wacked-out New Millennium Bible Camp had done this. Sid and Nancy had lived in Battle Lake for more than five years, and people had been drawn to their warmth, their knack for baking, and their humor since day one. I imagine there were those in town who didn't approve of their sexual orientation, but they at least had the sense to keep their ignorance to themselves.

No, this was the first outright hateful incident that'd happened at the café to my knowledge, and it didn't take a genius to see it directly correlated to the group at the Bible camp. Sodom indeed, and spelled wrong. You'd think if someone were going to slice letters from magazines one by one, they'd take the time to check their spelling first.

I folded up the note, shoved it in my back pocket, and stormed into the bakery kitchen to wash my hands and knees. Then I walked the whole building, bottom floor to top and back down again. I didn't see any more damage or vitriol. Convinced that the harm was contained to the main room, I called the Battle Lake Police Department and got through on the third ring.

"Battle Lake Police."

"Gary?"

"Hummph."

"This is Mira James. I'm over at the Fortune Café. Sid and Nancy asked me to open up for them this morning. I'm afraid we have an incident on our hands."

I heard a thump in the background and some scrabbling. Either Chief Wohnt had fallen off his chair, or he'd set down the phone. When he came back on the line, his voice was Sisyphean in its weariness. "Why am I not surprised?"

"I won't take that personally," I said, totally taking that personally. "Do you want to know what the incident is?"

"A dead body."

He said it so matter-of-factly that I couldn't help but snort. "Not even. Somebody hurled a rock through the café window. There's glass everywhere."

I heard a creak, like he was sitting up in his chair. "Was there anything on the rock?"

"Like lichen?" I'd decided before I called that I wasn't going to mention the note. I knew from experience that Battle Lake didn't have the means or the finances to fingerprint a piece of paper from a plain ole vandalism case. The only thing I would accomplish by telling someone about the note was to make Sid and Nancy feel bad, and possibly add fuel to the fire of the haters who'd tossed it.

Chief Wohnt's voice came over the line slowly, like he was trying to talk a three-year-old out of a tree. "No, not like lichen. Like *words*."

"Hm. Lemme go check." I marched in place so it sounded like I was striding toward something. "No. Nope. No words on the rock. Just some twine."

"What was the twine holding?"

Curse words. Why did I keep underestimating this man? "Maybe it was just put on there for purchase, so the rock could be hurled farther. But what do I know?" I shrugged even though he couldn't see it. "You're the police chief, not me. You better come down and look at it."

"Don't touch anything."

"Then you better get here quick because I have a coffee shop to open up."

A grunt was my answer. I went outside to water the front flowers while I waited. There was no wagon in sight, and I didn't know the combination to the storage shed, so I grabbed the empty five-gallon pickle bucket from next to the back faucet, filled it to the top with icy water, and hauled it to the front. The earth soaked up the water so fast I swore I heard slurping sounds. I made three more trips with the bucket for good measure and was back inside when Gary showed up.

"Chief Wohnt."

He wasn't wearing his sunglasses. I was startled by the blackness of his eyes, like they were two pools of oil swimming in his tanned face. It was unsettling and not his fault, and I wondered if his disconcerting eyes were the reason he usually wore the mirrored glasses.

"Where's the rock?" he asked.

"Over here." I gestured around the corner from the entryway and into the main room. Gary walked over, knelt by the rock, studied it, looked toward every corner of the room as if calculating distances, and clomped his way over to the broken window.

"You haven't moved anything?"

"I might have nudged the rock when I tripped over it in the dark, but that's about where it was."

He studied me, head cocked, and I had to turn away from his fierce gaze. "Do you mind if I sweep this up?" I asked, disconcerted. "I told Sid and Nancy I'd have this place open by six o'clock."

"Around here, people usually put notes on a rock before they throw it through the window," he growled.

This type of vandalism clearly happened far more than I knew. "You can check outside. A note could have fallen off before the rock was lobbed." I was careful to not *exactly* lie.

He was quiet for a beat. Then: "I'll do that."

"So I can sweep up?"

He was still studying the room. He apparently didn't find any reason to object. "You can, but keep your eyes open for anything out of place."

"Will do." The next words spilled out before I could stop them. "Don't you think it's weird, though, that this act of vandalism happens around the same time as the Creation Science Fair out at the New Millennium?"

Gary bristled like a dog that smells a deer. "What are you suggesting?"

"Just that it seems like an awful big coincidence."

His eyes pierced me like inky lasers. "A lot of people come through the area in the summer. Is there something you want to tell me?"

"Nah. Good luck searching outside."

Gary freed me from his penetrating gaze and stepped outside. As soon as I was sure he was out of sight, I pulled the note out of my pocket and hid it in the crack between the caramel and vanilla Italian syrups. It felt too conspicuous in my pocket, like my left butt cheek was glowing with a red X and the words "She's hiding it in here." When the chief returned, I had most of the front room swept. "You find anything?" I asked.

"No. And it's too dry for footprints."

My shoulders dropped. "So you might have to just write this one off?"

He ignored me, again studying all the corners of the room. "You didn't move *anything*?"

"I moved the glass when I swept it." I was such a good not-liar.

He saved me another black-eyed probe. "When Sid and Nancy get back, send one of them down to the station to fill out a report. In the meantime, call Boechler's to fix the window. With the August Moon Festival tomorrow night, we're sure to get some rain."

That sounded like a joke, but Gary Wohnt was as easy to read as a fish. "You going to the festival?"

He rubbed the back of his neck, and it made a scratching sound. "I'll be on duty. If you have anything to tell me, you know where to find me."

"Uh-huh." I made like I was real interested in a scabby piece of food crusted to the table nearest me. One beat, two beats, three beats, and Gary turned on his heel and headed out the door. I finished wiping down the counters, got some fresh coffee brewing, and had served about a third of Battle Lake by the time Sid and Nancy arrived.

Thankfully, Mr. Boechler was already installing the new window, and I'd returned the vile (and poorly formatted) note to my back pocket. After I made sure Nancy's sister's operation had gone OK, I brought them up to speed on the broken window. Neither one seemed particularly fazed.

"Kids," Nancy said, sliding her rainbow apron over her head and tying it at the waist.

Sid nodded in agreement. "I heard a couple were caught spray-painting the water tower last weekend. It's hot, the summer's getting boring, and they're being teenagers."

I put on a happy face and nodded.

It wasn't thrill-seeking teenagers. They wouldn't have bothered with a note, they wouldn't have referenced Sodom, and they certainly wouldn't have targeted one of their favorite hangouts. Battle Lake high schoolers were treated with respect at the Fortune Café, an unusual experience for kids that age.

The game and computer room was often full of study groups during the school year, and in the summer, the Fortune was a popular hangout for teens looking for relief from the heat. They drank their Diet Cokes and smoothies and bragged about how they couldn't wait to escape this ten-cent town.

"You guys need anything else before I head to the library?" I asked.

"We're good," Sid said. "We owe you one."

"Anytime." I slapped on my best smile, gathered up my iced coffee and breakfast bagel, and braved the molten day. The temperature must have risen thirty degrees in the three and a half hours I had been in the café. *Phew.*

I balanced my drink and sandwich in my bike basket and pedaled the three short blocks to the library, waving to locals I recognized on the way. When I arrived, Sarah Ruth had already opened up, her brown slacks and polo shirt a professional contrast to my T-shirt and jean shorts. I'd never been one to forgo comfort for rules.

Mrs. Berns was nowhere in sight, and I chose to ignore the distance that had developed between Sarah Ruth and me the last two days. We exchanged pleasantries before I planted myself in front of the computer and typed up my article on the Creation Science Fair. I used every passive-aggressive bone in my body to walk the line between responsible journalism and reckless make-funalism.

> On Thursday, August 20, the New Millennium Bible Camp in Clitherall hosted their first annual Creation Science Fair. The event had a real sense of community and drew over 100 people interested in the biblical view of science. Attendants were not disappointed. Featured displays included a rebuff of the theory of evolution featuring the irrefutable hypothesis "My Great-Great-Grandpa Was a Christian, Not a Monkey" and an examination into how capitalistic structures could have been successfully applied in biblical times.

In addition, the creationists looked to the pre-literacy era for inspiration on women's possible contributions to our current global economy. Entrants also tackled the sticky issue of teen sexuality and the hotly debated realm of thermodynamics.

All the exhibits in the Creation Science Fair displayed a bandwagon appeal and the ability to think inside the box. Pastor Mealy, host of the event, said, "I take my greatest pleasure in days like today, where I can touch the faithful . . ." Wednesday and Sunday services at Christ's Church of the Apocryphal Revelation, the church at New Millennium Bible Camp, are open to the public.

I sent the article off to Ron as a Word attachment along with a picture of the monkey exhibit, just to give him his second coronary this week. I'd acclimate him to me beating deadlines right before I skipped town.

Sarah Ruth and I made polite small talk throughout the day, which was uneventful except for a visit from Weston Lippmann, tick curator. As soon as I spotted the wilted wildflowers in his hand, I got an apprehensive, sour feeling in my belly.

"Hi, Mira!" he said cheerfully, flinging his cape over each shoulder so it rested on his back like folded bat wings. "These are for you."

He grinned his lopsided grin as he thrust the daisies at me. They were my favorite flower next to lilacs, but I was in no mood to be courted. Heck, I was in no *century* to be courted. "Thanks for the flowers. They're beautiful. I don't date."

"Oh, I'm . . . you're . . . I'm so sorry! I didn't know."

I tilted my head. "There's nothing to know. I'm not dating, but I can be your friend while you're here."

He smiled again, but it had lost its wattage. Having your offer of romance exchanged for secondhand friendship feels about as good as getting your leg humped by a raccoon. And I would know.

"They're just flowers," he said, "and you're the only person in town I know." He made that strange throat-clearing sound I remembered from our first meeting.

"I appreciate the gesture." I wanted to alleviate his discomfort. "Are you going to the August Moon Festival tomorrow?"

"I hadn't thought of it." Now he was pouting.

"Well, you should," I said, already souring on my friendship offer. If he was a manbaby, I wasn't interested. "It's a good time."

A squawky voice piped up behind me. "I'll take you to the festival."

Mrs. Berns popped up from behind the front counter. "When did you get here?" I asked, surprised.

She frowned. "Are you suggesting I'm not a hard worker?"

The clock told me it was quarter to three, and this was the first I'd seen her. "You've been here all day?"

"All I'm saying is that if the boy doesn't want to go to the August Moon Festival alone, I'd be happy to take him. Granny needs an escort." She smiled sweetly, her perfectly even dentures gleaming in the light.

Weston glanced at me, unsure how to respond. I kept my face smooth. "Sure, that would be fine," he said. "Thank you for the offer."

"Great, sonny. You can pick me up at five o'clock. I live over at the nursing home." She strode off to dust the bookshelves like she'd been doing it all along.

"You'll like Mrs. Berns," I said, trying to convince myself on his behalf. "She's nice."

"Yeah, she reminds me of my grandma."

"Hm. I wouldn't tell her that. She's pretty spirited. Just remember that no means no."

He blanched. "I would never!"

"No, I mean tell her that. Sometimes she gets a little too aggressive. But if you play dead, you'll be just fine."

Weston appeared momentarily uneasy, as if he wanted to trade in his capelet for body armor, and then he rallied gamely. "It sounds like tomorrow night will be an adventure. Can I count on seeing you there?"

Our new friendship was back on. Anyone who was open to appreciating Mrs. Berns deserved some kindness in turn. "You betcha. I'll be covering it for the paper."

"Wonderful. Good day." He did a little cape whisk, like a nebbish Zorro, and disappeared into the sunshine.

I spent the rest of my shift cleaning and avoiding Sarah Ruth. Or she was avoiding me. Either way, we didn't talk much, and at closing time, Mrs. Berns, Sarah Ruth, and I went our separate ways.

My bike ride home was not nearly as enjoyable as the trip into town. I felt like I was gliding over a dragon's tongue, down her throat, and into her fiery gullet. My face flushed as my body fought the humid, 103-degree heat shimmering up from the pavement like a mirage. My water bottle was full of tepid liquid, so I just kept my head down and biked as fast as I could. By the time I turned into my driveway, my hair was plastered to my neck, and even my toes were sweating. I bypassed the turnoff into my house and cruised down to the lake.

Luna followed, running alongside me down the shady driveway, her tongue lolling out the side of her mouth.

"Last one in is a fried egg!" I jumped off the bike, tires still spinning, shed my flip-flops, and plunged into the refreshing water, tank top, jean shorts, and all. I stayed close to the bottom, where the lake was a good ten degrees cooler. The water peeled off layers of grit and fatigue, and I popped to the surface a new woman.

"Whooo!"

Luna swam next to me, grinning. "Ever think of trying the breaststroke?" I asked her. "That doggy-paddling is getting old."

She just kept smiling and treading water. I swam to shore, found some driftwood, and waded back out to waist-deep water. We played water fetch for a good half an hour, my lower half cool as a cucumber. When both Luna and I were bored and hungry, I walked my bike up to the house, dripping water onto the dusty road. I couldn't stand thinking about not seeing her every day, so I didn't.

At the house, I filled Luna's and Tiger Pop's water bowls with fresh water and ice cubes and scooped food for them and the birds before trading my rapidly drying clothes for a loose cotton sundress. I scarfed down a bowl of Rice Twice cereal, popped some grapes into my mouth, and set to packing.

My plan was to bundle up my winter clothes and my meager decorations, including the photographs on the fridge, my cat-ears lamp, and a few watercolor paintings I'd picked up at a garage sale. I'd scrub out the bedrooms and bathrooms and pile my boxes in the living room. All I'd have left to do before I left town would be to pack up my summer clothes, my toiletries, my spices, my plants, and my pet, and the double-wide would be open to the next lucky occupants.

I packed and cleaned and almost managed to not think about how much this place felt like home and Luna like my dog. By eight o'clock, I was done. I fixed myself a pickle, provolone, and mustard sandwich on wheat, drank some bottled water, and changed into my sleuthing clothes.

Chapter 28

The summer version of my spying outfit was black china flats, a pair of black linen pants, a black tank top, and my hair in a ponytail held with a black rubber band.

I slid a flashlight into one pocket and the handle of my spider knife over my waistband. The knife was über-perilous and could be flicked open with one quick twitch of my thumb. That cocky accessibility was what made it dangerous, from my end. I'd already dropped it on my thigh when I was practicing my "menacing English major" stance on a camping trip and earned a good gash.

Despite my shortcomings as a gangster, I felt safer carrying the knife.

My plan was to drive out to Hancock Lake and park my car on the side of the road a half mile from the Golden Pond Road turnoff. Hancock had no public access, but it was full of bass, so some fishers got around that by putting their boats in at a low spot in the road. It would not be unusual to see a car parked there.

From that point, I would walk to where I thought Mrs. Mealy's sister's house was, sticking to the woods on the uninhabited side of Golden Pond Road. There, I would do a little spying to see if I could catch a glimpse of the sister. If she wasn't there, I might need to peek in some windows.

My heart hammered pleasantly at the thought, and the sensation was a nice alternative to sitting at home, waiting to move, trying not to drink. As the sun set, I hopped into the car and went to meet my destiny.

Hancock Lake was small and clean and about three miles from New Millennium Bible Camp as the crow flew, tucked away between Clitherall and County Road 6 running from Battle Lake to 94. You couldn't reach it on a blacktop, which was just as well. The isolation made the area beautiful, I thought, as I parked my car next to some cattails. Golden Pond Road was a one-mile elbow about four city blocks up and on my left, and the only length of Hancock's shores that was inhabited. The air was dark but not cool, and it smelled heavy and volatile, like gunpowder.

I strolled past what used to be Hendershot's Snowmobile Repair. A couple from the Cities had bought the place, and they looked to have a litter of children. I'd heard the couple kept to themselves, which worked for me. A walker on a warm summer night was not unusual, but I was a stranger to them, and so they'd remember me if someone asked them later.

Directly ahead of me, the road T-boned; if I went to the left, I'd end up at Silver Sage Riding Ranch, and if I went to the right, I'd end up at the blacktop that would take me to Inspiration Peak.

I took the left just before the T and crunched down the gravel of Golden Pond, smelling grilling meat as I crept farther to the uninhab- ited side of the road. The whole lane was heavily treed. On my left were summer cabins mixed with year-round houses, each sitting back from the road on one to three acres of land. On my right was a slough the size of a small lake, a little sister to Hancock on the other side. A welcome breeze licked at my short hairs, sending a whisper through the popple trees.

When I stood in front of the driveway to the house I thought Pastor Winter had described, the only year-round house next to the pink house, I crossed the road and melted into the woods skirting the driveway. The moon was bright enough that I could avoid stepping on sticks or rustling through leaves, and my passage was mostly silent.

Ahead shone a single light through what I assumed was the kitchen window, based on the high cupboards illuminated inside.

This side of the house looked like a single-story rambler with a two-car garage, but I assumed if I followed the driveway down its steep incline around the side of the house, I'd see it was really a walkout.

There was no noise except for a distant conversation carrying over the water, an occasional mooing from the dairy farm across the lake, and the far-off rumble of cars. I had walked as far as I could without leaving the tree cover, about twenty feet from the house. Now I could either wait and see if anyone passed a window inside, or I could scurry up to the house like a summer mouse and peek in the windows. Never a creature of patience, I'd just made to break my cover when I heard heavy footsteps from inside the dwelling.

I quickly ducked behind a tree and peeped out. The front door swung open, and a female figure stood in the doorway, backlit. A man came behind her, nuzzled his face in her back, and took off down the wheelchair ramp and toward me.

I concentrated on becoming one with the nearest tree, my face pressed tight enough against the bark to leave a pattern. I dared not move, even to pull my head behind the oak, so when the man walked five feet from me on his way up the driveway, I could see his face clearly.

It was Les Pastner, owner of Battle Lake's Meat and RV, and the local, freaky-as-a-two-headed-coot militia leader.

I stayed as still as a word on a page when Les passed, the whisper of breeze through leaves covering my shallow breathing. That was good, because the more I tried to control my breathing, the more impossible it became to get air. My breath was coming out in horsey pants. Les continued down the driveway, his hands shoved deep in the pockets of his camo pants, and headed out the way I had just come.

When I could no longer hear his boots shuffling down the dry road, I took a deep breath. If Mrs. Mealy's sister was the one I'd seen so empty but intense at the Creation Science Fair, and if this was her house, what was Les doing here? He'd been affectionate with the owner of the house, and I knew for a firsthand fact that he was as well balanced as a triple-scoop ice cream cone. Did that make her unstable, too?

I heard a rustle behind me and spun, expecting to see an army of militiamen advancing, their beady eyes glowing under greasepaint, glued-on branches sticking out of their shoulders and heads.

I didn't spy anything except moonshadows and flitting leaves.

It was only a squirrel, I told my cowardly heart. *I'm the only person in this forest.*

I decided that was one person too many. I turned to creep back the way I had come, my plan being to stick deeper into the woods so I didn't inadvertently run into Les. I made it five whole feet before my ankle was garroted in a whip-hot grip, and I was flung ass to stars, my flashlight falling from my pocket to the warm ground below.

Chapter 29

This booby trap had Les Pastner written all over it. I knew because the sapling the rope had been tied to didn't have the recoil strength to lift me off the ground and dangle me in the air, like the rope traps in the Tarzan movies or Looney Tunes cartoons.

When I had stepped into the circle of rope, releasing whatever contraption had been putting pressure on the tree, it ricocheted upright, yanking my feet out from under me and giving me one hell of a rope burn, but otherwise leaving me unharmed. I tried to undo the knot at my ankle with my hands, but it was too tight.

I was accosted by a surprise party of panic when I couldn't immediately locate my spider knife. Had it gone flying with my flashlight? Was all the circulation getting cut off from my foot? Would I have to gnaw it off and crawl to safety?

Then I found the knife, nestled warm and tight between my skin and waistband. I flicked the blade, slid it delicately underneath the ankle noose, and wiggled it until it was facing toward the rope. I sawed slowly, hyperaware of the razor edge of the blade and the fact that I was a sitting duck if Les heard my tussling and returned.

I panted anxiously, my heart beating rapidly against the tourniquet on my ankle. My knife cut through the rope like it was shredded wheat, and I massaged around the hot and raw skin underneath, listening for any movement around me.

The woods were quiet.

On a whim, I used the rope to pull the sapling toward me, cut the rope off at the tree end, too, and threw the fifteen-foot line over my shoulder. Better Les think he'd misplaced his booby trap than suspect someone had been caught in it.

I limped back to my car, the journey taking twice as long because I couldn't use the road or put all my weight on my left ankle. I didn't spot Les, and I sincerely hoped he didn't see me.

Once in my Toyota, I breathed out the jittery weight of a near catastrophe. I was a weird mix of angry and relieved—mad because I had walked into a trap like a dumbass, and thankful because I'd gotten out. As I drove home, I wondered who the trap had been set for. Les was well known for his militia ways; had he indoctrinated his girlfriend into the lifestyle? And was his girlfriend Naomi Mealy's sister? I wasn't any wiser for my trip. In fact, my spying goal had been completely thwarted, and more mystery layered on top of it.

At the home front, I tossed the rope into a shed, watered my "I think I can, I think I can" vegetable garden, dumped fresh ice cubes in Luna's and Tiger Pop's water dishes, and fell across my bed, still wearing my spy clothes.

I sat up long enough to point the fan on my face to keep the hot air circulating, then dropped into a restless sleep. It was peppered by dreams of floods, locusts, and Winnebagos driven by lasciviously grinning pork links.

Saturday announced itself bright and hot as a klieg light. Tonight was the August Moon Festival, and I had a lot to accomplish before then. Healthy or not, the Mealy family had become my new obsession, replacing mourning and drinking and moping. They'd marginalized my library and my friends and had some shady business going on at the New Millennium Bible Camp.

I didn't want to leave the town in their hands.

Where had they come from? Why had they left that place? Was that truly Naomi Mealy's sister living out on Hancock Lake, and was she the same woman I'd met at the Creation Science Fair? If so, what was the connection between her, Les, and the Jesus warriors I'd witnessed at the New Millennium? Between some internet searching and a friendly visit to the Senior Sunset, I was confident I could pick up some leads.

There was an unsavory task on my list as well. I was going to talk to Sarah Ruth and squish whatever bad vibe had developed between us. That would require an open and honest discussion, which wasn't my forte, but I'd do it for the sake of the library.

No biking for me today. It was too much work, and my ankle was still sore from the rope burn. I was in the library by eight a.m., seated in front of the computer. I started by searching "Pastor Robert Mealy." The first hit was the New Millennium Bible Camp's website. It was a stylish site that made the camp look like a fun summer getaway for God-lovin' kids.

On its pages, groups of teens canoed on Glendalough Lake, splashing each other with paddles and laughing. They also held hands around a campfire, singing, I had to believe, "Kumbaya." There was even a photograph of the outdoor pulpit and horseshoe seating down by the lake, but it wasn't underwater. In fact, the lake didn't start until several feet behind the setup in the photo. That was an oddity. Battle Lake hadn't had a drier summer than this in half a century, and the pulpit was currently in at least six inches of water. Had the scene been photoshopped to make the camp look more appealing?

I scoured the site for any other strange photos, or some indication that the camp was training Jesus's warriors for the apocalypse, but found nothing other than a short bio on Robert Mealy. It said he'd graduated from the Wisconsin Lutheran Seminary and found a home at the Our Father Lutheran Church in Buford, Georgia, before heeding God's direction to start Christ's Church of the Apocryphal Revelation outside Clitherall the previous year.

That he'd begun as a Lutheran surprised me.

I tracked down the Wisconsin Lutheran Seminary site. On the seminary's home page, I chose the "Graduates" link, and opened up all the graduating-class links starting with 1970. If Pastor Mealy was fifty to fifty-five years old, as I guessed, that would be around when he'd have graduated. Each year's link offered a grainy, black-and-white buffet of mustachioed white men in wide-collared suits. If I had a nickel for every thread of polyester on those men's backs, I could buy a small island.

I was growing bored by the time I reached the class of 1977, but I dutifully ran my fingers over the names on my screen until . . . voilà! Robert Mealy. The gray shades of the photo were unable to hide the odd mix of arrogance in his smile and insecurity in his eyes, protected behind his enormous shop-teacher glasses, the ones he still wore today.

I eyeballed the rest of the graduates, spotting only about three guys I'd trust my cat with on a long weekend, let alone my immortal soul. I was about to click out when my vision snagged on the last man on the yearbook page. His eyes were friendly.

And familiar.

Harvey Winter, current pastor of Nordland Lutheran in Battle Lake, Minnesota.

I bit my lip, trying to recall our conversation word for word. Pastor Winter had been generous in his assessment of the Mealys, and when I'd asked if he had met them, he'd said that they had introduced themselves when they first came to town.

I had to give Pastor Winter props.

Not only had he graduated from Wisconsin Lutheran Seminary, he'd also apparently graduated from the Mira James School of Non-Lying Half Truths. I didn't know where the connection between Pastor Winter and Pastor Mealy fit, but it stank like fish guts.

I exited the seminary page and searched for "Buford Georgia newspaper." The *Herald* appeared. Their webpage was standard newspaper layout except for the "Worship" and "Worship Directory" links at the bottom. Since when had church become news?

Both those links led to recent information and contained no mention of Mealy, so I went into the news archives and searched his name. Still nothing, except for a mention of a missionary trip to Mozambique he headed in 1985. I was losing hope and grabbed for a piece of printer paper and stubby library pencil. Sometimes distracting myself with doodling allowed an idea to escape past my common sense filter.

The air conditioner whirred, and an icy draft hit my bare calves. This inspired me to sketch a picture of a cow grazing in a field, twin calves at her side. I drew cartoonish daisies and some sprigs of grass around them.

Most of my drawings featured big oak trees that looked more like sloppy broccoli, and this picture was no exception. I was itching for crayons and so hopped off my swiveling stool, grabbed some from the children's section of the library, and returned to color the grass green, the cows black and white, and the daisies yellow. I used the brown crayon to color in the trunk of the tree and add a fence around the field, enjoying the warm and waxy scent of Crayolas. Behind the fence, I drew a road, and on it a pickup truck barreling toward the field. It was going to make the cows leave. Why would someone want the cows to leave?

Duh. Of course.

Leaving.

Why had the Mealys left Buford? Robert Mealy had started there immediately out of the seminary and appeared to have stayed for well over two decades, according to his bio.

I returned to the *Herald* web page, my heart skipping with anticipation. I checked the archives for local news from June, which was approximately when the Mealys had moved out of Georgia, give or take a couple months. I found little of interest. I then checked the July archives, and was disappointed to find that a local $3 million lottery winner named Judah Nelson was the biggest news.

I was about to give up when the August archives offered me a headline that made my heart freeze like a power line in a January sleet storm.

Chapter 30

The Bodies of Two Buford Girls Found

The bodies of Eliza Hansen and Paula Duevel, both 17, were discovered today, two miles apart. Both teens, missing since August 11, were shot in the back at close range. Neither girl knew each other, and police are searching for a connection and a motive in their deaths.

I read on, but it was hard through the tears blurring my eyes. It was the photo of their parents that got me. Both sets of families had been searching since the girls had gone missing, and a photographer had captured Mrs. Duevel's agony when she discovered that her daughter had been found, dead. Her husband held her up, her mouth open in a silent scream.

The photograph made me think of my mother, and how it would crush her if she lost me, too. She'd been a dinner-on-the-table-at-five-every-night kind of mom, reliable and ever-present. She'd worked as a part-time seamstress all through my childhood, specializing in sewing badges and names on letter jackets and sports uniforms.

She worked from home. I was never sure if it was so she could keep an eye on me or keep an eye on my dad. For the first time, I wondered what else her life could have been if she hadn't been saddled with an increasingly drunken husband and bullheaded daughter. It was strange to think of my mom like that, a person separate from me.

I turned back to the article and forced myself to read. The one fact that stuck with me, other than the manner of death, was the girls' appearance. They were both five foot six and around 120 pounds, both brunette, and both in their late teens. The physical description almost perfectly matched that of Lucy Lebowski, our dead cheerleader.

And, other than the age, Alicia Mealy.

The front door donged open, and I glanced up guiltily. Sarah Ruth. I swiped the tears from my eyes, logged off the computer, and crumpled up my cow drawing before she reached the front desk.

She slid a glance at me, but didn't slow. "Morning, Mira. I'm just going to go hang up my purse and umbrella in back."

The tension hung between us thick and murky like headcheese. I caught a whiff of her as she walked by and was struck by a familiar and masculine undertone to her scent. Where had I smelled that before? And more importantly: "Why do you have an umbrella? It hasn't rained in weeks."

"My neighbors assure me that the August Moon Festival tonight is guaranteed to bring a thunderboomer. I always like to be prepared." Her tinkly laughter was genuine, and I relaxed slightly.

At her interview a little more than a week ago, Sarah Ruth and I had hit it off right away. Maybe we were both just going through an adjustment period, me moving out and her moving in. I would talk to her and get to the bottom of this, but not right now. Personally revealing conversations were always better conducted in the afternoon.

The door chime went off again, and Mrs. Berns strolled through the front door, wearing her ultra-white old-lady tennis shoes, a white unitard, and a swim cap over her bony head. Apricot hair straggled out from underneath. She had the short end of a Power Rangers beach towel pinned around her neck. "Today's the day!"

I grabbed a tissue from the box on the counter and blew out the last of my grief. "What day, Mrs. Berns?"

"The day me and the superhero have our first date. Do you think he'll wait until it's dark to take me for a fly?"

"Huh?"

"Oh. Maybe you don't know." She lowered her voice to a whisper and put her arm around me conspiratorially. "The gentleman taking me to the August Moon Festival tonight? He's a superhero."

"Weston Lippmann?" My forehead wrinkled. "He's the curator of a tick museum."

Mrs. Berns tsked. "In a cape? Carrying a laser beamer?"

"What's a laser beamer?"

"Kinda like a flashlight, but for superheroes. I saw it up beneath his cape when I was hiding that mangy ferret under a table. He carries it in back, tucked in his pants. It's small and black. Only saw it for a flash. Come to think of it, it might have been a truthenator."

It occurred to me that Weston might have been carrying a gun, but the idea was too ludicrous. He was a tick curator who wore a cape. Plus, as a native Minnesotan, Mrs. Berns had been around enough guns to recognize one. "He wears the cape because he doesn't want birds to poop on him. He doesn't carry a laser beamer or a truthenator. He's a tick museum curator."

Mrs. Berns nodded sagely. "Probably best you don't know the truth. You'd give it up too easy if they caught ya. You've got the constitution of a newborn." She patted my cheek. "What're you crying about today, anyhow?"

"It's allergy season. My eyes water."

"Two facts don't make a truth, Mira," she said, puncturing my lies like a pro. "I'll be in back dusting."

"Fine."

"Kennie Rogers is looking for you, by the by," she called over her shoulder. "I ran into her at the Turtle Stew. I think she was heading over here next."

Crap on a cracker! I'd told her I'd come over to her house yesterday morning to look at her great new invention. If she found me here, I'd be a sitting duck. "I'm starving. I think I'll take an early lunch."

"Thought so," Mrs. Berns sang. "I'll keep an eye on that moody Sarah Ruth."

That moody Sarah Ruth was standing beside Mrs. Berns when she said that. I ducked outside and let the two of them work it out.

Or not.

My hair wilted immediately in the blazing-hot day. Waves of fire wafted off the pavement. I walked through the wall of heat, taking the long route back behind the old granary, so I wouldn't run into Kennie. Including my stop at Olson's Oil in town, it took me twenty minutes to get to the Senior Sunset, and I was sweating like a stripper when I arrived.

The nursing home had been built in the 1950s and resembled a cross between a bomb shelter and a high school. The drooping flowers skirting the building did their best to offset the institutional feel, but it was an uphill battle. I ignored the front door and came around to the back, where I was happy to see a fishing line coming down off the roof.

"Hey, Curtis!" I called up. "You catching anything?"

Curtis had lived at the nursing home for twelve years, and he'd been fishing off the roof for just as long. Never mind that there was no water down below, just a neatly manicured lawn, deck chairs, and a tiny garden plot that I tilled for the residents. His roof-fishing was a harmless pastime, and the nursing home staff usually turned a blind eye to it. Most thought Curtis was a couple face cards short of a full deck, but I knew better.

He peeked over the roof, his bright eyes shaded by the brim of a fishing hat. "Nah. Too hot. The fish like shady, rainy days."

"I brought you something. Wanna come down and see?"

"Might as well."

Five minutes later, Curtis Poling stood beside me in the shade of a basswood tree, smoking one of the gas station cigars I'd picked up for him. He was a rakish, good-looking old guy with cobalt eyes that didn't miss a beat. Between him and Shirly Tolverson, another nursing home resident, nothing happened in this town, past or present, that they didn't have a line on.

"Hot day," I remarked.

"Yup."

"You think the festival tonight will bring rain?"

"If not tonight, then soon. You feel that heaviness in the air, makes it hard to pull a full breath?"

I inhaled through my nose. He was right. I couldn't fill my lungs. "Yeah. What's it mean?"

"It means we're in for one fury of a storm. I haven't felt that thickness in the air for weeks."

I smiled. "The farmers'll like that."

He shook his head. "Not if it comes so fierce that it tears through their crops. But that's farming. It's always a gamble." The small talk out of the way, Curtis graciously led us both to the heart of my visit. "Damn shame about that Lebowski girl."

It hurt hearing her name, even though that was what I was here to talk about. "That's for sure. You know her family?"

"Good people," he said, nodding. "Her dad's a farmer out in Clitherall, one of the last ones doing it independently. He owns 160 acres, free and clear."

"How about her mom?"

"Farmwife. I think she's a substitute teacher, too. Lucy was their only child. She volunteered out here, Lucy did, as kind as the day is long."

I felt the pain like a cut across my heart. "Do you know what church the family went to?"

He trained his eyes on me, taking inventory. I held perfectly still. "You want to know if they went to that church out by Clitherall? At the Bible camp?"

I felt sweat slide down my back. "Did they?"

He pursed his lips. "Hard to say. They'd always been Nordland congregants, but they might have been checking out a new church. The funeral'll be at Nordland, with Pastor Winter."

"What do you know about Pastor Winter?"

Curtis cackled. "Are you interviewing me for a story, or just being nosy?"

I tried to smile. "Just being nosy."

"Then you better nose around with Ida. She goes to Nordland. Knows Harvey Winter and his family. He's from this area originally, you know."

"I didn't. Mind if we go track down Ida?"

Curtis stubbed out his cigar and led me into the cool shade of the nursing home.

Chapter 31

As always, the Senior Sunset's smell set me back a step. It was medicinal and syrupy and crept into your hair.

We walked down a long central hall cosseted with bland pictures of flowers to find Ida in her room, bejeweled reading glasses perched on her tiny nose. She smiled at me and batted her eyes at Curtis. I'd noted his Elvis-like spell over the senior set on previous visits.

I filled Ida in on what I was after.

"They don't come any nicer than Harvey Winter," she said, when I finished. "His family was one of the first settlers in Battle Lake, you know. Of course, he got around some as a boy, but look what he went on to make of himself."

I perked up. "What kind of 'getting around'?"

"The usual, for back then. Drinking, drag racing, and getting a little too familiar with the local girls. Nothing that landed him in jail or a wedding chapel." She removed her reading glasses and glanced off into the distance. "I do remember his parents being worried, but then he went off to seminary."

I rubbed the back of my neck, trying to keep the stress at bay. Harvey Winter was from Battle Lake. He'd been a troublemaker as a kid before going off to seminary. The same seminary as Robert Mealy, according to my earlier research. Robert Mealy then moved to Buford, Georgia, where he ran a church for a couple decades. When two teenagers were shot in the back in Buford, he packed up his family and moved to Battle Lake, the home of his wife's sister and his old classmate Harvey Winter.

Shortly thereafter, a teenage Battle Lake girl was shot in the back.

How did it all come together? More importantly, who'd killed Lucy, and why?

"What do you two know about the New Millennium Bible Camp?" I asked Ida.

Curtis and Ida exchanged a glance before Ida spoke. "Nothing good, just rumors."

"What kind of rumors?" I pressed.

Curtis spoke up. "That group's just a little too evangelical for this area. That's all. Supposedly, the minister's wife talks in tongues."

I sniffed. "That's no rumor. I saw her do it, though I'm not so sure it was anything mystical. It seemed like regular speech, but garbled. But if they're too evangelical for this area, where are they getting all their customers? The place was full up during their Creation Science Fair."

Curtis grimaced. "There's always plenty people looking for a place to belong."

I had a thought. "Speaking of, you guys know what Les Pastner has been up to lately?"

"The usual," Curtis said. "Running his store and bitching about the government, trying to make everyone forget he's a short guy with no friends."

"Not even a girlfriend?"

Curtis ran his hands through his wispy white hair. "Funny you should mention that, and in the same breath as the Bible camp. Seems Les is dating the sister of the wife of the pastor out there. He's not even hiding it that well. Ever since he ran for mayor, he's felt the need to spread the details of his personal life. Says the public has a right to know, but I ask, what about the public's right to not care?"

Cha-click.

A tiny piece of the puzzle fell into place. There wasn't enough for me to see a pattern, but I was getting close. "The sister live out on Hancock Lake?"

"Yes she does," Ida said.

"Thought so." Confirming suspicions is the *best* feeling. "I really appreciate your time, both of you."

Ida clasped my hand. "You come visit whenever you want. It gets boring here."

Curtis winked. "You say that, you make a man feel bad."

Ida giggled. "Nobody would ever call you boring, Curtis Poling."

They were starting to look a little too deeply in one another's eyes, which I took as my signal to go. I headed outdoors, pushing my way through the hot, thick air, Curtis's prediction about a storm close in my mind. The thought kept my mood upbeat, as did the fruitfulness of our conversation. I tucked away the information about Les, Pastor Winter, and the town's feelings about the new Bible camp like they were points on a treasure map. I just had to figure out how to read it.

Such was my good mood that, back at the library, I walked straight up to Sarah Ruth. "Got a minute?"

She fidgeted before summoning a smile. "This is about the awkwardness between us, isn't it?"

"Yeah. Can you come back into my . . . um, the office?" I was aware that it would belong to Sarah Ruth in under a week.

"Of course."

I turned to Mrs. Berns, who was practicing flying off a low counter in the kids' section. "You watch the place, 'kay?"

"Up, up, and away!"

Back in the office, I chose the position of authority behind the desk. This conversation was going to be uncomfortable, and I needed all the help I could get. "I don't know where to start."

Sarah Ruth sat across from me, her posture straight, her hands folded in her lap. I was again struck by her brownness. It wasn't her skin, which was as pale as bread dough, but it was in her permed hair, her clothes, her overall vibe.

"I think I do," she said. "Ever since you walked in on me on the phone in here, it's been strained between us."

"I didn't exactly walk in on you," I said, tensing. "I didn't know you were back here."

"I know." She drew a deep breath. "And I don't know why I lied about dialing a wrong number. I was actually calling the Bible camp."

I felt my eyebrows dip. "You can call whoever you want."

"It's not that easy. I've had God in my life ever since I was a little girl." She seemed to be searching for words. "I'm not ashamed of it, but I've learned that it makes other people uncomfortable, even suspicious." She squared her shoulders and looked me in the eye. "I have a close and personal relationship with Jesus. I didn't think you'd understand, so I've tried to keep my work life separate from my religious life, but I don't know if I can do that any longer."

"How do you mean?"

"I mean that my love of God is an important part of who I am, and I don't want to pretend otherwise." She tipped her chin toward me. "I don't want to feel like I have to lie about calling my church, or hide if I see you at the Bible camp."

A fire sparked in my rib cage. I messed up enough myself without taking on other people's mistakes. "Those are choices you made. I didn't tell you to lie, or to hide."

"Not in so many words, but you have to admit you're very negative about religion," she said timidly. "I don't want to hurt your feelings, Mira, but I have to tell you that you're incredibly closed-minded when it comes to God's love."

The fire flared and simmered up my throat all the way to my tongue. "If by 'closed-minded' you mean I lack blind faith, you're absolutely right. But I recognize you're entitled to your opinion, and your religion. I just don't happen to share it."

"Well, we'll have to agree to disagree."

I hated that phrase. It was code for "I know you're too obtuse to see how right I am, so to get any satisfaction out of this discussion, I'm going to pretend to be more reasonable than you. Oh, and get the last word in." I stood, my fists clenched, and then sat back down. After a deep breath, I measured my words. "We can definitely agree to disagree about what is a better use of our spare time. We can*not* agree to disagree about what's appropriate at work. Your religion, or *any* employee's religion, doesn't have a place at the library."

"What about your gardening?" she said, her timidity fading. "That's important to you, and you talk about it at work all the time. In fact, you're trying to convince me to take up gardening. How is that different from me talking about religion?"

Fish sticks. I hated it when religious people used reason when it suited them. And they were so good at it. You'd think all those sermons on unquestioning faith, virgin births, and people turned into pillars of salt would've dulled their skills. "You're right." And she was. "I've been judgmental, and for that, I apologize. Also, this is a library, and if free speech isn't welcome here, it isn't welcome anywhere. You can talk about your religion at work, and of course you can use the phone during your break time to call whomever you want."

She grinned triumphantly. "Thank you."

"But"—I held up my finger—"it's a two-way street. You need to be open to the interests of our patrons—"

"I always am."

"I'm not finished. Free speech isn't just about getting to say what you want. It's also about not harming others and knowing when to shut up. This library is not and will never be a conduit for any religion or person. Your job here is to make a wide array of literature available to a broad variety of people. If I ever hear that you're doing anything else, or limiting options based on your religious beliefs, or using this public institution for your private platform, I'll get you run out of town if it's the last thing I do."

Sarah Ruth's winner-grin wavered slightly, but she kept it on like a champ. "Understood." She stood up and offered me her hand. "We have different methods, you know, but I think we have the same goals. You're leaving this library in good hands."

"I'd better be," I grumbled.

I took her hand, shook it limply, and brushed past her. Our discussion seemed to have done her a world of good, judging by the spring in her step and whistle on her lips as she worked throughout the day.

For my part, I felt like I'd lost an important fight.

Chapter 32

After closing up the library, I stopped at Larry's Grocery to pick up a veggie tray for tonight's August Moon Festival potluck. Unfortunately, the deli had been picked over by like-minded festivalgoers. I settled for a family pack of Pringles and a bag of after-dinner mints.

As I turned west on 210 for the three-mile drive to Hershod's Corn Maze, I reached for the New Orleans Mardi Gras mask on the seat next to me. I didn't know who'd come up with the idea of wearing costumes at the festival, but I enjoyed the tradition. Being anonymous in a small town was a rare treat and lent an air of decadence to the gathering.

I crested the hill before the maze and realized I should have taken advantage of the shuttle bus ferrying attendees from Chip's Bait to the festival. I ended up parking three-quarters of a mile away and schlepping my Pringles and mints.

"Ah, the breakfast of champions."

I turned to the voice. It was a family walking alongside me to the maze. The father was nodding at the couch food I was bringing. "Larry's sold out of deli trays?" he asked.

"Yeah," I said sheepishly. "I should've planned ahead."

"Nothing wrong with Pringles," the mom offered. She had her hands full with a dessert tray of bars and cookies on top of a clear salad bowl filled with what looked like sliced cabbage, ramen noodles, and sunflower seeds. The family looked vaguely familiar, but I didn't know anyone's names.

"I guess not, except that I look like a freeloader next to what you're bringing." I smiled to show I didn't feel too bad. "Do you all have costumes?"

The four children, all boys ranging in size from toddler to teen, held up their masks—one ninja, a Superman, a grim reaper, and a Spider-Man. The father grinned at his brood and threw his arm around his wife. "We're hoping the festival brings us some rain. Our crops are thirsty."

"You're farmers?"

"Back three generations," he said, nodding. "We live over by Amor."

"Well, I hope it rains for you, too."

The crowd was growing thicker. I separated from the family, threading my way under the Hershod's Corn Maze arches, the closeness of the people intensifying the afternoon's heat. The grounds were vast, and the maze itself was nearly three acres resting in the center. To the right was a thick hardwood forest. On my left was an ocean of picnic tables covered with potluck offerings.

I slid my food onto the nearest table so it wouldn't be associated with me and took stock. I counted fourteen picnic tables laden with Saran Wrapped dishes, most of these thinly disguised vehicles for Cool Whip or Miracle Whip, the Whips being a west-central Minnesota food group unto themselves.

I estimated more than three hundred people here already, milling around the food, laughing, and making loud conversation. The ground was covered in straw as golden as liquid sunshine, and the air was rich with the smell of hotdishes, fresh-baked bread, and beer. I sidestepped the kegs and studied the maze entrance.

Corn mazes are a funny concept.

You take a field of close-planted, super-high, super-fast-growing, super-tough corn, the more acres the better, and you cut a series of four-foot-wide paths through it. Most are dead ends, but one of the paths leads out the other side. Tonight at nine o'clock, Bad Brad's band, Not with My Horse, would be playing at the "out" end of the maze.

I planned to avoid him. Run-ins with exes were bad, but run-ins with cheating exes with low IQs were worse. It meant second-guessing every choice you'd ever made.

The sun was beating iron-hot on my head even though it was pushing seven o'clock. The food appeared to be all set up, so I pulled on my mask and grazed from one picnic table to another until I'd tried at least one item on all fourteen tables.

The beauty of the Mardi Gras mask was that it covered only my eyes, so eating was easy. Pity the Richard Nixons and Power Rangers, who had to leverage their food under the plastic. As more people arrived, the combination of masks, unlimited beer provided by the chamber of commerce, and a white-hot summer made for a raucous mood. I was just about to steal away to a quieter spot where I could people-watch when a hand grabbed my shoulder.

"Mira! I was hoping I'd see you here."

Next to me stood Weston Lippmann wearing his trademark black cape over a red sweater vest and short-sleeved shirt, sweating furiously.

Mrs. Berns was leaning against him, all white in her superhero-support outfit. Neither wore a mask, but they were definitely in costume. "You two made it!" I said.

"We almost didn't." Weston shot Mrs. Berns an odd smile, the kind you give to a host who's just served you jellied clams. "Mrs. Berns wanted me to stop at the Senior Sunset to look at her room."

Mrs. Berns winked at me and took a chug off one of the two cups of beer she was holding.

Cripes. "You remembered what I told you about saying no, right, Weston?"

He swallowed dryly. "That worked, but it turns out running away works even better."

Mrs. Berns cackled. "Or it would have, if I hadn't lifted your car keys! It was just a little harmless fun, anyhow. You didn't have to scream."

Weston pulled on his collar like a practicing Rodney Dangerfield. "Of course not. I apologize. You caught me off guard when you put your hand in my back pocket."

"Just looking for your laser beamer."

Time for a change of subject. "What'd you bring for the potluck?" I asked brightly, indicating the pack of crackers stuffed into Mrs. Berns's utility belt.

"Communion wafers." She took one out and popped it into her mouth. "All Sarah Ruth's talk of Jesus makes me hungry."

I coughed on my own spit, and Weston nodded weakly in a *Do you see what I've been dealing with?* kind of way.

"Pastor Winter wouldn't give me any wafers to go, even though I've been attending Nordland for seventy-five years, and it's not easy to find these outside of a church," Mrs. Berns continued after she swallowed, "but Larry's has a new hippie section with all sorts of dried fruits and natural beans, like there's any other kind. That's where I got these glue-free Communion wafers."

"You mean gluten-free?"

"Whatever." She pulled the sleeve out of her holster. "Want one?"

"I'll pass. Thanks." Weston looked like he was about to faint, and I didn't have many safe conversational options left. "Are you two enjoying the festival?"

"I would be, if Party Pooper Man would start drinking." Mrs. Berns nodded at his empty hands.

"I don't drink," he said.

"That's another thing we have in common," I said happily. I kept to myself that I'd been a non-drinker for only three days. "We don't like birds, and we don't like drinking."

"And we like to read, listen to jazz, and spend our evenings engaged in deep conversation?" Weston asked hopefully.

Mrs. Berns appeared disgusted. "I think I hear someone calling my name."

"Huh?" he asked.

"Over there. Can't you hear it?" She pointed toward the keg, and when both Weston and I glanced that direction, she said, "Mrs. Berns! Mrs. Berns!" in a high, quiet voice. We turned back to her.

"Gotta run!" she said. "Thanks for the ride, Weston! If I need you, I'll call real loud, so make sure your super hearing is tuned in to my frequency."

She strolled off, her cape hung between her legs like a flashy dog tail. Weston appeared immensely relieved to see her go.

"She has a lot of energy for a grandma," he said.

Point of fact, Mrs. Berns actually *was* a grandma. Curtis Poling at the Sunset said she had twelve children and I-didn't-know-how-many grandkids, and I'd never met a one of them. "I warned you. Have you had a chance to eat?"

"I don't have much appetite this evening." He smiled weakly. "It must be this sun."

Or fending off the advances of an octogenarian in a white velvet unitard. "You must be hot. How many layers do you have on, anyhow?"

"The cape, a vest, and a shirt." He rumbled in the back of his throat, like he'd swallowed a bug. "I'm usually cold-blooded. Ever since I was a kid, I needed layers. Even growing up in the balmy South, I'd wear fleece pajamas at night. You know the kind with feet?"

I smiled at the mental picture of a grown, gangly Weston in footie pajamas. "I do, but I can't believe you're not burning up. It's pushing a hundred degrees, and this is the coolest it's been since noon. You sure you don't want to take off the cape, at least?"

"I'm good, thank you."

I shrugged. He didn't *look* good. He looked like he was melting. "Then you could try the corn maze. I bet if you stick to the sides, it'd be cooler."

Weston adjusted his John Lennon glasses with his index finger and shuffled uncomfortably. "I don't really like crowds. I don't suppose you'd like to take a walk in the woods with me instead? It looks like there're paths. Who knows? We could find a new subspecies of wood tick!"

If words were wine, Weston Lippmann was producing Boone's Farm. "I don't know. I should probably stay out here, to cover the festival for the newspaper, you know?"

"Oh, sure, I suppose," he said, his weak flirting attempt phlooshing to the ground like a popped balloon.

I gave him an *it's the best thing for both of us* smile and was about to make myself scarce when someone slapped me on the back. "Mira James, so pretty she gives you heart pains! How's it going? I haven't seen you in weeks."

Cheese and rice, if it weren't for bad luck . . . was I emitting some sort of loser pheromone? Had I been secreting it my whole life? I was a nice person. I held doors for old people and said my pleases and thankyous. I even considered myself fairly intelligent. Of course I loved to read, and I stayed on top of current events by perusing magazines at work. I was a little clumsy and for sure a dork, but what had I done to end up as a librarian and reporter in Battle Lake, Minnesota, mysterious-murder capital of the Midwest and home to one too many exes?

I turned to glare at the body attached to the hand. "Hi, Brad."

"You come to hear me sing? My new band is the fox's socks! We do a techno-punk-grunge cover of 'God Bless the USA' that'll make you cry. People around here love it. Can't get enough."

I grimaced. "I can only imagine."

"Say, who's your friend?"

I looked reluctantly to Weston. I wanted to get away, not make introductions. "Weston, this is Brad. Brad, this is Weston. He's in town for a couple weeks doing scientific research."

"What's up with the cape, dude?" Brad hooted. "That's so weird!"

This from a guy who wouldn't eat blue cheese the whole time we dated because he thought it would make him sad. "Don't you have to do a sound check or something?"

"Totally! You want to come with me? It'll be like old times." He grinned, counting on his Jim Morrison–good looks to sway me.

Frying pan or fire? I chose frying pan. "That's a great offer, but Weston and I were just about to take a walk in the woods to search for wood ticks."

Weston's eyes lit up. "Yeah?"

"Yeah." I grabbed him by the elbow and led him away. This town was getting much too small.

Ironically, that's exactly what I was thinking as I bumped into Kennie with a fire burning in her eyes.

Chapter 33

"You said you were going to come to my place yesterday morning." Kennie wore a flowing bohemian cotton top over a pair of stretch pants that were earning their name. One sneeze from her and we'd all be covered in spandex.

"I'm sorry." I didn't even have the guts to lie, and that had a lot to do with the three coffins lined up behind her. They were simple pine boxes on four legs that stood two feet off the ground. The tops were closed. I preferred to imagine them empty. "What's with the boxes?"

She placed her hands protectively on the one nearest her. "These *boxes* are pure money, but it's too late for you to get in on it, so don't even ask."

Bullet dodged. "Get in on what?"

"The entrepreneurial deal I've been trying to offer you a cut of all week."

I saw at least one problem with this "deal," and I didn't mind telling her. "Coffins have already been invented."

"These aren't just coffins. They're coffin *tables*." She moved aside and showed me the sign she'd been blocking, outlining it with a Vanna White flourish.

BEAUTIFUL CENTERPIECE WHILE YOU'RE ALIVE, ETERNAL RESTING PLACE WHEN YOU'VE GONE ON TO THE NEXT PLACE. CUSTOM MADE TO YOUR SPECIFICATIONS. BUY THE ONE PIECE OF FURNITURE THAT NEVER GOES OUT OF STYLE.

Behind me, Weston coughed uncomfortably. The poor man had now been in close range with Battle Lake's two most notorious women in less than an hour. He was probably going to get the bends. "The wood grain is very nice," he offered.

Kennie smiled proudly. "I had a local carpenter make up these demo models. See the legs? They fold up when it's time for you to be buried. We're even offering a glass-topped one so you can fill it with potpourri or magazines while it's in your living room. Then, at your final viewing, your loved ones can polish the glass so everyone can see you as they say their farewells."

I shivered despite the heat. "Who would put a coffin in their living room?"

"Not a coffin. A coffin *table*."

"Who would put a coffin *table* in their living room?"

At that moment, Chief Gary Wohnt materialized out of the crowd. He wore his impenetrable sunglasses and his law enforcement uniform. "Kennie."

"Chief Wohnt," she said icily, planting her hands on her hips.

"Do you have a license to sell those?"

The energy between them was flinty. Gary used to be Kennie's number-one supporter, and to have him embarrass her like this was painful to witness.

"They're not for sale," Kennie said arrogantly.

Gary removed his pot of lip balm, frosted his mouth, and stuffed it back into his chest pocket. "You're not selling these?"

"Not right now."

"You'll get a license when and if you do decide to sell." This was a statement, not a question. I wanted to kick him in the knee for how he was treating Kennie, like she was a stranger. I wasn't ever going to be the president of Kennie's fan club, but she'd grown on me. A little.

She didn't seem to care for his treatment any more than I did. She covered the four feet between them, slow and dangerous. "I am the mayor of this town. I follow the rules. I recommend you do the same. Mira, watch the coffins for me, please. I have a date that I can't miss."

If her words affected Gary, he didn't show it. She stormed away angrily, slipping on her high madras heels but not slowing her pace.

I turned to Gary. "You didn't have to be so hard-core."

He trained his black-mirrored gaze on me, twisted his lip as if to speak, thought better of it, and stalked off in the opposite direction of Kennie.

"What was that all about?" Weston pushed his glasses up his nose and stared wonderingly from disappearing Kennie to retreating Gary.

"I'm not exactly sure," I said, concerned with how flushed he still looked, "but we better get you in the shade."

He thrust a thumb over his shoulder. "What about the coffin tables? Don't you need to watch them?"

"Nah. Kennie just needed to save face. Nobody's going to take three pine coffins with legs, particularly if they have her name on them."

Weston grinned happily. "To the shade, then. Onward, Christian soldiers!"

The phrase struck me as odd. "You're a religious man?"

"Oh, no. It's just a figure of speech."

I remembered the caped figure I'd seen entering the New Millennium Church the other day. I wasn't sure if all my run-ins with organized religion had made me paranoid or if Weston was suddenly sending off a weird vibe, but the night was young, the air was festive, and the shade of the woods to the east of the corn maze entrance looked mighty nice.

"Gotcha. Looks like there's a main path here. I'm pretty sure it leads down to the lake." As far as I knew, Hershod's owned the land the festival was on and about ten acres of the woods, but their property stopped at the small and expensive lakeshore lots. I thought I remembered a public access down there, though.

"We could dangle our feet in the water!" he said.

I was navigating the crowd, and I had to raise my voice to be heard. "I thought you were cold-blooded."

"Usually, but I'm beginning to feel a little overheated." Weston cut his eyes at me, and I purposely ignored the look.

"I'd like to stay close to the festival," I said, as I strode into the jungle-thick forest. "I love to people-watch. How about right over here? I think I see a rock we could . . ." My words trailed off as I spotted a naked white butt rear up on the other side of the large fieldstone. It was just a flash, but it looked wide and hairy.

Then it flashed up again.

And again.

"For the love of Pete!" Weston drew up behind me and clapped his hands. "There is a festival going on out there, and there are children not fifty feet away. Whoever is behind that rock better stop what they are doing, or I'll come over and break it up myself."

I, for one, wanted to see what sort of man was attached to that hairy ass before I made any threats, but I admired Weston's forcefulness and wondered what reserve he'd pulled it from. Regardless, it worked. There was some shuffling behind the riding mower–size rock, followed by fierce whispering. Then two meaty hands appeared, followed by a meaty head and a meaty body.

When I saw it was Tom, of Tom and Tina's Taxidermy and Trinkets, I felt the heat rise on my face. The last thing I wanted to do was catch two people I knew going at it.

"Sorry. Guess we got a little carried away in the night air. You know how young love is."

Young love? I spotted a flash of blonde hair followed by a woman crawling away. The shade of the oak forest made it hard to make out the face, but I knew the Amazon body, even without its neon clothes and expensive jewelry. "Annika?"

She whipped her head around before dashing off deeper into the woods, toward the lake, clothes in hand, but I'd seen enough. Smoke began curling out of my ears. Tom had been boinking the new employee, which explained the disappearing cash from 4Ts. Either Annika was taking money to buy herself expensive jewelry and Tom was turning a blind eye or Tom was taking money to buy her expensive jewelry, and probably more. The affair would also explain why Annika was coming in when it wasn't her shift.

I suddenly felt greasy. Annika was of age, but barely. It was creepy of Tom to take advantage of a young employee like that, not to mention what he was doing to Tina. I knew what it was like to be cheated on, thanks to Bad Brad, and it was an awful feeling.

"What in the hell are you doing, Tom?" I demanded.

He chuckled ruefully. "Making a jackass of myself, apparently."

I wasn't swallowing his aw-shucks act. "That wasn't Tina."

"Really? It's so hard to see in these woods." His deeply poor joke contained a dark edge.

"Weston, I think we should get back to the festival."

He grabbed my arm protectively. "I agree. After you."

Weston kept his eyes on Tom until I was nearly out of the woods, and then he followed. "You know, this town is an odd place."

He didn't know the half of it.

Chapter 34

Once we stepped out of the forest, we were immediately back in the world of family and fun. I did a head-to-toe shake to release the bad vibes.

"Did you know that guy?" Weston asked.

"I know who he is. His wife is a friend of mine, but that wasn't his wife."

"I see."

I sighed. "Me too. I saw too much, in fact, and I don't know what I'm going to tell her."

"You want my advice?"

I glanced up at Weston's face, tall enough to block the sun from my eyes. His untamed flop of hair fell over his glasses, which were sliding down his nose. "You know what? I really do."

"Don't tell her anything. Nobody wants to hear that they're being cheated on."

"You wouldn't want to know if your wife was sleeping around on you?"

His eyes darkened for a moment, and I wondered if I had hit a nerve. I glanced at his left ring finger—empty, just like I thought. His eyes cleared so fast I decided I'd imagined it. "I bet that guy's wife already knows. If she wants to talk to you about it, she will."

I thought back to Tina's convincing me to spy on her store. Had she suspected Tom was cheating and used me to find out? Nah. She didn't have a duplicitous bone in her body. "You might be right. I'll have to think on it. You want to walk through the maze with me?"

He glanced at the crowd bottlenecking the entrance. "Sure. It looks like we might have to wait awhile, though."

He was right. More than a hundred people had formed a circle between us and the entrance, the sun baking their heads and shoulders. Behind them, tall green cornstalks stood as still as sentinels. "That's odd that everyone is standing in a circle. Usually, people here are pretty good about making lines. Should we go see what's going on in the middle?"

"I don't know." He shoved his hair back. "I don't do so well in crowds, and I'm still feeling warm."

He did look a little green around the gills. "Why don't you wait over there, by the edge of the woods, and I'll pop in there real quick. After I see what's going on, I'll grab us both a couple cold sodas and we can wait it out in the shade until there's fewer people. Deal?"

"Deal," he said gratefully.

I watched him wobble off into the sparse shade and hoped he wouldn't stumble across any more forest-lovin' locals. The crowd around me was drinking beer and laughing pleasantly, but the farther into the circle I pushed, the less drinking and joy there was.

Also, I noticed more and more people holding their masks instead of wearing them, their faces tight. The nearer to the center I got, the easier it was to make out the shouting that held everyone's attention. I elbowed my way to the very front and was dismayed to see Robert and Naomi Mealy holding court.

Robert was dressed starkly in a black button-down shirt and slacks, his dark shoes as shiny as a mirror. His 1970s shop-teacher glasses made his eyes appear big and ominous. One of his fists pumped in the air, and the other held a sign: No False Religions! The Time to Repent Is Now. He had one foot resting on his wife's wheelchair, as if she were a piece of furniture.

She was staring fiercely up at him, her thin hair tied back, her face makeup-free. She was also dressed in a dark top and had a lap quilt peppered with an autumn leaf design covering her from the waist down. They were as overdressed for the heat as Weston.

There was no sign of Alicia.

"Leave this heathen festival and return to the waiting arms of God! He will provide!" Robert Mealy thrust his sign into the air as he spoke, swiveling to make eye contact with the guilty faces surrounding him. I didn't look away when his gaze lit on mine.

"'Be sober, be vigilant; because your adversary the devil, as a roaring lion, walketh about, seeking whom he may devour,' says Peter! And I say to you, the devil is about at this festival. Is he going to devour you?"

A shiver slid down my spine, giving me vertigo in the crowd and heat. I was distracted from my queasiness by a glimpse of a mousy-haired woman three back in the crowd. She looked like the rapturous woman I'd seen staring at Naomi at the Creation Science Fair, the one I was sure was Naomi's sister and Les's lover, but when I threaded my way through the crowd, she'd vanished. I pushed my way back to the front of the gathering to observe Pastor and Mrs. Mealy.

Naomi was still watching her husband intensely, an inner light burning like a fever behind her eyes. On her left hand she wore the gaudy ring I'd noticed when we first met, and from this angle, it appeared to be a cross, or maybe a crucifix, set on a band. Was it the same design as the strange necklaces Alicia and Sarah Ruth wore?

I was jostled before I could get close enough to verify the design. I made my way farther around, so Mrs. Mealy was directly in front of me and her husband was behind her. Unfortunately, I was on her right side, and she'd tucked both her hands under the quilt, so I could no longer see the ring. She stared up hungrily at her husband.

"From the Galatians, we know we should 'be not deceived; God is not mocked: for whatsoever a man soweth, that shall he also reap.'" Pastor Mealy thrust his fist with every syllable.

"It's just a party!" a heckler yelled from behind me.

"And we got a drought!" someone seconded.

Pastor Mealy yelled back, his neck veins popping, "'He that obser-veth the wind shall not sow; and he that regardeth the clouds shall not reap'—Ecclesiastes, chapter 11, verse 4!"

The feel of the crowd was dangerous. Those here for a good time, a reprieve from this dry summer and their long workdays, were growing agitated, but a fair number of people appeared shamed by the pastor's words. I was wondering where Gary Wohnt was when I noticed some-one in the crowd flip a lit cigarette toward the two in the center. It arced and landed on Naomi Mealy's lap, not five feet from me. I was the only one who appeared to notice it except for Pastor Mealy, who flicked a glance at the thin wisp of smoke snaking up from his wife's blanket, glared balefully at me, and then went back to yelling.

I waited for Mrs. Mealy to spot the smoke, but like the rest of the crowd, she was transfixed by her husband. I was loath to put myself on center stage, but the cigarette had quickly burned a hole in the fleece lap quilt and was working on whatever layer she had underneath, whether that be skin or cloth. I jumped forward and ripped the quilt off her lap. The butt flew off with it, but I saw that the ember had already melted through her slacks, leaving a red mark on the skin of her undernour-ished thigh. "You're burned!"

Naomi snatched the quilt from my hand and covered her legs up quickly. "I'm fine." She looked back at her husband with fierce adoration.

"What?" Had she noticed that her leg had been on fire? "Your leg is burned. You need to get some ice on it."

"We're fine." Pastor Mealy took his foot off the wheelchair and glared at me.

"I don't think you are. Your wife is injured. A lit cigarette landed on her leg."

The unintentional intermission the butt had caused woke the crowd from their reverie. They began to glance around, at the masks in one hand and the beer in the other. A couple shook their heads ("If they were in charge of evolution, we'd still be monkeys," I heard someone mutter), and all but a few zealots turned back toward the maze and their friends and family.

"I said, we're fine," Pastor Mealy said.

I scowled. "Shouldn't you ask your wife if she's fine?"

Naomi spoke without meeting my eyes. "'For the wife does not rule over her own body, but the husband does,' 1 Corinthians 7:4."

"What's going on here?" Gary Wohnt elbowed his way next to me.

Pastor Mealy dropped his angry expression and offered his hand. "Gary! Welcome!"

Gary shook it, turned back to me, and repeated himself. "What's going on here?"

"Well, these two were picketing the festival, and I came to see what was up when I saw someone flick a cigarette that landed on Mrs. Mealy's lap. I brushed it off her, but wanted to make sure she was OK."

"She is," Pastor Mealy said firmly. "And now, I think we'll be on our way. I believe we've conveyed our message. If we can turn away even one person from this ungodly exercise, we will have done our duty. Good day to you both." He pushed his wife's wheelchair toward the main entrance.

"You go to their church," I said accusingly. Gary didn't respond. "And *you're* at the festival. Don't you see a conflict?"

"I'm on the clock." He took off into the crowd.

For my part, I stared longingly at the keg of beer across the commons. If Weston hadn't been waiting for me, I might have put my mouth to the hose. I settled for two Diet Cokes and a handful of salami, cream cheese, and pickle tubes and made my way back to the woods. We munched and talked and traveled around groups of people as the sun set and the air became bearable.

I didn't much like small talk, but Weston was good at it, as long as it was with only a few people at a time, so I played shadow. The highlight was when I caught a glimpse of Alicia Mealy, who must have expertly avoided any run-ins with her parents, dressed like a Fly Girl and holding hands with a flop-haired brute. I smiled to myself, a titillating hunch taking shape in the back of my head.

When I heard the sounds of Not with My Horse warming up on the north side of the festival, I asked Weston if he was ready to brave the maze with me before the sun was completely off the horizon.

"Do you mind going without me?" he asked apologetically. "You know that guy I was talking to about the correlation between rainfall and mosquito reproduction? I told him I'd wait here for him. He had to run and pick up his girlfriend, and then he was going to finish telling me about a wood tick he pulled off his dog last week. Said it didn't look like any other tick he'd ever seen."

I rolled my eyes. "Not a problem. I'll probably head home after I get through the maze. See you around?"

"Deal." Weston squeezed my arm and then turned back to wait for the inside track on a wood tick, his fingers quivering in anticipation like he was playing little pianos at his side.

I strode firmly past the keg, grabbed an apple out of a bowl, and entered the maze. Most people had already gone through, so I was alone in the entrance, with only the play between the setting sun and burgeoning full moon for company. The first fork appeared at twenty feet, and I chose left. I followed that winding path for ten minutes before I realized it was a dead end. I could hear distant chatter and the squealing riffs of Not with My Horse's opening number when I returned to my initial starting spot, choosing right this time.

The clean, peppery smell of corn tassels tickled my nose as I marched across the hay lining the ground. I considered for a moment turning back. It was going on full dark, and if the rising moon went behind a cloud, I wouldn't be able to see. Glancing at the clear sky, I decided to continue on. If nothing else, I could yell for help if I got lost.

Hopefully, I would be heard over the cranking of the band.

My fingers trailed over the smooth leaves and rough stalks of the six-foot-tall, thick-as-thieves corn. On a whim, I tried to bend one. It was like a steel rod. I didn't know what sort of genetically modified corn went into making a maze, but it was solid. I gave a yank to the stalk, and the ground didn't move. I couldn't even push it far enough apart to squeeze through and cheat. I guessed the only way out of the maze was to follow the paths. As I walked, the sound of the band grew louder. The techno-punk-country fusion was painful to listen to, but it served as a beacon for the exit.

I had just taken what I hoped was my last right when I was brought up short by a scream, long and shrill like an animal being butchered. It sounded close, maybe twenty feet straight ahead, and it turned my blood to ice. I rushed forward but met a wall of corn, planted so close together it felt like a bamboo jungle. I had to take a run at it to break through the first three layers with my shoulder, but behind it were more layers.

I darted back and around, and then around again, searching frantically for a way to reach the scream. When I heard another shriek, this one so full of terror it made my stomach turn, I realized I was getting farther away, not closer.

I raced back, and then left, and forward, and right, and forward, and right again. I was just about ready to scream myself when I saw a wide opening ahead, a lighter black than the corn walls surrounding me. I charged forward and stumbled out of the maze.

Straight ahead was the stage, but most people were turned toward a sobbing teenage girl crumpled on the ground not far from the exit I'd just run out of.

"They took Jennifer! They just grabbed her and pulled her out of the maze!"

Chapter 35

Jennifer, the bubble-nosed brunette from Tom and Tina's Taxidermy, Lucy's pal and fellow cheerleader, had been abducted.

According to her friend, Julie, two men dressed in black had grabbed them inside the maze and dragged both teens to a hole cut into one of the outside walls. Julie had escaped by biting her captor's arm and running, but Jennifer had not been so lucky.

As Julie sobbed inconsolably, a pall hung over the crowd, everyone thinking the same thing: Jennifer was going to be shot in the back, just like Lucy Lebowski. Parents ushered their crying children away. Men and women exchanged worried glances before buzzing into action. Gary Wohnt called the state police, and a search party began forming out of the gathered townspeople.

I listened to all this, feeling like one of those firecrackers that spins on the sidewalk, pointlessly shooting sparks. Instead of waiting for instruction, I took off around the east side of the corn maze until I spotted the hole a couple hundred yards up. Gary was already standing there with one of his deputies, and I cut into the hardwood forest on the maze's perimeter before he spotted me.

The abductors couldn't have gotten far, and they must have taken off into the woods.

I wished I had my flashlight and spider knife on me, but I would have to make do with the full moon and a big stick I kicked up. The woods were fairly cleaned out, which made walking easy, especially when I found the path Weston and I'd been on earlier. I walked it back toward the maze until I was about twenty yards south of the cut-out exit. I stepped in something mushy and glanced down. Someone had spilled a large amount of liquid where the trees met the field, and they'd done it after Weston and I passed over this spot. Two evenly spaced tracks ran through mud, each about two inches wide and half an inch deep.

I stuck my fingers into the ooze and smelled it—water and dirt.

I backtracked on the path searching for more clues. Trees loomed over me, casting long-limbed shadows. I felt like I was in another maze, only larger, and my senses were heightened by a blend of fear and anger. How dare someone terrorize the festival! Would another mother have to learn that her daughter had been murdered, that nowhere was safe?

I had an idea that I'd keep going until I came out at the lakefront property in the hopes of finding some evidence of Jennifer having been dragged this way, but the deeper I walked, the less able I was to see amid the trees. I was about to turn around when a shaft of moonlight through the trees outlined a figure, maybe six feet tall, his arms out.

He was headless.

I froze, my heart knocking around in my chest. Was it Jennifer, shot through the back and hung in the trees? Was it one of the kidnappers? I was too afraid to tear my eyes away.

I opened my mouth to yell, but nothing came out. In the distance, I could hear the rumble of people shouting Jennifer's name, searching, agitated, but they were all too far away to help me.

I stayed frozen to my spot. A breeze rippled through the treetops. The form did not move. A larger gust blew, raising the figure's arms. When the wind died, so did the arms. I stepped cautiously toward it and reached up.

It was a dark, empty coat, caught in a branch. I exhaled heavily, tugging it down. I felt inside. The pockets were empty and the interior was smooth except for a rip in the left shoulder. I forced my breathing to slow and relaxed ever so slightly. I scanned the immediate area and found nothing else.

I made my way back out of the woods and straight to Gary Wohnt, who was still standing at the hole the girls had been dragged from. He was taking notes and barking orders.

When he took a breath, I said, "There's something I want you to see."

He raised his eyebrows but followed me without complaint, motioning to one of his deputies to finish assigning tasks. When we reached the tracks in the mud, I pointed.

"What?" he asked.

"Those tracks. See them? They're the same tracks I found outside the Fortune Café after it was vandalized." I had a theory forming in my head. The vandalism at the Fortune, Lucy Lebowski's murder, and Jennifer's kidnapping were all connected, and I was working on an idea of who was behind it.

"Wagon tracks," Gary said brusquely. "They brought the kegs through here to avoid the crowds."

Not good enough. "And the tracks at the Fortune?" I asked.

"Was the ground wet there, too?"

"No," I said reluctantly. "It wasn't. They were just faint tracks in the dry grass. But they were the exact same tracks that are right here. What made them?"

"I don't know. Another wagon?" He rubbed his jaw. "Why didn't you point them out to me when I was there?"

"It didn't seem important then. It does now."

"I don't see how." Gary abruptly turned on his heel and walked away.

We weren't friends, but he had never been this dismissive of me. What was going on? I looked at the coat I'd found in the woods, now draped over my shoulder. It was either navy blue or black.

I stared at Gary's retreating back, remembered him shaking hands with Pastor Mealy as the pastor picketed the festival. I wasn't sure any longer which team Gary was playing for. I would keep the coat to myself for now.

I made my way back to my car. After a quick stop at home to grab my knife and flashlight, I was driving directly to New Millennium Bible Camp.

Chapter 36

The traffic was light. Almost everyone had stayed at Hershod's, knowing they wouldn't find Jennifer but unwilling to go home without trying to help. When I drove back past the corn maze, I saw proof of it in the hundreds of flashlights bobbing in the night like fireflies, or the torches of villagers hunting a monster.

My radio wasn't on. I needed to think, and the clean night air and buzzing bullfrogs were enough background noise. I knew in my gut that Robert, Alicia, and Naomi Mealy were responsible for the vandalism, one dead girl, and one missing girl. I had a hunch that the tracks I'd seen outside the Fortune Café hadn't been made by a wagon.

They'd been made by Naomi's wheelchair.

They were also the same tracks I'd just seen near the corn maze.

Lucy Lebowski's body had been dumped in Clitherall, not far from the Bible camp, and if it had been wet enough, I was sure there would have been wheelchair tracks there as well.

The two men in black Julie said had pulled her and Jennifer out of the maze had actually been Robert and Alicia, I was sure of it. Naomi probably waited in the background while they did their dirty work, and then they piled the body on her and wheeled it away. I didn't know why they'd done it or how they'd known the dead girls, but I guessed it was related to the God's Army they were forming.

With Gary in their thrall, though, I needed irrefutable proof.

That's what I intended to find at the Bible camp.

I turned on the gravel road leading to the New Millennium and continued on past the camp entrance, parking my car next to the Glendalough Lake public landing. I hoofed it back, my senses on alert for any sign of Jennifer.

The camp was dark. None of the six cabins had lights on, and the assembly hall was as black as a haunted house. The only spark I spotted was a dim glow off the back of the Mealys' house. I scurried to the nearest cabin, my heart pounding in my ears, and crouched down. From there I had a clear view of the central yard, a vast, moonlit sea separating me from the Mealy house and the main hall. I was about to leave my safe spot and dart toward their house when I saw someone lurking around the assembly hall.

I pressed myself to the cabin, a shrub partially obscuring me from view. The person was not much taller than me, and slightly stooped. He or she *also* appeared to be heading toward the Mealy house. My mission changed on the spot from looking inside the Mealys' to finding out who else was trying to look inside the Mealys'. I concentrated on making my heart stop hammering until the lurker was out of sight, and then I dashed across the open space before my common sense had time to haul on its work clothes.

I crouched next to the building for a moment, catching my breath, and then slipped soundlessly around the moon-shaded side of the great hall and tiptoed toward the Mealys' house. At the end of the building, I peered around the corner and peed my pants a little when the shadow appeared not twenty feet in front of me, glancing over his shoulder back toward the house.

With his face turned toward the moon, I saw it was Pastor Winter.

My heart lurched. What could he possibly be looking for? Cribbing a sermon for tomorrow's service? Searching for a kidnapped girl, like me? Or maybe hiding an abducted teen's body, or planting evidence of a kidnapping? He scurried across the open grounds to one of the sheltering cabins, and then disappeared from sight.

He wasn't trying to search the Mealy house after all. Had he just wanted to look inside?

When I heard the distant rumble of a car starting, I prayed it was Pastor Winter heading out. I gathered my resolve to take my turn spying on the dimly lit Mealy house.

I walked lightly and low to the ground, avoiding the gravel so as not to make noise. My calves ached at the effort, and every sound, from the song of the bullfrogs in the slough to the snap of a branch in the woods, made my hackles quiver. When I was within twenty feet of the Mealys', I dropped into a crawl, my knife in hand. This close to the grass, I smelled dryness and dirt. The unwatered sod crackled under my hands and knees.

A light spilled out the back of the house, and I followed it around to Pastor and Mrs. Mealy's bedroom. Crouching under the lit window, I took a deep breath and slid up the side of the house, facing in. Not for the first time in my life, I wished my forehead were smaller. If they were looking out, they'd have a full view of two inches of noggin before I could lay eyes on them.

Fully erect, I was just able to peer over the sill. Pastor Mealy lay in bed holding a Bible, a glass-shaded lamp casting a circle of yellow light around him. Next to him was a prostrate form completely covered in a quilt. I assumed the body was Naomi, probably in bed early at her husband's command.

I continued around to Alicia's window. Her room was dark, so I had to peer in for several minutes before my eyes adjusted. It appeared as though the bedroom was empty, so I took a risk and shined my flashlight around. The door was closed and the room was person-free. That was significant, but how, I didn't know. Was Alicia somewhere, in charge of guarding Jennifer?

If so, where?

I crouched on my haunches, contemplating my next move. I considered searching the other buildings, but they were all open to the public and would be busy bright and early tomorrow, on a Sunday. I couldn't imagine that the Mealys would be foolish enough to hide a girl where she'd be certain to be discovered. Really, there was only one logical place besides the Bible camp where the Mealys could stow a body, and it was only a couple miles away: Naomi's sister's house on Hancock Lake. I shoved my knife into my waistband and jogged back to my car.

I reached the Toyota in under seven minutes. I was fairly certain no one had followed me, but I drove with only the light of the moon until I reached the blacktop. I knew there was a minimum-maintenance road that would take me directly to Hancock Lake, and after several missed attempts, I found it and bumped along. I parked at the same spot near the lake where I had on my original visit and walked up to Golden Pond Road, knife once again in hand. I knew Les Pastner patrolled these woods, and it was better to be prepared.

I followed the perimeter of the woods, the lonely sound of an owl hooting overhead. I shivered. Night birds were worse luck than day birds. I was sure of it. They had *stealth*.

When I reached Mrs. Mealy's sister's driveway, the front kitchen was ablaze in light. A figure inside zipped past the window, too quick for me to be certain who it was. I made my way closer, on guard for some more kindergarten rope traps. My ankle burn from the first one was just starting to heal.

I stepped closer to the house. There was also a light on in the lower level coming out of those little half windows high on basement walls. The yellow glow shone through the snowball bushes in front of the windows strangely, flickery and golden. I wanted to get closer to see what was making that light.

I was forced to cross an expanse of naked driveway, the moon barreling down like a headlight. I steeled myself and strode steadily forward. I was fifteen feet from the basement window, the light strobing out, when the front screen door of the house crashed open.

"Who's out there?"

An icy claw grabbed my heart and my feet. If I ran forward or sideways, I could hide in the woods. If I ran back, I could stay on the road and get to my car the quickest. My mind was quicksilver, but my feet were lead.

The ratchet of a shotgun being cocked came on the heels of the woman's harsh voice. "Show yourself!"

Her command broke through my fear, and I turned and beat cheeks. I ducked in the woods first, remembering a conversation I'd overheard between some hunters at the Turtle Stew. They said that if you zigzagged from someone who was shooting at you instead of running straight, the shooter would have only a one in ten chance of actually hitting you. Even then, they'd likely miss a vital organ. So I darted around trees, in and out of ditches, until my car was in sight. Then I ran straight as an arrow, fumbling for my keys, so I had the car running before I was all the way sat down.

I waited until I was a mile away to lock all my doors. As a resident of Battle Lake, I'd been threatened by worse than a woman with a gun, but the creepiness of the Mealys combined with Jennifer's kidnapping made the whole night menacing, from the trees to the moon's liquid reflection on the lake to the raccoon scuttling across the road.

I kicked myself for still not getting a good look at Mrs. Mealy's sister, but there was no help for it now. I'd need to come up with a way to slip inside that house in the daylight.

Tomorrow.

Chapter 37

Sunday morning was as hot as the devil's armpit, and draped in a cottony funk. Heavy clouds locked elbows in the sky, but even without a visible sun, the oppressive heat wasn't letting up. The temperature and uneasy weather riled the already-stressed folks of Battle Lake. Jennifer was missing, and if she wasn't yet dead, she would be soon. The town buzzed with people whispering their worst fears, locking their doors, not letting their children walk next door to play. A mandatory curfew had been enacted, and word was the FBI was in town, which made the crime's seriousness inescapably visceral.

For my part, I was out of Battle Lake in a week, and I didn't know if that would be enough time to find Jennifer or to pin Lucy's murder and the vandalism at the Fortune Café on the Mealys. I needed a way to weasel into the Mealy inner circle, and to also steal into Mrs. Mealy's sister's house. The opportunity to accomplish my first goal presented itself nicely at the café over breakfast.

"Hey, Sid, what's this?" I held up the nub I'd just ripped off the flyer thumbtacked to their community bulletin board.

Sid glanced up from the designer coffee she'd been crafting. "I don't know. That young Elizabeth Taylor look-alike from the Bible camp stuck it up this morning."

"Alicia?"

She shrugged. "If you say so."

The flyer had said "Save Your Soul" across the top in gothic lettering. It was an invitation to the public to visit New Millennium Bible Camp to "Cleanse Your Soul of Pagan Residue and Get Right with God or Pay the Price in Eternal Damnation." The nubs included directions and a phone number.

The front door opened, and I heard soft-tennie footsteps stop behind me, followed by an old-lady voice. "If you're thinkin' of joining, remember that Jesus wants spiritual fruits, not religious nuts."

"Mrs. Berns?" I turned. "What're you doing here?"

"I was on my way to church. Right outside the door, in fact. That's when I realized I didn't wanna go in. I think it's all the glue-free communion wafers I ate yesterday. They didn't sit quite right." She patted her tummy. "I coulda pooped through a sieve last night."

I wrinkled my nose. "Maybe that's why they only distribute one wafer a week."

"Maybe. How'd your date with Weston go?" She nodded over my shoulder, and I spotted him leaning toward a computer screen in the next room. I hadn't noticed him when I first walked in, being too distracted by the flyer.

"It wasn't a date," I said, turning back to Mrs. Berns. "He's not my type."

"Too nice, huh?"

I rolled my eyes. "He's a sweet man. I'm just not dating right now."

"Too bad. I bet your kids would be able to fly." She cupped her hands around her mouth. "Hey, Weston! You see Mira over here? Maybe you should come say good morning."

Weston's head popped around, and he quickly shut down his computer. When he stood, he had a strange expression on his face; it reminded me of the look Tom the taxidermist had had last night when we'd caught him stuffing a different kind of animal—guilty and defiant all at once. I realized there was a lot I didn't know about Weston.

"Good morning, Mira. Mrs. Berns. How are you two?"

I took his offered hand and shook it, though the gesture seemed oddly formal. "Fine. I didn't see you after we separated last night. Did you hear that a local girl's been kidnapped?"

His eyes cleared and turned serious. "I did. I joined the search party."

"They find anything?" I asked.

"Nothing. The FBI has been called in. At least that's what I heard one of the local police say."

"I wonder if they need any help?" Mrs. Berns asked. "I always enjoy a special investigation."

I raised my eyebrows, envisioning Mrs. Berns with a badge, a gun, and a license to kill. "Good luck with that. I've gotta get going."

"Where're you off to?" Weston asked.

I held up the flyer tearaway. "To get saved."

"I didn't think you were the religious type."

I reeled back mock-defensively. "Why not?"

"Because you're a librarian, and you swear, and you're so curious."

"Nice save," I said, giving him a salute. "I'm actually going because I have a hunch that the pastor and his family out at the Bible camp have something to do with the recent bad luck in Battle Lake, and I want to check it out more." I wasn't sure what drove me to reveal my conspiracy theory. I usually played my cards much closer to my chest, but Weston was giving off a weird vibe, and I wanted to call him out.

Weston looked at me sharply. "What makes you think that?"

I was protective of my clues, the few that I had. "Just a hunch. Anyways, I'm off."

He was suddenly earnest. "Bring me with."

"I don't think so. I work best alone."

"If you two are going," Mrs. Berns said, "I'm going, too. I just gotta lay some cable first."

I glared at her.

"What? Pretty girls poop, too. I'll be right back."

I looked her up and down. She was dressed normally today—no superhero suit, no toy sharpshooters. "Fine, I'll buy a scone and some tea and meet you two out front. If you're coming along, though, you can't blow my cover. We're all going to get saved, no questions asked."

Mrs. Berns saluted and turned smartly toward the bathroom. Weston grinned and shrugged. For my part, I walked to the front counter to order my breakfast. Sid gave me the *who's that guy?* question with her eyes, nodding toward Weston, and I tossed her back the *I'll tell you later* look.

Once I had breakfast in hand, I headed out, Mrs. Berns and Weston on my heels. I ignored their chatter as I drove, the route becoming so familiar I could cruise it in my sleep.

I sensed it was a bad idea to bring these two, but hope springs eternal. Plus, and here was the truth, I was still unsettled from last night's foray. I didn't want to be there alone. When we reached the Bible camp driveway, I warned them again that we were undercover.

"What's our code name?" Mrs. Berns asked.

"We don't have code names," I said, using all my willpower not to slap my forehead. "We're ourselves, pretending to be here to get saved."

"Okey dokey, artichokey." She nodded thoughtfully. "But if you're in trouble, I'm the Green Lantern, he's Aquaman, and you can be Snow White."

I shook my head. "I'm not going to be Snow White."

"Fine. You can be Dyna Girl."

"No, we're just us," I said, louder than I would have liked. "Weston Lippmann, Mrs. Berns, and Mira James. We're here for salvation. If you can't stick to that, you need to stay in the car." Mrs. Berns appeared hurt, and I immediately regretted my harshness.

"Fine," I grumbled. "I'm Dyna Girl, you're Green Lantern, and Weston is Aquaman. But *only* if we're in trouble. OK?"

The sun rose on Mrs. Berns's face. "Ten four, good buddy."

The parking lot was packed, as usual. People streamed in and out of the cabins and the assembly hall, and a crowd was gathering around the pulpit in the water. All the benches in the horseshoe around the pulpit were taken, and the congregation was seven deep. In the center stood Pastor Mealy, up to his ankles in slimy water. As the three of us marched toward the outdoor gathering, I searched everywhere for Alicia and Naomi. They were nowhere to be seen.

For the first time, I wondered about the soundness of this idea. I'd been so excited to have an in at the Bible camp that I hadn't considered what getting saved might involve, and how I was going to come off as a sincere, repentant sinner. If Mrs. Berns and Weston hadn't been with me, I might have turned around. Two missing teens in a week, one dead. Those weren't the kinds of odds a normal person would stick their nose in.

"Get a move on!" Mrs. Berns prodded me. "You're the leader. Show us the way to the Lord." She cackled as she followed behind.

I reluctantly led us to the pulpit in the water, where we hung out on the border of the crowd. I had just about decided this was a waste of time when an opening parted. "You are here to be saved?"

There was no mistaking that Pastor Mealy was pointing at me. It was now or never. "I am."

"Then come to the front and give yourself to Jesus."

I walked shakily through the crowd and noticed that both Gary Wohnt and Sarah Ruth were seated toward the front, facing the pastor. Gary Wohnt, sunglasses-free, peered at me impassively. Sarah Ruth looked apprehensive. I flashed both a weak grin, and cringed as the lukewarm water rushed over my leather sandals. The lake bottom was squishy underneath, and my feet made sucking noises when I pulled them up. The hot air smelled like peat moss.

When I was standing directly in front of the pastor, I looked into his eyes, and strangely, my fear melted away. I knew he was taking responsibility for whatever happened next, and it felt good to share the load. Besides, what could happen in front of a crowd of people?

He took me by the wrist and led me until we were at an open spot away from the pulpit, now up to our waists in water. He placed one hand on my forehead and the other at the small of my back and pushed me toward the murky lake. My back arched, and the bathwater-warm water caught me. It was happening so quickly that I only had time to be thankful I'd worn a bra.

Pastor Mealy pulled me back up, his eyes closed, whispering fervently. "May God take her safely to his Kingdom."

I glanced around, relieved. That hadn't been so bad.

I was turning to give Weston and Mrs. Berns the thumbs-up when Pastor Mealy took his hand off my forehead, grabbed my upper arm firmly, and ground his shoe-clad foot into my ankle. It was the same one that was still raw from Les Pastner's trap. I whimpered and went down, twisting to escape. I felt his hand on the back of my neck as I dived underwater, the fleshy bottom of the lake allowing me to spin out from under him. I didn't surface until I'd stroked several feet away, sure I was going to feel the full body of the pastor pin me underwater.

When I came up, I wiped my eyes quickly, ready to dive down again if need be. Pastor Mealy was where I'd left him and Gary Wohnt was striding toward us, knee-deep in water. Everyone else was humming rapturously and swaying with their eyes closed, with the lone exception of Mrs. Berns, who had hawk eyes trained on the pastor and the police chief.

Weston was nowhere to be seen.

I tried to put pressure on the foot Pastor Mealy had crushed, moaning at the icy-hot pain that shot up my leg. My ankle was severely sprained, or broken. I swam toward shore as far as I could and hopped the rest of the way to Mrs. Berns, dripping filthy water.

No one offered me a hand.

Mrs. Berns offered me a surprisingly strong shoulder to lean on. "Are you all right, Dyna Girl?"

"No," I said, trying not to cry. "I think my ankle is broken."

"The pastor dirty-dogged you, didn't he?"

"He stepped on my foot." I brushed dripping hair out of my face. "I suppose it could have been an accident."

"I suppose walleyes can fly, too. Let's get you to a doctor."

I looked around. "Where's Weston?"

"He disappeared about the same time you got all moony-eyed and went into the lake." She let out a puff of air. "He can find his own way home."

"I don't want to leave him here."

"Have you seen your ankle?"

I purposely had not. It felt hot and pulsed like a migraine. When I let my eyes wander down my mud-streaked leg, I was rewarded with the sight of my left ankle as wide as a rabbit in a snake's throat, the skin purple and stretched. "Yeah, Weston can probably find his way home. Can you drive?"

"Is the Pope Catholic?"

"I'm pretty sure he is, but can you drive?" Don't ever deflect a deflector.

"Not in the eyes of the law, but that doesn't stop me from getting where I'm going."

"Good enough." We hobbled back to the car. I mostly limped, using Mrs. Berns for balance, and my ankle throbbed with every jolt. I periodically glanced back at the congregation, but they took no notice of us. The air was hot, but I was wet and in shock, and I shivered as we made our way.

Once we reached the car, it took Mrs. Berns a couple tries and painful grinds to figure out my stick shift, but soon we were headed to the Douglas County Hospital in Alexandria. When we arrived, Mrs. Berns ran in for a wheelchair so I didn't have to walk. She pushed me in with a flourish, and we spent the next several hours waiting next to sunstroked tourists, a guy with a fishhook stuck in his lip, and other assorted emergencies.

By the time we were seen by a doctor, my ankle had gone numb. My overriding sensation was of being covered in sticky, dried swamp water. An evil poking session and several X-rays later, my ankle was declared sprained but intact. A kind nurse cleaned it off, wrapped an

ACE bandage around it tight as a tourniquet, and gave me an ice pack for the ride home. She offered crutches, but I didn't take them. I wasn't planning on being out of commission long enough to learn how to use them. In fact, thanks to a Paul Bunyan–size dose of ibuprofen, I'd decided I was going to drive us home. One trip on windy back roads with Mrs. Berns at the wheel had been enough for me.

"Hey, Green Lantern, you mind if I drive?"

"Suit yourself, but the doctor said you should stay off that ankle."

"It's my left foot. I hardly need it. Can you help me find a sweat-shirt, though? I think there's one in the trunk, and I'm feeling chilly."

Mrs. Berns studied me doubtfully. "It's ninety-seven degrees. You sure you're OK to drive?"

I shivered. "Positive. I just want a sweatshirt."

"OK." She took my keys and walked around to the back. "Will this do?" She held up the black coat I'd found in the woods at the festival last night.

"No. That's not mine."

She peered at the inside. "Hell of a rip here on the left shoulder. My aunt used to have rips in all her parkas just like this. She was a free spirit, and all her big, sharp rings tore the shoulders of every coat she had when she put them on. Boy, could that woman belly dance, though."

The sudden thought was almost too big to fit inside my head. Naomi Mealy wore a big, sharp ring on her left hand. Could it have torn the inside shoulder of this coat? Had I found her coat at the corn maze, stuck in the trees as if she could walk out of it?

What if Mrs. Mealy could walk?

But then how come she hadn't pushed the burning cigarette off her leg? Was she that unhinged? Or was I the unhinged one for even thinking she could use her legs?

I thought back to Naomi talking in tongues, and her reverent adoration of her husband. No, the more I thought about it, the more it made a sick sense. Naomi and Robert Mealy had some twisted reason for kidnapping and killing teenage girls, first in Georgia and now in Minnesota, and Mrs. Mealy's sister was their partner in crime.

But no one would believe me if I told them my bonkers hunch, least of all Gary Wohnt, who was under the Mealy spell.

No, it was up to me. I would take my flashlight, my knife, and a digital camera and find Jennifer tonight, if she was still alive.

Nothing would turn me away.

Nothing.

Chapter 38

It was almost seven p.m. when I finally dropped Mrs. Berns off at the Senior Sunset. She didn't want to let me go home alone. She said it was because she was worried about my ankle, but I think she sniffed a showdown in the air and didn't want to miss it. Part of me wanted to bring her along—she'd been a fantastic bodyguard—but I didn't know what I was walking into and couldn't in good conscience let her tag along.

At my house, I played fetch with Luna so she could exercise without me needing to move, and then I hobbled around, filling both pets' food and water dishes. I also fed and watered myself, though I was too jittery from anticipation to swallow much more than fruit and juice.

I showered and rewrapped my ankle, only this time I made it so tight it felt like a club. I couldn't have bent it to save my soul. I hadn't had time to wash my summer spying outfit since my last mission, but it didn't smell too bad, and the linen pants slipped on easily over my mummified ankle. I added my stun gun to the knife and flashlight in my waistband.

I'd bought Z-Force, as I'd fondly christened the weapon, in June, and had a couple good opportunities to see it in action. The little gizmo looked like a black hair trimmer but stung like a scorpion, if said scorpion could deliver several thousand volts of electricity off one charge. Z-Force was a passive-aggressive, commitment-avoidant weapon—you zapped and ran, and no one was hurt for very long—and it fit my lifestyle like a glove.

I wasn't stupid. If my instincts were correct, two of the Mealys were kidnappers and at least one was a murderer. They were dangerous, and the odds weren't on my side in a direct confrontation. However, the chance of convincing God-struck Gary Wohnt that they were culpable was even poorer. All I needed was one shred of concrete proof that the Mealys were guilty—Lucy Lebowski's pom-poms squirreled away in the assembly hall kitchen, or Jennifer locked in the church basement, or a recording of Pastor Mealy confessing to God that he murdered the Lebowski girl as a way to redirect his inappropriate feelings about his daughter.

If I didn't find that evidence at the Bible camp, I would uncover it at the Hancock Lake house, even if it took me all night. I could find that proof and slip away without being seen and let Gary take it from there. If I didn't come up with that proof, though, Jennifer was a dead girl, guaranteed.

If she was even still alive.

I pushed the thought away. Jennifer had to be alive, though what the poor girl was suffering now was impossible to imagine. Better action than fear. I was the only person who suspected the Mealys, and I took that responsibility seriously.

Before I drove to the Bible camp, however, I had a hunch that needed following up. A short drive brought me to the curiously named Makeout Point, odd because there was no point, just a lot of making out in a field next to an abandoned farmhouse. All the local teens parked and partied here, even though the Battle Lake police regularly busted them up. Whoever owned the land had finally caved to reality last summer and placed a porta-potty next to one of the decaying sheds.

I counted four cars and a minivan as I pulled in. Knocking on the windows of the first two brought embarrassment for all involved—it's hard to tell one brunette from another when she's got a blond farm boy attached to her face—but the minivan contained the pot o' gold.

I'd knocked on one of the back seat windows, impressed with the amount of heavy breathing it must have taken to fog up every pane of glass in a seven-passenger Dodge Caravan. My initial knocks didn't break the pace of the writhing mass I could make out through the misty window, so I rapped with the nice end of Z-Force. "Police!"

What fun. Wild shuffling took place inside the minivan. Minutes later, the sliding door rumbled open, and I was face-to-face with a flushed young man with saucer eyes and an underbite.

"You saw a cop car?" he asked, looking over my shoulder.

"What?" I asked innocently. "No, I said, 'Puh-leez.' Who makes out in a Dodge Caravan?"

He ducked his head sheepishly. "It's my parents'."

"Figured. I'm looking for Alicia Mealy. Preacher's daughter?"

A batch of tangled brunette hair peeped over his shoulder, followed by two angry eyes. "Whaddya want with me?"

Bingo.

Anyone who's grown up in a small town knows that nobody parties like the pastor's kid. I liked Alicia about as much as a cold sore, but I had a feeling she was too whiny to be a murderer and too manipulative to follow her parents' lead except when it benefited her. I'd started work on this theory when I'd discovered the bag of weed in her drawer. When I spotted her holding hands at the August Moon Festival with Knute Anderson, last year's star senior quarterback and lover of the ladies, I knew exactly what type of person I was dealing with.

No way would she give up a Saturday night to kidnap a teenager. A little early-morning vandalism as revenge for some imagined slight, maybe. A crime that involved getting dirty and didn't have boys around? *Never.*

Now to follow up on the second part of my hunch. "I need to talk to you."

"Don't care," she said, buttoning her shirt.

"You *will* care. Either you answer a couple questions, or I tell your parents you were making hot monkey friction on the Sabbath."

She rolled her eyes, adjusting her boobs under her now-buttoned shirt. "They'd never believe you over me. They think I'm an angel straight from God's hands."

Probably true. I had another ace in the hole, though. "I know someone else who would think you're a heavenly angel."

She snorted. "Who?"

"You know the band that played at the festival last night? Not with My Horse?"

"Do I know them? Gawd, do I wish! They were smokin'!" Alicia said this with no consideration for the hurt-looking minivan driver whose mouth she'd most recently visited. He was, incidentally, not the former star quarterback she'd been holding hands with last night. Someone really should do a study on the direct correlation between proximity to God in your childhood and affinity with beer, bongs, and boys in the teen years.

"The lead singer is a good friend of mine," I said with only a little regret.

Her eyes grew wide. "The one that looks like a blond Jim Morrison?"

And screws like a blond Andy Rooney. But she didn't need to know that. "Yeah. His name is Brad. How about we do a trade? You answer a couple questions for me, and I set you up with him."

Her eyebrows knit together. "How do I know you'll follow through?"

I shrugged. "You don't, but what've you got to lose?"

She shoved her hair back, looked like she was about to slide the door closed on my face, and then must have realized she'd just been making out in a minivan. What *did* she have to lose? "Fine. Make it quick."

"You know Lucy Lebowski and Jennifer Henderson?"

"I know who they are."

"Their parents go to your church?"

She weighed the question and must have decided it was information I could find out elsewhere if I wanted to. "Yeah. At least a couple times."

"Did Lucy and Jennifer attend church with their parents?"

"Hell no!" This was the minivan driver, apparently finally awoken from his lust-stupor. "You couldn't get Lucy within a mile of a church. She said she'd go up in smoke!" He laughed at the memory. "Jennifer wasn't as much of a partier, but she stopped going to church her junior year. Stopped eating meat, stopped curling her hair, the whole deal. It was really weird. We thought maybe she was joining a cult."

Ah, yes, the cult of freethinking. Scary stuff. But between Alicia and her boy toy, my questions had been answered and my theory confirmed. "Thank you both. You've been a big help."

"You're not going to introduce me to Brad, are you?" Alicia pouted.

"Oh, I most certainly am," I said truthfully. "You two will make a perfect pair. I'll be in touch." I'm not sure if they were able to get back in the mood after I left, but I didn't much care. I was on to bigger and scarier things.

As I pulled out of Makeout Point road, the full moon stared down at me, as round and myopic as a saucer of milk. There was an ominous, electric feeling in the air. It reminded me of the day in fifth-grade science class when our teacher, Mr. Bowden, brought in a Van de Graaff generator. The static electricity machine looked like an aluminum ball on a pedestal. I wasn't sure what his teaching goal had been, but what I took away from the experience was that you didn't want to be the last person in a Van de Graaff chain.

The shock you'd receive would singe your toenails.

Even if you didn't touch the silver ball, your arm hair crackled up whenever you stood within five feet of it and your blood felt lighter than normal. That's how I felt now as I stared down empty County Road 8, heading south. Heat lightning flashed across a field to my left and I shivered, the night air smelling as lonely as a wolf's howl.

As I drove, I weighed my situation. I knew I couldn't bring anyone with me tonight because it was too dangerous, but if something happened to me, my theory could disappear forever, and teens would continue to disappear from Battle Lake. Settling for a compromise, I backtracked to Clitherall and wrote my theory on a sheet of scrap paper that I folded like an envelope. I grabbed a stamp from the sheet I kept in my checkbook and stuck it on the outside but was at a momentary loss for whom to send it to. Suddenly the name and address came like a flash, and I added an extra two lines to the end of the note.

There was one blue metal mailbox outside the Clitherall post office, and I heaved open the top and dropped my letter in. It would go out with tomorrow's mail, come hell or high water.

Back in my car, the light-blooded feeling was still with me, but I didn't feel quite as lonely. Too nervous to listen to the radio, I hummed and played "Would You Rather" with myself. It was a childish game that Mrs. Berns loved, and it involved giving a person two horrible choices, like "Would you rather wake up next to Jerry Springer or Geraldo Rivera?" I was mulling over the merits of working the fryer at McDonald's versus personning the complaints desk at Walmart when I took a right onto the dirt road leading to New Millennium Bible Camp.

When I heard my tires chew the gravel and realized I was actually doing this, my blood drifted even farther north. I deliberately kept up the inane mind chatter. I couldn't afford to talk myself out of this, as perilous as it felt. I was imbued if not with confidence, then at least with faith in the rightness of my actions.

I believe I would have made it all the way to the Bible camp if not for the bloodied woman dragging herself across the dusty road in front of me.

Chapter 39

The glimpse I caught was of a female figure in bloody rags, army crawling, pulling heavy legs behind her. Then came a hurricane of fear too big for my body, screams that were mine or hers, and pure, ice-cold adrenaline as I pumped my brakes. Because she was so low to the road, my headlights hadn't caught sight of her until I was almost on top of her.

I dragged backward on my steering wheel as if I could stop the car by sheer force of will, and I squeezed shut my ears and hoped like I had never hoped before that I wasn't about to hear my car thump over a body.

Silence.

Dust drifting through my headlight beams like snow.

A full, bright moon.

The sweaty, sour smell of fear.

But no thump.

I realized my car had killed itself, either out of terror or my inability to remove my bandaged left foot from the clutch before I buried the brake. Shakily, I reached for the door handle and let myself out. My legs quivered as I limped around to the front of the car.

"Hurry." The feminine voice was raspy and sad, not at all commanding.

My heart skipped. "Jennifer?"

Her face and body were to the road, her hands stretched in front of her as if in supplication. Her dark hair was long and matted, part of it underneath the passenger-side tire of my Toyota, itself just inches from her head. The scene was surreal, a tableau of horror coming and going.

I hobbled over and knelt next to her. "Jennifer? Can you talk to me? I'm going to turn you over, OK?"

When she didn't answer, I slipped out my knife to gently cut the hair neath my tire and turned her away from my car. I was irrationally worried that the Toyota was going to roll forward that handbreadth and pop her skull like a summer squash. Her head lolled as I turned her on her back, and I had to bite my lip to keep from yelling. Her face was black with dried blood and swollen beyond recognition. I'd grabbed her left hand to feel for a pulse when I saw the gigantic rings.

Click. Click. Click.

"Mrs. Mealy?" I drew back, scared all over again. "Mrs. Mealy? Is that you?"

Her lids fluttered open. She didn't move anything but her eyes, which darted around like birds trapped in a house. "Where am I?"

"You're just outside the Bible camp, Mrs. Mealy. I'm going to run up there for help. Don't worry. I'll be right . . ."

She pushed herself up with her hands, not minding her legs, which lay at awkward angles. Her eyes burned like coals. "Don't! Don't go back there! Please, don't." Tears that obviously hurt her cut cheeks rolled down her face.

"I'm sorry, Mrs. Mealy, but I don't have a cell phone. I need to get you to a hospital. It's just a jog up the road. I won't leave you alone for long."

She grabbed my arm with desperate strength. "He did this to me. Do you understand? Robert did this to me. If you go back up there, he'll kill us both. He's out looking for me right now. We have to get out of here!"

She threw frightened glances into the woods, and her terror was contagious. The forest was thick and ominous on each side of the road, barely containing the evil within it.

I made up my mind on the spot. "If we work together, can I get you into my car?"

Naomi nodded mutely and offered me her arm, raw from pulling her body along. Talk about being wrong about a person; I couldn't believe I'd thought for a moment that she could walk. Lifting her up as best I could, oblivious to the pain shooting through my ankle, I towed her to the passenger door. She was nearly as light as a child, but the drag of her legs made it hard to maneuver. I tried to be gentle with her battered body, but I was as tense as a razor wire, waiting for the wicked hand of Robert Mealy to reach out and grab me.

Once I had her buckled in, I shambled around to my side and crossed my fingers that I hadn't done any permanent damage to my car. The first three starts were grinding failures, and as my headlights flickered, I thought I saw a shape slide in the woods to our right. I leaned over and slammed the lock on Naomi's door and then locked mine.

"Please please please," I begged.

My Toyota listened.

She fired up on the fourth attempt, and I executed the sharpest 180-degree turn on record. When I shifted from reverse to first, my bandaged ankle protested. I'd pay for this tomorrow, but I had more important matters to deal with now. "I'm bringing you to the hospital in Alexandria, Mrs. Mealy. If I drive fast, I can get us there in a half hour."

She'd drooped like a doll when I set her in the car, but my words brought back the fight in her. "You can't! Robert will kill me if you bring me to a hospital!"

I rubbed my face. "It looks like he just about did already."

"You don't understand, do you?" She shook her head and studied her raw hands, reluctant to reveal private details. Well, she didn't have to, not to me. She could tell it all to the police once I got her to safety.

When I turned right toward Alexandria, she made up her mind. "He's a murderer," she said softly.

I lifted my foot off the gas. "What?"

Her voice was soft, furred with tears. "It started in Georgia, when Eliza Hansen and Paula Duevel went missing. Their parents both attended our church. When their bodies were found, I suspected Robert was involved, but he wouldn't talk to me. We moved to this area right after. Then it started happening here. First Lucy, and now Jennifer. I tell you, it's Robert."

My head was throbbing. "Why? I mean, why would he do that?"

She made a choking sound deep in her chest, like a child crying in a well. "Our baby."

"I'm sorry?"

"We lost our baby."

It occurred to me that Mrs. Mealy might have a head injury. I needed to speed back up. I tried to shift into fourth, but my ankle failed me. I pushed the car to forty-five in third gear. "I don't know what you're talking about, Mrs. Mealy."

"When Robert graduated from the seminary, we had a baby. Only we weren't married." Her shoulders were shaking, but it didn't sound like she was crying. "Do you know how terrible that is, for a man of God to father a child out of wedlock? Do you?"

I could only imagine. "And you lost the baby?"

She was quiet for five long seconds. Her voice, when it came, sounded like a saw cutting through wood. "She was nine months old. She died in her crib."

"I'm very sorry." My mind raced back to the birth certificate I'd seen on the Mealys' dresser, the one with Alicia's name but not Alicia's date of birth. "Your first daughter was named Alicia. You named your second daughter Alicia, too?"

"Yes." The word was clipped, and her shoulders no longer shook. "We did. Second Alicia was adopted. After we married. Robert says she looks just like I did when I was her age."

Second Alicia. Did they actually call her that? If so, that'd mess a girl up good. "And so now he's killing girls who look like Alicia and, apparently, like you did at that age?"

A sob broke free from her chest. "The loss of a child will unbalance a man. You have no idea. His sorrow has turned him into a murderer."

Something wasn't adding up, but I couldn't get the headspace to figure out what. "Do you have any evidence?"

"I do. I do." She sounded very tired. "But not tonight. I need to clean myself up, and then I'll go to the police tomorrow. I swear to God."

I blinked. If Robert was the murderer, then who was his accomplice? Julie had said two people tried to abduct her and Jennifer. "Where's Jennifer right now?"

She looked over at me, her expression hollowed out, one eye almost swollen shut. "I don't know. I honestly don't."

I squeezed the steering wheel. I wasn't sure I believed her, but I got the sense she was scared enough to jump out of the moving car if I tried to take her to the hospital. "Where do you want to go? Do you have friends?"

"My sister will take care of me. She lives on Hancock Lake, and she knows how to protect her house." Naomi laughed, but it was humorless. "He's having an affair, too, you know. I suppose you can't blame him, what with me being like this." She indicated her immobile legs. "If only he had been more discreet."

I took a right at the next stop sign, heading back the way I'd come. Apparently, I was going to drop her off at her sister's, though it didn't seem right. I couldn't fathom the level of abuse a woman as traditional and God-fearing as Naomi would have had to suffer to reach this point. I guess I didn't have to. I was sitting next to it. She looked like she'd fallen into a meat grinder.

I was going to go to the police as soon as I dropped her off, obviously. If there was any chance at all that Jennifer was alive, the police needed to search the Bible camp immediately. We couldn't wait for Naomi's evidence.

She trembled next to me as I drove. "You want me to pull over and grab you a blanket?" I asked. "I have one in the trunk."

"Please don't. You've done enough already. Just get me to my sister."

I followed her orders quietly. When I turned onto Golden Pond Road, all the houses were dark, including her sister's.

"What's your sister's name?"

She didn't answer.

"Mrs. Mealy? What's your sister's name?"

"I've always called her Sissy."

I wasn't sure why that seemed creepy, on top of everything else that had transpired tonight, but the way she said it made my skin crawl. I pulled around the circle of the driveway and turned off my car, sitting in front of the house I'd spied on twice. "It doesn't look like anyone's home."

"She's always home. At night."

"OK, then. I'm going to knock on the door and ask her to help me get you into the house. Are you OK with that?"

Naomi's head fell against the seat. "Fine."

I wasn't so sure but didn't see any viable choices. My car ticked as it cooled down. I could hear bullfrogs singing. Other than that, the night was silent, though still heavy with that electric scent of charged moisture. I closed my door quietly and limped toward the door.

I was nearly to the wheelchair ramp when a heavy hand clamped down on my shoulder. I squealed and turned, tipping sideways as my sprained ankle gave out.

I would have fallen to the ground if Weston Lippmann hadn't caught me in his arms.

Chapter 40

"What are you doing here?" I demanded.

The moonlight reflected off his John Lennon glasses. I couldn't read his eyes. He held me while I steadied myself, my heart beating a warning.

"Because I'm so far away from Buford, Georgia?" He made his faint southern accent stronger. "Is that what you mean?"

I felt like someone had dipped me in a tub of icy lard. Of course he was from Georgia. He'd come right out and told me that when we first met, but I had fallen for his nerdy-professor act. I didn't know how he was connected to Robert Mealy, but I knew he had seventy pounds on me and two good feet. "I have to get something out of my car."

He chuckled softly. "You're absolutely transparent, Mira. It's clear you're as scared as a sheep on shearing day."

I yanked myself clumsily out of his arms and glanced toward the house, which was still as dark as a tomb. I forced myself to hold his stare while I reached for my stun gun with one hand and my knife with the other.

"You won't need either of those," he said, not breaking eye contact. "We're on the same team."

How'd he known that I had two weapons and was reaching for them? "I'm not really a team player," I said, stalling as I fumbled at the tangled spider knife hooked in my waistband.

Quick as a rabbit, he pulled a Taser from under his dark coat, held it up for me to see, and then holstered it as he pulled out a wallet and flashed his identification.

I scowled. "It's too dark to read that."

"I'm a detective from Buford. I was sent up here to follow Robert Mealy, who is a person of interest in an active investigation."

Wood tick says what? "Then why are you carrying a Taser instead of a gun?"

He laughed again. "Mrs. Berns already talked to me about that, only she called it a 'laser beamer.' I told her it was so I could time travel. The truth is, Pastor Robert Mealy has a habit of shielding himself with people. You never see him alone. I have a gun in my car, but the Taser is the better choice."

Something about his story didn't sit right, but that might have been because he was now telling me he'd been lying all along. Where should I start believing him? Since his zapper trumped mine, though, there was no harm in at least pretending that I bought his story. "I have Mrs. Mealy in the car. She's been beaten up pretty badly by her husband, and she claims to have evidence that he's responsible for the killings in Georgia as well as Lucy's death and Jennifer's disappearance."

He reeled back. "Why didn't you take her straight to the police?"

"She was adamant about not going to the police, and I was afraid she'd do something wild, like jump out of the car and kill herself, if I didn't listen. I figured I'd go as soon as I got her safely to her sister." I darted a glance at the car. Naomi looked like she was out cold.

Weston sighed and ran his hands through his flop of hair. "Let's get her in the house and check out her injuries. We'll decide where to go from there." All business, he went to the passenger door and lifted Naomi out. The movement roused her, and she let out a groan.

"Mrs. Mealy? My name is Weston Lippmann. I'm going to get you into your sister's house."

She didn't respond. I walked ahead and reached to knock on the house's door, but it was opened before my hand touched it. In front of me stood the same mousy-haired, pear-shaped, fever-eyed, poorly permed woman who'd been staring at Naomi with rapture at the Creation Science Fair. "Are you Sissy? I mean, are you Mrs. Mealy's sister?"

"I am."

"She needs your help." I stood aside, and Weston walked forward.

Sissy blanched when Naomi was carried past her.

"She said her husband did this to her," I said. "She insisted that I bring her here instead of the hospital. Can you take care of her?"

"Does she have any broken bones?"

"Not that I can tell."

"That stubborn mule." Sissy shook her head. "I'll end up bringing her to the hospital anyway, you know. She needs a doctor."

I nodded, relieved. "I was hoping you'd say that. You need help getting her into your car?"

"No, I've got help here."

I looked around, finally seeing the inside of the house I'd spent a couple good nights spying on. I stood in the entryway with the kitchen to my right, a main hall straight ahead, and a cavernous main room to my left. Weston was gently laying Mrs. Mealy on a couch in the great room, talking to her quietly.

I wondered if Les was in the house, if that was the help Sissy was referring to. I didn't have time for random thoughts, though. "Can I use your phone?"

She smiled apologetically. "Don't have one. I value my privacy."

Weston came up and gave me a reassuring look before turning to Sissy. "Your sister doesn't have any broken bones, just a lot of surface abrasions. I'm sorry to leave you like this, but we have to get going. You're sure you can handle this?"

Sissy walked over to her sister, who was stirring. "I'm sure."

"OK."

I followed Weston out the door. When it closed behind us, I looked at him out of the corner of my eye, not sure what our next move was. "You drove here?"

"I did."

"Do you have a cell phone in your car?"

"Yes, but it's not much good in these woods. No reception." He smiled. "Good thing I have a police radio."

I relaxed an inch. "So you can call in what I told you about Jennifer?"

"Yes, and get an ambulance here. You're going to drive back to town?"

This felt wrong, all wrong. "I suppose."

"Go straight to the Battle Lake Police Station," Weston said softly. "Don't stop for anyone."

"Deal."

He tipped his head curtly and strode back through the woods. As I walked to my car, a bright glint in the passenger's side seat caught my eye. I opened the door, reeling at the coppery smell of Naomi's blood. In the seam of the seat was her giant crucifix ring. I held it up toward the sky, and it caught the moonlight in a thousand glinting shards.

There were lights on in Sissy's house now, and I heard a door slam, presumably the one leading to the garage. I'd quick drop off the ring, return to my car, then head to town like a bat out of hell.

Back inside the house, I was surprised to see that Naomi had already been moved off the couch. I glanced around. The kitchen and hallway were also empty. Back and to my left were the stairs to the basement, and a trail of blood led down them.

I stopped at the top of the stairs. "Naomi? Sissy?"

Something heavy crashed to the floor downstairs, followed by a pitiful whimper. I dashed down the wooden steps as fast as my sprained ankle would allow. I entered a finished basement with Sheetrocked walls and a floor covered in linoleum designed to look like wood planks. The main room was set up like a den with marble-eyed animal heads hung on the wall, two uncomfortable-looking chairs, and a small television. Three doors led off this den, and another soft cry came from the one catawampus from me.

I rushed to the door and yanked it open. My intestines turned light and icy as I realized I'd lurched right into the spider's web.

Chapter 41

The room I'd stumbled into was decked out like a small, gory church lit only by candles. Along the far wall were hung larger-than-life figures of Jesus on the cross, each one showing him progressively bloodier, his eyes bottomless pools of betrayal and sadness. The abutting wall held the true horror, though: Jennifer and Pastor Mealy bound and gagged on the floor, between them a life-size statue of Jesus with nails driven through his hands and feet. To the immediate right of the door was a full-size nativity scene, shocking in its innocuousness.

My eyes picked up these details in a millisecond, which was a hair longer than it took for my ass to say, "Run!" I twisted toward the door, fully aware that the only chance I had at saving the three of us was escaping before I was discovered.

But when I turned, I was confronted with an even more horrific sight. In the middle of the basement den stood Mrs. Naomi Mealy, herself a gruesome ghost of a woman, a soft smile on her pulped face, her body still covered in blood and rags.

She could walk, and she held a gun.

I swayed between the ghastly church behind me and terrible apparition in front and fought the urge to faint with all the desperation of a woman hanging on to a cliff wall by her fingernails. I stomped down on my sprained ankle, and pain shot up my leg like an electric shock. With it came focus.

"You call that hurting yourself? Beginner." Naomi smiled, and one of the scabs on her face cracked. A thin trickle of blood rolled down her chin. She really had beaten herself up, or had someone else do it, just like she'd really let a cigarette burn on her leg, her living, feeling leg.

I moaned and darted a glance at the stairs behind her. I couldn't get to them, not with my twisted ankle, not when she had a gun on me. I had a door to my right and a door to my left, but I didn't know where either one led. It was me, Mrs. Mealy, and dead stuffed animals.

I had no idea what to do.

That's when I heard a creak at the top of the stairs. Mrs. Mealy didn't turn to look, but I saw feet coming down the carpeted steps.

I recognized them. "Weston?" I spat out, shocked.

He came into full view and smiled at me apologetically. The room spun, or maybe it was my eyes. I grabbed the doorjamb.

Weston was in on this with Naomi.

Chapter 42

How naive had I been?

As tears filled my eyes, Sissy appeared behind him. She held a mean-looking snub-nosed pistol to his back. My heart soared. He hadn't betrayed us! The situation was bad, but at least there was a law enforcement officer down here now.

My hope of him performing some slick police move to get us out of this was quickly squashed, however, when Sissy darted her hand forward, snatched his Taser out of his holster, and zapped him with it before he had a chance to change expressions.

He slumped to the ground.

"Tie him up and put him with the rest." Naomi didn't take her eyes off me as she spoke. "Make sure you do a good job this time. We don't want any getaways like we had at the pagan festival."

Sissy ducked her head in shame. She was clearly the follower on this team. The intense adoration I'd seen her shower on her sister had been real. Sissy leaned her sturdy farmwife body down, hooked Weston under his armpits, and began dragging him toward the horrible church room.

I stared back into Naomi's unhinged eyes. "You lied about Robert. *You're* the one who's murdering girls who look like you used to. Why? Why would you do that?"

"'As a jewel of gold in a swine's snout, so is a fair woman which is without discretion.' Proverbs, chapter 11, verse 22."

"What? You killed three teenagers and kidnapped a fourth because they were without discretion?"

She shook her head. "Because they were fornicating harlots. I tried to show them the righteous path. I gave them a chance to repent. They didn't, not until I had them in my own small church." She indicated the horror show behind me, running her hands through her hair, ragged where I'd cut it to release her from my tire. "It's my duty to turn girls off the trail that sullied me. That's why our Lord let me walk down that sinful path with Robert, so I could prevent others from making my same mistake. Because of me, they will not despoil themselves. They will not know the searing pain of losing a beloved baby."

There had to be a way out of here. If I could keep her talking, it would come to me. "If they repented, why didn't you let them go?"

She laughed, tightly. "Because it was too late. Those girls were too far gone. They had cavorted with Satan and could not be turned back. I had to do the Lord's work."

"The Lord's work?" Bile burned at the back of my throat. "Kidnapping and murdering young women?"

"I have fought a good fight, I have finished my course, I have kept the faith: Henceforth there is laid up for me a crown of righteousness, which the Lord, the righteous judge, shall give me at that day: and not to me only, but unto all of them also that love His appearing."

"Amen," Sissy seconded, as she stripped off a loud piece of duct tape from a roll on the floor and bound Weston's wrists. She grunted and strained as she dragged him roughly to the horrific tableau behind me, pushing me aside as she struggled past. Weston was still out cold, though I thought I saw his eyelids flutter.

When Sissy passed directly behind me, I could see sweat leaking through the back of her blue-flowered cotton dress. I wanted to jump on her and make her stop, but she had arms like Popeye and would make short work of me if Naomi didn't shoot me first.

Naomi scowled at her sister's interruption. "I can't imagine you would understand what it's like to lose a child and to find forgiveness and peace only by agreeing to do God's bidding. Robert pegged you as a heathen from the first. That may have been the only thing he was right about. He always came up short, though, my Robert."

I shook my head. "What was all that about him being the head and you only being the neck?"

Her words smiled. "The neck turns the head, my dear."

Sissy returned to the den and stood alongside me, breathing heavily. She aimed her thumb at me. "What are we going to do with her?"

Excellent question. "I could convert."

Naomi gestured with her gun. "Tie her up and put her with the others."

Sissy shoved me roughly.

"And then what?" I asked. A mental picture of Lucy Lebowski, her perfect young back marred by a murky hole big enough to put a fist through, flitted behind my eyes.

"'If thine enemy be hungry, give him bread to eat; and if he be thirsty, give him water to drink. For thou shalt heap coals of fire upon his head, and the Lord shall reward thee.' Proverbs, chapter 25, verses 21 to 22."

Sissy's head shot up. "You're going to burn my house down?"

"It's the only way. I already wrote Robert's suicide note and left it at the camp. Apparently he couldn't stand the shame of kidnapping and killing four teenage girls. He beat his wife within an inch of her life and went to his sister-in-law's house to kill himself and destroy all evidence."

"This was your plan all along?" I asked. "To frame Robert, throw yourself in front of a moving car so that you couldn't possibly be a suspect, and then murder him and Jennifer?"

"God's plan," Naomi corrected. "I was surprised when it was *your* car he sent me to crawl in front of, but I do not pretend to know his ways. I am but a follower."

I shook my head. "But that plan will never work. Robert'll be found tied up. And how will you explain me and Weston being here?"

"The fire will burn his bindings off before they find your corpses." She shrugged. "They can think what they want about you and your fornicating friend. The Lord is calling you home."

"What about Sissy?" My mouth was dry with desperation. "The police will think she was in on it."

"Sissy is officially at the Holiday Inn in Saint Cloud. She made a great point of telling me, Alicia, Robert, and the entire congregation that she'd be gone all weekend and wouldn't be back until Monday morning. She already checked in yesterday. Robert would certainly have taken advantage of that to finish his dirty work in her empty house."

An unsettling, joyful agitation burned in Naomi's eyes and was reflected in Sissy's. They had both tumbled over the edge of sanity and were operating on adrenaline and misplaced faith. Standing together, one sister solid as a silo and plain, the other bloody and wasted but oddly striking, I could see just a hint of a resemblance, a glimmer of what they may have looked like, young and hopeful, before this religious fervor had consumed them.

"What about Alicia?" Panic made me lightheaded. "You'd kill her father?"

"Not her true Father," Naomi said scoldingly. "This is all for Him. 'If God be for us, who can be against us?' Now, tie her up."

I put up a fight with Sissy, who stuffed her gun in her waistband, but she was as quick as mercury. She had me trussed like a Christmas pig and on the floor within minutes. She dragged me into the little room of horrors, dumping me against the enormous crucifix.

The giant nail driven through Jesus's foot dug in my back. Weston lay on his side, eyes closed but one foot twitching, like he was chasing rabbits. Jennifer and Pastor Mealy were on each side of me, their hands and feet tied and their eyes closed.

Sissy, ever the workhorse, appeared with a five-gallon can of gasoline and an armload of cotton rags. She doused them with gasoline, the wicked, heavy stench of fuel slipping into my nostrils. The metal can made a chugging-sucking sound with every splash of gasoline she poured. She backed out of the room, dropping a trail of rags that she'd doused with fuel. I heard splashing outside the room, up the stairs, and on the floorboards above as she spread out the last of the fuel.

The smell was suffocating. When Sissy returned to place the empty can near Robert Mealy's slumped and trussed figure, I pleaded with her. "You don't have to do this. You can stop it all right now."

"It's too late." Her voice sounded disconnected, robotic. "I have to leave."

I would have given all the gardens in Minnesota to do the same. The binding bit into my wrists, but the pain kept me focused.

"Is it all set?" asked Naomi, following her sister into the room. If I'd been hoping for a twinge of guilt or a last-minute reprieve, it wasn't coming. Her eyes were as hard as obsidian chips.

"We should be able to light it from the wheelchair ramp out front," answered Sissy. "We better get the car on the road first, to be safe."

"Come on, then. You've got to get back to Saint Cloud, and I have to get back to the woods by the Bible camp. I'm going to have to throw myself in front of someone else's car."

Not even a backward glance from either woman as they walked up the stairs. The stench of gasoline was so thick that it coated my eyes with a greasy sheen. I tried to shift, but the metal nail in my back scratched at my spine. I endeavored to push it away, but it snagged on the duct tape holding my wrists.

I got an idea—a tiny, desperate idea.

I pushed the duct tape against the nail and felt it snag again. I scooted my whole body back toward Jesus's legs and began to rub the tape furiously against the nail. Robert Mealy and Jennifer were both lying still, in the same spots and position as when I had first seen them. I could touch them with my foot if I stretched. Weston had stopped twitching near the door and was now motionless.

I returned my focus to the task at hand—getting this damned duct tape off my wrists. It was hard to return to the right spot without being able to see what I was doing, and several times my wrists slipped and the gargantuan nail sliced me.

I didn't stop, the smell of gasoline pushing against the back of my throat like a finger. The front door slammed, and I imagined I could hear the whoosh of a gas stove firing—first the doused rags leading up the wheelchair ramp, through the entry, down the stairs, across the floor, and into this room. We'd probably suffocate before we cooked, but it would be a race.

I rubbed, harder and harder, until the tape grew hot. Harder and harder I rubbed, ignoring the blood trickling down into my cupped fingers.

I heard it before I saw it, the whistle of oxygen being removed, followed by a fiery tongue licking down the stairs as fast as a snake. In desperation, I stretched out my leg and kicked over part of the nativity scene. The manger fell on the cotton rags, disrupting the chain at the door. Still, when the flame snarled toward our room, it lit the gas fumes, creating a searing sonic boom that left me without eyebrows. My heart raced, and I felt every remaining hair on my body stand up.

From this angle, I could see that the rug and one of the chairs in the den had caught fire. The manger had bought me some time, but not much. I rubbed with even more gusto, telling myself that my wrists could not feel pain, that they were just instruments.

I felt eyes on me and looked over to Jennifer to find her eyes wide, scared, and young. I wondered if she'd been alert but in shock the whole time. Tears were coursing down her face, but she didn't say a word, even though her mouth wasn't bound. Across the room, Weston was beginning to shift, but Robert Mealy remained still as a statue, his eyes closed.

One monumental tug on the nail, and there was suddenly give in my wrists. I pulled them apart at an angle and was able to free them of the duct tape. Sweat coursed down my face as I tried to draw oxygen out of the heated air. I felt like a roasting turkey on preheat.

I turned to the Jesus statue and used my tender and bleeding hands to wiggle the railroad-size nail out of his feet. When it was free, I plunged its sharp point into the tape binding my ankles.

From the corner of my eyes, I saw the couch go up in flames that were now licking hungrily at the walls. In the center of the main room, the rags burned ineffectually, their gasoline power long gone, but the linoleum at the edges of the walls was curling and blistering.

I pulled my legs apart, but the duct tape was still too tight to rip. I plunged the nail twice more into the spot between my ankles, trying not to notice how difficult it was to breathe. Across from me, Jennifer whimpered, her first sound.

"Mira?"

"Weston? Are you awake?"

He moaned and sat up drunkenly. I ripped viciously at the duct tape, and suddenly, I was free.

I stumbled over to Weston and ripped off the tape at his wrists. He was still groggy. I slapped him across the face hard enough to leave a mark.

"Get out now, Weston! Get Jennifer and go!"

He stood up shakily. "What about you?"

The flames were kissing the doorframe, little pecks at first, but it would take only seconds for the fire to become a towering demon, its tongue darting lasciviously into the room and along the ceiling. I coughed out orders. "I can walk out of here. Go now! There isn't time to get her bindings off."

He scooped up Jennifer, and for a terrible moment, I thought he was going to pass out. He rallied himself, wrapped his cape around both of them, and then charged through the flames and up the stairs.

I crouched low, but the smoke was everywhere. Using the nail, I had Pastor Mealy free in less than six seconds. "Get up! I know you can hear me. If you don't get up now, you'll die."

The pastor's voice, deep and sad, rumbled out of his body. "But God is the judge: he putteth down one, and setteth up another."

There simply wasn't time.

I reached over and grabbed the nativity scene baby Jesus that had rolled out with the manger, and I conked Robert over the head with it. It was a good, solid noggin-bonker, and it laid him out cold.

"The Lord helps those who help themselves," I whispered hoarsely.

I was able to drag him all of three feet before my ankle gave out. Fortunately, Weston had returned down the fiery stairs, a wet blanket over his head and another in his hands. He shoveled Robert Mealy onto his shoulders, and together we scuttled clumsily up the stairs, the flames caressing our legs, begging us to stay.

Free of the house, I was confused by the complete and utter darkness of the outdoors. "Where's the moon?" I croaked through a smoke-seared throat.

Thunder answered my question, followed by raindrops as big and heavy as grapes. Fresh water poured down on my shoulders, a sweet balm that cooled my raw wrists and hot skin.

The farmers would say the August Moon Festival had worked its magic.

Sarah Ruth would say it was the Lord.

Me? I just said thanks.

Chapter 43

Ironically, the torrent of rain kept Sissy's house on Hancock Lake from burning to the ground. The gory church-room, the den, and the stairs were the only areas to suffer real damage.

Weston Lippmann was as good as his word about the radio in his car. He had an ambulance, a fire truck, three state troopers, and two unmarked cars at Hancock Lake within twenty-two minutes of sending out the word.

Jennifer was traumatized, but she'd heal.

Robert Mealy came to shortly after the ambulance arrived and was pronounced physically healthy except for a concussion. His immortal soul was a different matter.

After Weston gave instructions on where to find Sissy and Mrs. Mealy, he and I were driven off in the ambulance. On the ride he told me Sissy's real name was Constance Penwick, long-suffering older sister of Naomi Mealy, née Penwick. Likely, Sissy was the reason the Mealys had chosen to move to Battle Lake. In the course of his investigation, Weston had found no other connections tying them to this area.

I took wicked pleasure at the thought of Mrs. Mealy, lying in wait in the woods, a smirk on her twisted, puffy face as she heard the police sirens blaring toward the Bible camp.

She'd think they were coming to tell her her husband had gone up in smoke; they would really be coming to handcuff her and toss her to the mercy of very human judges.

All her self-flagellation would be for naught.

The ambulance delivered Weston and me to the Douglas County Hospital in Alexandria, where the same nurse who had originally treated my sprained ankle—telling me sternly not to put any pressure on it—was still on duty.

When she saw the grass and dirt stains on the bottom of my straggling bandage, surface burns on both feet, charred hair, missing eyebrows and eyelashes, and wrists rubbed raw, she looked at me like I didn't even deserve ankles.

This time, I took the crutches.

Chapter 44

I took eight days off to recover and made a new moving plan in light of my injuries and a couple key realizations. While I was laid up, Mrs. Berns and Sarah Ruth were in charge of the library. Sid and Nancy took turns running baked goods out to me and tending to my lawn, garden, and animals. It'd been raining steadily and pleasantly since the rock-and-roll thunderstorm the night of the fire, and all of Otter Tail County grew brazenly lush and as humid as a greenhouse.

I healed along with the parched ground.

The burns and abrasions mended quickly, but it took days before my ankle went from pumpkin-size to merely swollen. I had to chop off a couple inches of hair, my lungs weren't yet at full capacity, and it'd be a few months before I'd have eyebrows again, but I was alive.

When I returned to the library, I had a new writing assignment for the paper: cover the affirmation celebration Pastor Winter wanted to hold the coming weekend.

"Tell me again why Pastor Winter was out at the Bible camp the night Jennifer disappeared," I asked Mrs. Berns. She and I were alone, as Sarah Ruth had failed to turn up for work.

She leaned her face into the palm of her hand, her elbows on the front desk across from me. Her eyes were sparkly, like they always were when she had some dirt.

"He knew they were up to no good," she said. "He was looking for Jennifer, just like you."

"Why'd he suspect the Mealys?"

She smiled. "He'd been at that Wisconsin seminary with Robert when he and Naomi lost their baby. Said it was a real scandal. Well, not so much said it, but I could tell that's what he meant. Said it was a tragedy, broke Naomi in half. She just stopped walking, eating, started talking in tongues. The Mealys disappeared after that. When they showed up in Battle Lake last fall, Pastor Winter wahooed them."

The spot where my eyebrows used to be shot up. "What?"

Mrs. Berns rolled her eyes. "It's called the internet. You want information, you *wahoo* it. Welcome to the twentieth century."

I rubbed my ankle, feeling no need to correct her about the difference between "wahoo" and "Yahoo." "And what'd he find out? When he wahooed them, that is?"

She shrugged. "Same thing you found. They went to Georgia, started a church, but Mrs. Mealy just kept spiraling until she talked him into founding that wacky Christ's Church of the Apocryphal Revelation. Then a couple teenagers get shot in the back, the Mealys skip town, and next thing you know, they're in Battle Lake. When Lucy turned up murdered the same way, Winter figured there was a connection, but didn't know what. He was trying to find that out when you saw him at the Bible camp the night of the festival."

I stretched, enjoying a comfortable silence with Mrs. Berns as we both chewed our thoughts. I realized I still had an unanswered question. "So how'd the Mealys know the teenagers in Georgia?"

"Robert Mealy didn't. Naomi Mealy confessed to meeting them both at a girls' after-school center she volunteered at. Said when she saw them, she knew she had to save 'em."

I shivered. "With help like that, you almost don't want to leave the house."

Mrs. Berns nodded agreeably. "Pastor Winter feels terrible he wasn't able to prevent Lucy's death."

Pastor Winter hadn't been able to save Lucy or find Jennifer, but he'd done what he could to heal the town. He'd started by initiating a calling chain in his congregation, arranging for members to be with Jennifer and her family at all times. They would be up to their ears in hotdish, ham, buttered dinner rolls, and Jell-O salad until Jennifer was comfortable and the family felt safe once more.

Lucy Lebowski's family would never feel safe again, but I knew Pastor Winter would make sure they felt the support and comfort of their community for as long as they lived here.

Once he was satisfied he was doing everything in his power to care for the town, he'd turned to his religion. Calling together some of his most active congregants in an emergency meeting, he put forth the need for some large-scale event to restore faith in the church. He wanted to call it the "Apologies, Not Apostasies" Festival and hold it as soon as possible.

He envisioned closing down Lake Street, bringing in a Christian band, and having arts and crafts booths, bake sales, and profuse literature highlighting the "upbeat" parts of the Bible along with walking, talking pastors from other communities called in to support the town through Jesus's words.

Sid and Nancy talked him down from the lofty pulpit, gently arguing that people may have had enough evangelizing for a while and that an encore to the August Moon Festival, which'd been sadly interrupted, would be the way to go. After all, they pointed out, Pastor Winter had often told them that our goodness is seen in our actions, not our words.

They agreed on a town-wide potluck with arts and crafts, bake sales, and Not with My Horse playing in the afternoon. All proceeds from the bake sales would be divided evenly between Lucy's and Jennifer's families. Kennie agreed to close off Lake Street from 1:00 p.m. to 6:00 p.m. this Saturday, and I'd agreed to write an article promoting the event.

After I zipped off the community festival article, I edited the *Recall* police log. Although this was an activity I always enjoyed, I took particular pleasure in the third item.

WEDNESDAY, August 19

10:01 p.m. Denny Warner called in, reporting that neighbor has fire in fire ring. Dispatcher said that was legal. Mr. Warner said fire is too big. Dispatcher advised as long as it's in ring, it's legal. Mr. Warner said neighbors are making too much noise. Officer en route.

THURSDAY, August 20

9:43 a.m. Nelson family reports their grandmother, Louise Nelson, is locked in their car outside the nursing home and refuses to go back in. Officer en route.

SUNDAY, August 23

11:11 p.m. 17-year-old male minor pulled over for suspicious driving in 1993 Dodge Caravan, license plate GH 857. Alicia Mealy, 19-year-old female, found, apparently hiding, under blanket in rear of vehicle. Reported bruises on her neck. She declined to press assault charges.

Ah, hickeys. The calling card of young lust wielded by sons of farmers all over the Midwest since time immemorial.

And what did Alicia expect, making out with a high school kid in his parents' minivan? He probably begged her to wear his letter jacket and she was so excited that she wrote his name in hearts and wondered what it'd be like to marry him. Or maybe I was confusing my brief, sad adolescence with her protracted one.

I had no doubt that life had just bumped Alicia out of the self-involvement she'd been enjoying for so long. She was now on her own, with her three nearest relatives in jail for serious crimes: her mother for three counts of murder and multiple counts of kidnapping and attempted murder, her aunt for one count of kidnapping and multiple accounts of assault and battery, and her father for accessory to murder. Robert had declared that he hadn't known what had been going on, or even that his wife could walk, but he'd have to prove that in court.

Now Alicia needed to figure out what she was doing with her future and how she was going to define herself, free of her parents' rules. It was hard to be a rebel when you were the only one who cared what you did. I hoped she ended up making some good choices for herself; my money was on cosmetology school. When she met me for coffee—hey, I was willing to cut her some slack, now that I knew she had been Second Alicia her whole life—she said she was staying in Battle Lake for the time being. I gave her a heads-up about Brad's cheating ways, which she didn't see a problem with, and then we agreed to go to his next show together. After that, my debt to her would be settled, and I planned to avoid her.

When someone shows you who they are, believe them.

I had one more job to complete. Weston—who'd stopped by my hospital room to say thanks before returning to Georgia to work on extradition papers for the senior Mealys—had advised me not to tell Tina what we'd seen in the woods at the August Moon Festival, but I couldn't sit on that. It might ruin our friendship, but that was a price I was willing to pay if it would help her escape an abusive marriage. I hobbled over to her shop on my lunch break and described the scene in the woods at the festival as clinically as possible, omitting the whiteness of Tom's rear as he pumped in the moonlight, but making clear that I'd witnessed him and Annika being unquestionably intimate.

"That's not possible." Tina's eyes grew shiny with tears.

I wanted to be anywhere else in the world. "I'm sorry."

"Are you sure they weren't just talking?"

"They were on the ground, naked."

Tina shook her head repeatedly, like a dog with water in its ears, and then broke down sobbing. Part of me had figured she'd be relieved to get out of a relationship with that clod, but that just went to show how much I knew about relationships. It took me a half an hour to calm her down. Finally, she asked me to leave and shambled into the back room like a broken woman.

Back at the library, I felt like a heel, but knew I'd done what I had to. I'd just settled into my seat, grateful to put my battered ankle on the front counter, when the front door slammed open. In charged Kennie, murder in her eyes. Her hair was plastered to her head from the rain that had been drizzling pleasantly on and off all morning. Her clothes clung to her like honey on a spoon.

"Nice weather," I said, to no one in particular.

Mrs. Berns had sidled up next to me for a front-row seat. "It is if you're a seed," she said agreeably.

"Mira James!" Kennie called out.

"Hi, Kennie."

"Gary Wohnt is gone!"

I sat back. "Where'd he go?"

"A four-week leave of absence." She slapped a typed letter on the counter. "Four weeks!"

"He didn't say where to?"

"No." She looked distraught. "He just wrapped up his end of this murder-and-kidnapping business and hit the road."

I put my elbows on the counter. "What're you going to do?"

She peeled a straggle of soggy platinum hair off her forehead and tossed it back. "Find a replacement to head the police department, I suppose."

"Who'll work at the job for just four weeks?" I grabbed Mrs. Berns's hand as she began to raise it.

"I don't know," she wailed. "This is just terrible for the town."

More likely, it was terrible for Kennie. She clearly still carried a torch for Gary, even though he'd cheated on her with God. *Come to think of it, Gary's absence might be bad for me, too.* As much as our personalities clashed, he had always come through for me. This might be a mystery I'd need to look into more. "You'll fix this, Kennie. You always do."

Kennie humphed and strode back out. I supposed she could simply promote one of the three deputies until Gary returned. But where had he gone? Suddenly, I had a tickly feeling along my hairline as I realized I knew exactly why Sarah Ruth was not at work today.

I should be getting official word in the next day or two.

Chapter 45

The on-and-off rain of the past week soaked deep into the earth, massaging roots and worms all across Minnesota. In its wake were a lush greenness and air almost too thick to breathe. If you listened hard, you could hear plants humming "Hallelujah" in high, squeaky voices.

The moisture had broken the hot snap, but the Battle Lake First National Bank thermometer declared this Tuesday morning to be anything but cool. Seventy-seven degrees, and it was only nine a.m.

I'd slept in, fed and watered my animals and myself, and left for work with barely enough time to open the doors, water the plants, turn on the lights, and dust. I'd leave shelving the books to Mrs. Berns, who was in the back room primping before our first patrons arrived—getting ready for the show, she called it.

The return bin was overflowing, however, so I grabbed some books off the top to move to the counter. I had a hard enough time balancing my own body without adding cargo, and two tomes slipped out of my hand. That's when the note fell, drifting to the ground like a feather.

It was simple, and not at all surprising: it was, after all, Gary Wohnt I'd smelled on her two weeks ago.

> Dear Mira:
> Thank you for all your hospitality. You made me feel welcomed in Battle Lake, and you run a wonderful library. I don't think you know how much you are

admired and respected. If I had stayed at the library my whole life, I don't think I could have met the standard you've set. However, the Lord has chosen a different path for me. He has thrown love in front of me, and it would be a crime to refuse this Gift. God has brought Gary Wohnt and me together, and together, we are going to explore this beautiful earth. I'm sorry I am not able to give you two weeks' notice. I hope you understand.

Yours in Faith,
Sarah Ruth O'Hanlon

The note gave me mixed feelings.

Sarah Ruth was a hard worker, but she also had a vague shiftiness about her. I was thinking specifically of her hiding that she'd been dating Gary and not telling until she was asked that she was a Christ's Church of the Apocryphal Revelation congregant. That crooked quality was certain to interfere with her job and our friendship down the line.

I decided I was better off without her.

Gary Wohnt, though? He just might be irreplaceable.

I took comfort in the fact that he had taken only a four-week leave of absence and not quit his job altogether. He might be hedging his bets, or not as serious about the relationship as Sarah Ruth. There was hope he'd be back. Anyhow, the fact that they had been dating explained their weirdness for the past two weeks, the secretive phone calls, awkward encounters, and odd behaviors. Guess you *could* keep a secret in a small town.

"I knew that God groupie was never going to last," Mrs. Berns said, peeking around my side. "No spine."

I crumpled up the note, but it was too late. "Don't sneak up on me like that."

She made a pooh noise. "I'm eighty-nine. I got nothin' but sneak. What's that part about you being a great librarian?" She tilted her head at the letter balled up in my hand.

I tossed it in the nearest wastebasket. Perfect shot, no rim. "She's just stroking me. You know how it is when you quit a job. You don't want to feel like a heel, so you try to make your boss feel better."

She snorted. "So now you've got nobody to replace you. Somebody up there must really want you to stay on in Battle Lake." Mrs. Berns pointed at the sky.

"If that's the case," I said, hands on hips, "he certainly does move in mysterious ways. Psychotic, passive-aggressive, mysterious ways."

"Speaking of heavenly bodies, is that Johnny Leeson coming up the sidewalk?"

I glared at her, not at all in the mood for bad jokes. When the door donged open, I turned, expecting to see Les Pastner, or some other repellent human being.

When my eyes connected with Johnny's tentative, cerulean, bottomless, thick-lashed peepers, I started to fall off my crutches.

Chapter 46

He rushed to my side and put one muscular arm around my waist and gently pulled me up. "Are you all right? Why are you on crutches?"

His thick, dirty-blond hair brushed against my neck, and I was bathed in his signature scent, a mixture of green earth and something clean and natural, like a fresh-cut cucumber.

"I'm technically not on crutches at the moment," I said. "I'm on you."

He smiled, his face inches from mine. My heart was pumping so hard that I blushed. I pulled away, reset my crutches, and hobbled over to take a seat behind the counter.

He followed. "I'm gone for a few weeks and you manage to break your ankle."

"It's not broken, it's sprained. And you've been gone for nearly eight weeks." So nice of my harpy shrew desperate alter ego to come calling. It got so lonely in my head without her.

His voice was quiet. "The U-Mad project ran over schedule."

I pushed my hair behind my ears, taking silent inventory of my appearance. Clean, sporadically brushed hair, no makeup, white tank top, fading bruises circling my wrists like bracelets, cutoff shorts, and flip-flops.

Oh, and no eyebrows.

Yep, just like he'd left me, give or take a wound and some hair. "You're just back to get some stuff, then?" My voice arched high and squeaky with the last word. Sniffing out killers, vandals, and secret lovers, I was good at it. Talking to men I really liked, not so much. And the sad truth, impossible to deny with him across from me, was that I *did* really like Johnny.

Oh boy, did I.

He scratched his head and glanced over at Mrs. Berns. "Can I talk to Mira alone for a minute?"

"You could, but she says even stupider things when I'm not around to keep an eye on her. I'll stay and coach her, if you don't mind." Mrs. Berns nodded encouragingly. "It'd be the best for both of you."

"Um, OK. I brought you something, Mir." He walked back to the door and picked up the two potted plants he'd set just outside it. "It's a pepper and a tomato plant. I went to your house and saw someone had trashed your garden." He looked from my wrapped ankle to my wrists and back to my face, silently asking if there was a connection between the violence to my garden and the violence to me. I didn't offer any insight. "Anyhow, I can help you plant these."

"Thanks, but I can do it—"

"With your sexy-hot body right next to my side. Please don't wear a shirt, and oil your chest like you're about to cook some eggs on it," Mrs. Berns suggested.

I glared at her, but she kept her eyes on Johnny.

He laughed. I forgot how nice his laugh was. It was open and friendly, and had the same huskiness as his voice. "I'll see what I can do," he said to Mrs. Berns, before turning back to me. "But first, I wanted to tell you something."

Both Mrs. Berns and I leaned forward, me anxious and her curious. Before Johnny could finish his thought, the door banged open, and Kennie slunk on in, dressed in a Halloween stripper-cop uniform.

"I have an announcement!" she yelled.

As one, Johnny, Mrs. Berns, and I looked her over, from her five-inch patent leather pumps, to her fishnet stockings, to her hot pants, to her button-down shirt complete with silk tie and badge. Around her waist she wore a belt with a flashlight, gun, and billy club, and on her head was perched a police hat of a design not seen outside of 1980s cop shows or the Village People.

"You're going on a doughnut run?" Mrs. Berns asked.

"That was quotable," Kennie said sarcastically. "Somebody get me an embroidery pillow. No, I have wonderful news. Since Gary Wohnt is leaving town for four weeks, I've stepped in as the new Battle Lake chief of police, so look out, crime!" Kennie opened her arms and twirled, using her beauty pageant background to keep upright in her stilt-like stilettos.

Oh my. I shook my head. "Can you just do that?"

"Sugar, I can do it all."

As if responding to a song cue, Tina of Tom and Tina's Taxidermy strode through the door, only it took me a couple beats to recognize her. Her head was high, her shoulders were straight, and there was a touch of cockiness in her step. She had morphed into a redhead since I'd last seen her, and the auburn color complemented her skin and eyes nicely. Without waiting for her turn to speak, she set herself in the center of the group. "I won't take much of your time. I just stopped by to say thank you."

My head was reeling from the revolving-door morning. "For what?"

"For shoehorning me out of a terrible relationship. I always hated that store. Dead animals and jewelry? It's stupid. Plus, it always smelled like a morgue. I put it on the market this morning."

I smiled at her sassiness. "Tom's OK with that?"

"Doesn't matter. I owned the store before we were married, and I kept it in my name. I've been squirreling money away for years, too. I've got a house in Florida in my mom's name, and I'm moving there for good. Tom wasn't the only one with tricks up his sleeve." She chuckled. "I'm going to be just fine, and I can't thank you enough."

Mrs. Berns and Kennie eyeballed me suspiciously. I knew they were going to hammer me for details later. Johnny just stood back and took it all in, the plants still cradled in his tanned arms. Every time I noticed anew how white his T-shirt was against his sun-kissed body, I felt a little shiver in an area I thought I'd consigned to a life of lonely darkness, interrupted by only the occasional bike ride. "You're welcome, but this is all you, Tina."

"You bet it is. It's all me, finally." She gave us all one great wink and sashayed back out the way she had come, humming "These Boots Are Made for Walkin'."

"That bitch stole my thunder."

"Kennie," I said, "no one will ever steal your thunder. I promise."

Mrs. Berns and Johnny nodded in acknowledgment of the plain truth.

"I suppose you're right," she said, turning her attention on me in a manner I found very alarming, "but before I go, I want to ask you if you'd be my paid consultant. You'd be reimbursed out of city funds. You know, for solving the odd mystery."

I winced. I could still smell the burn of gasoline in my nostrils. "I'll get back to you on that."

"Just don't wait too long," she said. "Battle Lake gets busy, and I need the help."

When she left, Johnny seemed reluctant to pick up where he'd left off. He settled the plants on the broad front counter and made a show of pinching dead leaves. Mrs. Berns and I waited not so patiently. He turned around when he was ready. "Mira, what I wanted to tell you is that I'm not going back to Madison. Not this year, anyhow. My mom deserves to have me close right now.

"I feel bad about leaving the way I did. Not just leaving my mom, but leaving you. I had every intention of coming over to your house that night, and I was really looking forward to spending time with you." He looked at Mrs. Berns, who gave him the *And . . . ?* look. "And I really like you. I want to see if this can go somewhere between us. I realize I have to earn your trust back. I'm hoping you'll give me a chance."

"Not only will she give you a chance, she'll give you a b—"

"Mrs. Berns!" When she didn't leave right away, I pointed toward the back of the library. "The books need to be shelved. Now."

"Fine," she said, shrugging, "but don't blame me when you can't get that hoof outta your piehole."

When she was out of earshot, I looked back at Johnny, but it was difficult. I was suddenly shy. "We're going to have to back it up. You know, back it up to friends. For a while."

He looked relieved. "That's fair. I can do that."

Suddenly, I smiled. It *was* fair, and it felt right, with an undercurrent of pleasant anticipation. "How is your mom doing?"

"Good, but she needs me closer until she gets her feet back under her."

"It does feel good to be needed, doesn't it?"

I had decided in the ambulance on the way to Alexandria that I was going to stay in Battle Lake, at least through the winter. This place had its problems, don't get me wrong, but I felt like I belonged and like I mattered, and that was a new sensation for me. I took Johnny's unexpected arrival as confirmation that my choice to stay was a good one. "Say, what would you think about you and your mom having dinner with me and my mom? She's going through a tough time, and it'd be good for her to have more friends."

That would give me an excuse to call my mom and explain the strange letter she was about to get, postmarked in Clitherall, ranting about a pastor who was kidnapping and murdering teenage girls, and ending with an apology for how I'd acted when she told me that she had breast cancer.

I leaned back in my library chair, once again queen of my domain. I was warm with a confidence in myself as alien in my life as hangovers had become familiar.

Maybe a little faith wasn't such a bad thing.

Book CLUB Questions

1. Can you relate to any of the characters in *August Moon*? To what extent do they remind you of yourself or someone you know?

2. How does Mira evolve throughout the story? What events trigger these changes?

3. Who did you think killed Lucy? What clues supported your speculation?

4. Did the surprise climax to the story catch you off guard? Did you find it believable?

5. What themes did you see throughout the book?

6. What role does humor play throughout the novel?

7. Do you think humorous mysteries, which are predominantly considered entertainment as opposed to highbrow literature, should be free of the topics of politics and religion? Why or why not?

8. If you could create the perfect boyfriend for Mira James, what would he look like? Act like? Smell like?

9. The Murder by Month mysteries are set in 1998. What were the clues that this wasn't a present-day mystery?

10. Scenario: You, Mrs. Berns, Kennie Rogers, Mira James, Johnny Leeson, and Gary Wohnt are on a ship in the middle of the ocean. The ship is sinking. The life raft has room for only five of you, so one of you has to go down with the ship. Who is it, and why that person?

Visiting the Real Battle Lake

All the characters in the Murder by Month series are truly fictional and truly characters, every one of them. This is not to say that Battle Lake doesn't have memorable folks of its own, being a lovely and quirky real town situated in a beautiful puff of rolling hills and crystal clear lakes in west-central Minnesota.

The town, like the mystery series I've located there, has a great restaurant named Stub's and a full-service drugstore called the Village Apothecary, where, last time I was in town, you could buy creamy, crunchy Nut Goodies. I'm tickled to say that the Chief Wenonga statue, featured prominently in *Knee High by the Fourth of July* and making cameos throughout the series, is also 100 percent real. Thank god for small favors.

The little gingerbread shed where you can buy vegetables on the honor system also exists, as do the Dairy Queen, Larry's Foods, and Granny's Pantry, and over in Clitherall, there's Koep's and Bonnie & Clyde's.

Although there's probably a Bible camp or two near Battle Lake, I've never attended one, and am sure they have nothing in common with the fictional Bible camp in *August Moon*. Likewise, the Turtle Stew, the Last Resort, the library, and the Fortune Café are all figments of my often-embarrassing imagination.

Thank you for the opportunity to let it out to play.

About the Author

Photo © 2023 Kelly Weaver Photography

Jess Lourey writes about secrets. She's the bestselling author of thrillers, comic caper mysteries, book club fiction, young adult fiction, and nonfiction. Winner of the Anthony, Thriller, and Minnesota Book Awards, Jess is also an Edgar, Agatha, and Lefty Award–nominated author; TEDx presenter; and recipient of The Loft's Excellence in Teaching fellowship. Check out her TEDx Talk for the true story behind her debut novel, *May Day*. She lives in Minneapolis with a rotating batch of foster kittens (and occasional foster puppies, but those goobers are a lot of work). For more information, visit www.jessicalourey.com.